"FINISH HIM, BOY," SOMEONE SHOUTED.

Barclay took the knife in his hand and held it to Boggs's throat. He was flooded with feelings he had never encountered before. He wondered if he really could kill another person. That had never been a question before; he had always just assumed that when the time came, he would do what he had to. Now he was not so sure.

More than that, though, he questioned whether he wanted to kill Boggs. He could see no reason to do so, even though he was certain the trapper would kill him without a qualm if the situation were reversed.

Voices filtered into him, almost all calling for him to kill Boggs. With the rush of adrenaline and the prodding encouragement of the small crowd, he felt he had made up his mind. Besides, he wanted to see if he had it in him to kill someone. Now was a good time to test himself.

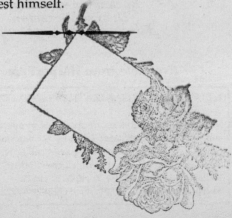

Dear Reader:

Just a moment of your time could earn you $1,000! We're working hard to bring you the best books, and to continue to do that we need your help. Simply turn to the back of this book, and let us know what you think by answering seven important questions.

Return the completed survey with your name and address filled in, and you will automatically be entered in a drawing to win $1,000, subject to the official rules.

Good luck!

Geoff Hannell

Geoff Hannell
Publisher

By the same author

Mountain Country series:
Southwest Thunder
Winter Thunder
Mountain Thunder

Buckskins and Blood
The Frontiersman
Fire Along the Big Muddy

Available from HarperPaperbacks

FIRE ALONG THE BIG MUDDY

JOHN LEGG

HarperPaperbacks
A Division of HarperCollins*Publishers*

For Aunt Pat (Taylor).
For all your kindness and help since as far back
as I can remember.
I love you.

HarperPaperbacks   *A Division of* HarperCollins*Publishers*
10 East 53rd Street, New York, N.Y. 10022

Copyright © 1995 by John Legg
All rights reserved. No part of this book may be used or
reproduced in any manner whatsoever without written
permission of the publisher, except in the case of brief
quotations embodied in critical articles and reviews. For
information address HarperCollins*Publishers,*
10 East 53rd Street, New York, N.Y. 10022.

Cover illustration by Tony Gabrielle

First printing: September 1995

Printed in the United States of America

HarperPaperbacks and colophon are trademarks of
HarperCollins*Publishers*

❖ 10 9 8 7 6 5 4 3 2 1

PROLOGUE

Heavy mist drifted lazily through the confines of the Fort Atkinson stockade, clinging to the wood barracks and seeming to catch on the sharpened logs of the picket walls. The wind whistled through the cracks in the walls, and made the mist dance across the parade ground. The temperature was expectedly chilly in the gloomy dawn that struggled weakly to rise.

Miles Barclay thought the gray, cold morning was appropriate as he was taken out of the guardhouse. His clinking shackles added to the surreal trappings. "Seems like a good day for these proceedin's, don't it, Harley?" Barclay said to one of the six privates escorting him.

"Lordy, but you're a mite cheerful for a man goin' to his death," Private Harley Wilkinson said, somewhat unnerved by Barclay's cavalier attitude.

"Well, that might be true, but what the hell, if you can't enjoy your impending doom, what kind of man are you?"

Wilkinson glanced at Barclay as if he had lost his mind, then looked away, dumbfounded. He had served here with Barclay for more than a year—until Barclay had deserted—and thought he had known him, but now he realized he hadn't known him at all.

Barclay was not a big man—five foot ten, perhaps

one hundred sixty pounds, but he had a wiry strength to him. He had a lean, hungry-looking face and even in chains he retained a cocky attitude, which was seen in the way he carried himself, the way he walked, the particular way he cocked his eyebrows, and in his shining brown eyes.

Wilkinson knew that Barclay's cockiness would get him into trouble—hell, had gotten him into trouble with distressing frequency. But he had never thought it would lead to this. He took another surreptitious look at Barclay. He thought he could detect just a hint of worry amid the sparkle of his eyes. That made him feel slightly better. At least Barclay was showing a minimal sign of being human.

The small contingent finally stopped, and Barclay stared at the solitary log stuck into the dirt two feet in front of the wall. "Ain't much of a place for a man to meet his Maker, is it, Harley?" he said, more than asked. His voice had lost just a touch of its normal haughtiness. "Well," he added, "best get the ball rollin' here. I ain't gettin' any younger, you know."

His guards stifled chuckles, their admiration for Barclay rising.

"Ye're nae gonna run on us now, are ye, Miles?" Corporal Mac Dunnigan asked. He was in charge of the small detail.

"You gonna let me free?"

"Aye, we thought it'd be easier if we just tied ye to the pole."

"Easier on who?" Barclay asked, almost laughing.

"The rest of us lads, of course. It'll be bad enough haulin' your carcass out for the buryin' wi'out havin' to do it wi' ye havin' chains hangin' all over ye." There was no malice in his words.

"I'm happy to see you ain't gone sentimental, Corporal," Barclay said, lips twitching in the beginnings of a smile.

"We all have to think of oursel'es, lad," Dunnigan said with a shrug. "After all, ye'll be gone to your Maker—or the other way—while we here still on this glowin' gem of earth have to get on with our lives."

"Can't say as I blame ya. If I was in your place, I'd do the same."

"Remember yer promise now, lad," Dunnigan said. "No runnin' or causin' trouble."

"I ain't goin' nowhere, Mac. Just get on with it before I die of old age—which, come to think of it, wouldn't be such a bad thing, at least from where I'm standin'."

"I can see that," Dunnigan said with an understanding nod. "But if ye hadn't killed Captain Pennington, ye'd not be in this position." He didn't sound like he missed the officer much, but duty was duty.

The chains and shackles were removed, and Barclay stood a moment, rubbing his chafed wrists. Then he turned and backed up to the pole. Through the mist he could see the gathering of the troops, more than three hundred of them, made eerie by the haze. "Looks like Colonel Shithead is goin' all out to entertain the boys, eh."

"Aye," Dunnigan agreed. "But I dunna think most of the lads want to be here watchin' this."

"That's comfortin'," Barclay said dryly.

Dunnigan shrugged. "We take comfort where we can get it, lad."

Two privates wrapped thick rope strands around Barclay's chest and the post, then one of them knotted it tightly. When they stepped back, Dunnigan checked their handiwork. He walked around and stopped in front of Barclay. "Aye, me lads did a fine job. Ye'll nae fall to the ground when ye get pumped full of lead balls."

"That's heartenin' to know," Barclay said sarcastically. Then he sighed. "Get on with it."

Dunnigan marched his six soldiers off about thirty feet and began forming them into the firing squad.

Barclay watched with almost a detached air as the troop prepared. But the enormity of his situation was finally beginning to sink in. He had seen all this as a lark of sorts. As if they would get to this point and then the fort's commander, Colonel Henry Leavenworth, would put a stop to it and everyone would enjoy a good laugh. He knew in his head that such a thing was ludicrous, but in his heart he had hoped. After all, he had always managed to get out of tight spots before. He just assumed this would be another one.

But now, with the six men arrayed before him, just waiting for the order to end his life, he began to realize that there would be no miracle this time. That saddened him, but in a way it interested him, too. A natural curiosity had him wondering just what the death experience would be like. It was morbid, he knew, but he couldn't deny his interest.

Suddenly someone shouted "Fire!" and Barclay jerked against the tightness of the ropes, figuring his end had come. He thought perhaps that, in his interest in what the coming of death would be like, he had not paid attention to it happening.

Then he realized that the soldiers were still standing there, rifles at their sides. They looked as confused as he did.

Another shout flickered through the hanging mist: "Fire in the barracks!"

Men began to turn, looking in befuddlement. Then flames could be seen, colored pink in the mist, leaping from the log barracks at the far corner diagonally from where Barclay was tied.

Moments later, Dunnigan had dashed off with his small troop in tow. The sound of orders being shouted drifted over Barclay, and soon the entire post was in action, heading toward the fire.

Then, Barclay sensed someone coming up behind him. Then he heard the voice of Private Klaus Schellenberger, his best friend at the fort.

As Schellenberger sliced through the ropes with a large knife, he spoke softly, but swiftly. "When I haff cut you loose, run for the stables. There is a large pile of olt hay. It's full of dung, but it's better than the alternative, yah?"

"Yep."

"Sometime after dark, I vill come for you."

"Long wait," Barclay said sarcastically. "Then what?"

"Then you vill get out of here."

"How?"

"Don't ask me that now."

"You start the fire?"

"Nein. Dot vas Jay Vatrous who did dot. I asked him to."

"I should've known that tall, skinny, disreputable feller'd be involved in this." Barclay felt the last of the rope fall away from him. He breathed a sigh of relief.

"Yah. Now go. I'll come for you tonight."

Barclay ran for the stables, thankful for the heavy mist. It would shroud him from prying eyes if anyone happened to look his way. Puffing, he stopped at the stables and made sure no one had remained there. No one had. With a feeling of distaste mingled with resignation, he burrowed into the fetid pile of urine-soaked, manure-tainted hay.

"What the hell've I gotten myself into now?" Barclay mused as he pulled the hay around him a little, so that it would look natural from the outside, and made himself a sort of a den there.

It was going to be a long day, and he did not look forward to it. On the other hand, even this fetid, stomach-turning haven was a lot better than the short future he had faced just minutes ago.

Sitting there in his stinking little cave, Barclay had plenty of time to contemplate the many wrongs he had committed in his short but active life. While he really did not regret any of the specific incidents, taken as a whole he knew he could have done a lot more with his life. Had he just used more common sense, he would not be in this predicament.

Much of his trouble—as he saw it—started when he had gotten to this dismal post almost three years ago. He had joined the army six months or so before that. He had been looking for adventure, and a chance to fight Indians. He had been regaled by his father and two uncles for as long as he could remember about the fighting during the war with the British back in 1812. So he had figured it was his turn. But the army had turned out to be a lot more boring than he had thought it would be. And so he began getting into trouble.

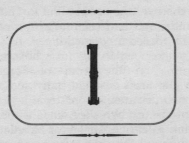

1

It was spring; anyone could tell that. The grass was sprouting, flowers were blooming, the trees along the Missouri River greening—and the young men's blood was running high.

After an overly long, dreadfully dull, bitterly cold winter, Miles Barclay was about fit to bust. So bust he did.

There had been nowhere to spend money during the snow-swamped winter, even if the men had been paid. But now the payroll had arrived, and Barclay was flush with cash. Well, as flush as he ever had been. When a small-time trader showed up at the fort two days later, Barclay bought a quart of whiskey from him at the "bargain" price of only ten dollars, after Barclay dickered him down from thirteen.

The whiskey was as bad as any Barclay had ever swallowed. It felt as if it were eroding his esophagus on the way down and his stomach when it got there. But he didn't care, he just guzzled it, sharing it with Schellenberger. The rotgut was as potent as it was rank, and by the time Barclay pitched the empty bottle away, he and Schellenberger were three sheets to the wind.

Feeling invincible, the two troopers began prowling the confines of the fort, singing poorly and looking for trouble wherever they could find it. They had been here for months and had seen no action of any kind, and they were primed for something.

It didn't take long to stir up a hornets' nest, the trouble coming in the form of Sergeant Sven Noordstrom, the fort's resident bully and already the bane of the two privates. Noordstrom had also gotten ahold of some putrid whiskey, and, while he wasn't quite as drunk as either Barclay or Schellenberger, he had had enough to make him even more cantankerous than usual.

It took perhaps thirty seconds of taunting by Barclay and Schellenberger before Sergeant Noordstrom flung himself at the two, opening the battle.

Noordstrom was a big man—six foot three and two twenty—which was the primary reason he had become a sergeant. While he could handle himself quite well in a brawl, Barclay and Schellenberger weren't so bad with such activities either.

The three soldiers scrabbled around in the dirt, punching and kicking. They stirred up a heap of dust, but, being as drunk as they all were, they did little damage to each other.

Finally, though, a squad of troops moved in and separated the combatants. A furious Captain Willard Pennington glared from one to another of the three, before fixing an angry stare on Barclay.

Pennington was a short, pudgy man who tried to make up for his lack of stature with a streak of meanness. He had an undeserved patrician air about him, with a face like week-old bread dough in consistency and color. He lacked respect for his men and held his superiors in barely restrained contempt. And for reasons unknown to Barclay—and probably to himself—Pennington had a particular loathing for Barclay.

"Won't you ever learn, you dumb bastard?" Pennington demanded, still glaring at Barclay.

Barclay was keenly aware of Pennington's deep dislike for him; he reciprocated the feeling, and then some. He had known immediately upon Pennington's fixing that baleful glare on him that he was going to be blamed for this entire incident. Because of that, he was in no mood to be polite. The rotgut whiskey still pulsing through his veins didn't do much for his judgment either.

"Not when I got an ass like you doin' the teachin'," Barclay retorted.

"That'll get you another fortnight in the guardhouse, Private," Pennington said with a sneer. "On top of the two weeks you're getting for starting this ruckus."

"What ruckus?"

"You opting for more time, stupid?"

Barclay shrugged. "Anytime I can knock the crap out of your sweetheart over there," he said, pointing to Sergeant Noordstrom, "is worth a little extra time in the guardhouse, Numb Nuts."

Noordstrom strained against the men holding him, trying to get at Barclay. The private grinned insolently at him.

"You're an even bigger fool than I thought, Barclay," Pennington said. "And that'll get you another week in the lockup." Pennington was not insulted by Barclay's insinuation, rather he was enjoying himself in heaping punishment on Barclay.

"I'm surprised you can think at all," Barclay said sullenly. Some of the alcohol was beginning to wear off, and his thinking, while still pretty muddled, was getting a little better. He realized he could not win this battle of words, and that annoyed him.

"Hope you like the idea of bread and water, Private," Pennington said, still relishing the moment. "Once a day. That's all you're going to get."

Barclay shrugged again. He had mostly come to

his senses, at least where this was concerned. Opening his mouth again was only going to get him in more trouble.

"Lost your power of speech suddenly, have you, Private?" Pennington gloated. He was disappointed when that drew no response from Barclay. "Take him away, men," he finally ordered. Then he looked at Private Schellenberger. "I think a month in the guardhouse is enough for you, Private." He paused. "Unless you'd like to try for more time, like your idiot friend."

"Nein," Schellenberger said carefully. He was about as drunk as Barclay had been, but some innate sense of self-preservation managed to keep him from worsening his situation.

"Too bad," Pennington muttered barely audibly. Aloud, he said, "Take him away, too."

"Vhat about him, Captain?" Schellenberger asked, pointing to Noordstrom.

"What about him?" Pennington countered.

"I vas just vonderink if he vas goink to be joinink mein freund und me in the guardhouse."

"Not that it's any of your business, Private, but why would you think that?"

Schellenberger had his answer. He shrugged. "Just vonderink."

"Well, I see no reason to chastise Sergeant Noordstrom for defending himself against two drunken louts."

With a shake of the head, Schellenberger turned and allowed himself to be escorted off by several soldiers.

The guardhouse was a dismal log building in one corner of the fort. Two of the walls also formed the walls of the fort itself. There were three cells, each separated by iron bars. The fronts of the cells were iron bars also. Each was equipped with a blanket on the packed-down dirt floor and a bucket for personal business. In front of the cells was an open area for the guards on duty. There was a battered desk, two cots, a rifle rack on one wall, and a set of keys hanging from a peg. Light was provided by several candle lanterns in wall sconces, and by sunlight coming through the cracks between the logs.

Barclay was in the far corner cell, and the guards put Schellenberger into the middle one.

"I don't suppose Noordstrom's followin' you?" Barclay questioned when all but the guard on duty had left.

Schellenberger snorted. "Not vith Captain Pompous runnink things."

"So I figured. How hard was he on you?"

"Just a month." Schellenberger grinned. "I had enough sense to keep mein mouth shut. Unlike somevon else I know."

Barclay nodded, ashamed now for the way he had acted. It was always so. He acted cockily and without thought during the heat of things. Then, when he had time to consider his actions, he almost always regretted what he had done, since it almost invariably had gotten him into deeper trouble. There was many a time he wished he was different, but he wasn't, and he knew that. He figured the best he could hope for was to someday learn how to control his impetuousness.

He sighed. There seemed to be little chance of even that, he thought, his whiskey-fogged brain still struggling for rational thought. He lay down on the dirt and pulled the blanket over him. He was asleep almost instantly.

Standing in the next cell, Schellenberger decided Barclay had the right idea. He, too, stretched out his long, sturdy frame and nodded off.

Barclay felt poorly in the morning, but not as bad as he had feared he would. He did hope that he looked better than he felt—and better than Schellenberger looked. The blunt German's eyes were bloodshot and puffy, and his nose laced with red. Barclay figured his face was about the same, and he was glad he didn't have to look at it himself.

Private Jay Watrous was the guard on duty, and he was the one who had roused Barclay and Schellenberger. Once he saw that they were awake, he brought them their breakfast.

Barclay took the tin plate and tin mug, then looked at Watrous in surprise. "What's with this?" he asked, nodding at the heap of bacon, biscuits and single egg, and the steaming coffee.

"You don't want it?" Watrous asked. He was almost as close a friend to Barclay as Schellenberger was.

"Hell, yes, I want it," Barclay said enthusiastically. "But Captain Numb Nuts said I was only going to get bread and water, and only once a day at that."

"You don't see that righteous fool standing here, do you?" Watrous asked rhetorically, grinning. He ran long, bone-like fingers through his long, lank hair. "And you can't find a half-dozen men on this entire post that'd give Pennington the time of day. You know that."

Barclay nodded, smiling a little despite the hangover.

"I don't know how much you can expect this, but when I'm on duty here you'll eat fairly well."

"I'm obliged, Jay," Barclay said sincerely.

"No need for that. Now eat up before Pennington shows up and takes your food away."

Barclay did so. As did Schellenberger in the cell next to him. Barclay felt considerably better with hot food and coffee in him, and he was determined to enjoy his forced vacation, even if it would be short—he didn't expect Pennington to let him sit here long. Not when he could be out on some work detail breaking his back in the warm spring sun. Still, he figured the Captain would let him languish for several days, allowing the boredom to set in.

Watrous gave him a deck of cards, and he and Schellenberger spent much of the next two days playing poker. When they weren't doing that, they generally were sleeping or just talking.

But, as Barclay knew, it didn't last. Four days after Barclay and Schellenberger were locked up, Pennington and a troop of ten soldiers stomped into the guardhouse. Barclay and Schellenberger were shackled to each other, with a four-foot length of chain from Barclay's left ankle to Schellenberger's right. Then the two were marched outside into the snapping sunlight, and down to the river. The rickety little wood pier that edged out into the water was sagging, and weeds and brush had partially covered it.

"The keelboats will be coming upriver soon," Pennington announced, as if everyone didn't know that. "Both those with supplies for us and those of the fur traders. In anticipation of their imminent arrival, the pier needs to be repaired, and the area around it cleared of weeds, brush and logs." He grinned rather devilishly. "That's where you two fools come in," he added. "To ensure that this punishment has some beneficial effect on your behavior, you will do this work."

"Going to be a little hard to do when me'n Klaus are chained together like this," Barclay said evenly. He was trying hard not to react in his usual manner to Pennington's goading.

"That's your problem, men," Pennington pronounced. His entire being seemed to exude smugness. "But you'll certainly have to learn to work together—in tandem, sort of like oxen or mules."

Pennington's grin infuriated Barclay, and he tried to contain his rage. But he could not. "You get any more goddamn pompous, you overstuffed bag of wind, and you'll likely explode," he snapped. "And then we'd all be covered in skunk shit."

The oily smile fell off Pennington's face. "That'll cost you another two weeks," he said, regaining some of his humor as he doled out more punishment. "Plus a month's pay."

Barclay shrugged, some of his usual cockiness returning. "Hell, General," he said sarcastically, "sooner or later we're gonna have to do some Injin fightin' or something, and you'll need all the troops you can find. You can't keep me locked up in the guardhouse or out here doing hard labor forever."

"We'll just see about that, Private," Pennington said with a satisfied smile. "Now get your asses to work, both of you," he commanded, suddenly trying to look stern.

"Go to—" Barclay started.

"Dot's enough, mein freund," Schellenberger said in his sonorous voice. "If you vant to get yourself into more trouble, dot is your business. But vhen you are chained to me, und your troublemaking also vill affect me, I must draw the line. So, now ve vork."

Barclay glared at his friend for only a moment, then nodded.

As the two clanked down the bank toward the pier, Schellenberger wondered again that they had ever become friends. The two were so different in so many ways. Where Barclay was a swaggering, smart-mouthed barbarian who seemed to have few, if any, cares in the world, the German was rather more intro-spective and quiet. Not that Schellenberger couldn't raise hell with the best of them; it was just that he didn't too often go out looking for trouble. Barclay seemed to court trouble, almost as if wooing a woman, starting slow, and coaxing it along until it flared into a bright white heat. There were too many times for

Schellenberger's liking that he had been burned in the flames Barclay had created. Because of that, Schellenberger had considered severing the friendship on numerous occasions, but he never did, since he found a sort of deranged comfort in Barclay's antics.

"Vell," Schellenberger said as they stopped along the water's edge, "vhere do ve start?"

"Hell if I know, Klaus," Barclay responded. "But I expect we ought to do something lest Numb Nuts over there gets all excited."

2

The work was hard on the two men, especially having to do it while chained together. But that was not the only problem with the labor. The river water was frigid, and the two had to spend a fair amount of time splashing around in it just off the bank, as they cleared out a winter's worth of debris that had collected among the rocks there. In addition, the bank was slick with mud, the brush often thorny, the logs heavy and unwieldy, and the mosquitoes thick and hungry.

Though it was yet early spring, the midday sun grew quite hot, and the humidity worsened the sun's effect. Twice in the next five days it rained for the better portion of the afternoon, drenching the two involuntary workers, and making their task even more perilous, what with the lightning and the freshly slicked mud.

The only bright spot—and a mighty small one at that—for Barclay and Schellenberger was the fact that they were left alone. They couldn't get far being chained together. Under the command of Captain Pennington, eight soldiers marched the two out every morning in full view of the rest of the fort, and left them to work. Pennington would show up now and again, to stand there up on the bank and gloat as he issued orders, all of them meaningless and given simply to humiliate Barclay and his friend a little more.

Each evening the small troop under Pennington's command arrived to escort the increasingly filthy prisoners back to the guardhouse. They were allowed to wash in the freezing river just before returning.

Pennington wondered how the two were faring so well on a diet of bread and water only once a day, at least in Barclay's case. He did not, of course, know that a number of the other soldiers who pulled duty at the guardhouse had, like Private Watrous, made sure they got some decent food in them.

Almost three weeks after they had started their enforced project, Barclay and Schellenberger spotted two large keelboats coming upriver. The two men had made considerable progress in clearing the pier, though they had not yet gotten around to repairing it. However, with the boats just about here, the rickety landing would have to suffice. Still, they had smoothed out the wide path up the bank, and packed brush into the slick mud to give visitors some traction on the walk.

Barclay and Schellenberger continued working, though they stopped for a few moments every now and then to check the keelboats' progress. It was slow, and Barclay figured the low, heavily loaded, curved-bow boats wouldn't arrive until well into the afternoon.

They weren't the only ones who had noted the keelboats coming, and soon any men who were not on duty began lining the bank to watch the boats. The cordellers strained against the ropes, walking along the shore when they could, or in the bitterly cold water when they couldn't. Barclay was amazed—as he had been every time he had seen a keelboat being towed up the river that way—at the strength and endurance of the cordellers. Now that was truly backbreaking work, he thought, and he regretted having felt a little sorry for himself with the work he and Schellenberger had been doing here.

"Come on, Miles," Schellenberger said, tugging on Barclay's sleeve at the shoulder. "Ve better get back to vork."

Barclay glanced at his friend, and behind Schellenberger he could see many soldiers lining the bank. While most of the enlisted men and even the lower-ranked NCOs were friendly to them, there were always a few who disliked them and would take any opportunity to report them for not working. He nodded.

The two men having been shackled together for three weeks now, they were pretty adept at their work, and their labors went more smoothly. Still, they took time once in a while to check on the keelboats. Finally the two ungainly vessels were there, and Barclay and Schellenberger stepped back. The cordellers tied the two boats up and then scattered along the bank, keeping mostly to themselves.

Colonel Leavenworth, with a troop of soldiers and officers—including Captain Willard Pennington—came down to the makeshift wharf to greet the traders.

The first one off the *Yellowstone Packet* was General William Ashley himself. He was a rugged, fierce-looking man with a thick, neatly trimmed beard. He was dressed in dark wool pants and short matching jacket. All in all, Barclay thought, Ashley cut an imposing and authoritative figure.

Even more imposing to Barclay, though, were the men who followed Ashley off the *Yellowstone Packet* and the *Rocky Mountains*. Nearly all of them were men who had made the journey upriver with Ashley the year before. They were a rough-looking lot, almost savage in appearance. Most of them ignored the two military prisoners standing there, just off the wide path leading up the bank toward the fort on the bluff. But one stopped. "What the hell did ye two fellers do to be in chains sich as ye are?" he asked.

"Got drunk and kicked the living bejesus out of a

damn fool sergeant," Barclay said with a full dose of his old arrogance.

"And so they locked ye up?" the old man—one of only a couple over the age of twenty-five along on the expedition—cackled.

"Captain Pennington is a right pain in my ass, and is out to get me," Barclay said flatly.

"Sounds like a cursed devil to me," the man said.

"He's that for damn sure."

"What's your name, young feller?"

"Miles Barclay. My chain-mate here is Klaus Schellenberger."

"Pleased to make your acquaintance, boys," the man said. He held out his hand and shook with each of the two prisoners. Despite his age, his grip was strong. "Name's Jethro Greathouse."

"You're a mite long in the tooth for such an expedition as going to the Upper Missouri, ain't you?" Barclay said with some guile.

"What would ye rather have me do, sonny?" Greathouse asked. The high, wavering cackle had been replaced by a deep, more serious tone. "Set on a rocker somewhere watchin' the pigs waller or some sich?"

"Well—"

"Hell, sonny, I been trappin' now for nigh onto forty years. From the Chattahootchie country and the Smoky Mountains to the headwaters of the Mississippi. I don't know nothin' else. So's when I heared General Ashley was headin' to country I ain't ary seed afore—and country that's jist teemin' with beaver and sich, or so's I heared—I jist had to join up. He seemed right pleased to have an experienced hand with him."

"I still think you're too old for such a thing," Barclay said. It was not really accusatory; it was more curiosity.

Greathouse laughed. "Damn, sonny, wait'll ye git to be my age—if ye ary make it that fur. Mayhap ye'll

understand then. Now, I admit I'm minus a many of
my teeth now, and my joints ache more than occasional, but I still got a prime man's juices in me, sonny,
and don't ye doubt it."

"I can see you're a hardy old fart," Barclay said
with a partial grin. "But why ain't you takin' your
leisure somewhere, instead of takin' on such a trip?
I've heard it's a mite dangerous up that way."

"Well, it's like this, sonny," Greathouse said
calmly, "I'd rather go to meet my Maker from a Ree
arrer or a Pawnee lance than sittin' on my ass dyin' a
little bit at a time."

That made some sense to Barclay, but he had no
time right now to give it any real thought. "Ain't you
afraid of those Injins out there?" Barclay asked, a little
surprised. "Everything I've ever heard about them says
they're pretty fierce."

Greathouse shrugged. "Nah, I ain't afraid. I ain't
ary met any of those Innians, but I've fought some
pretty hard Innians afore. Shawnee, Creek, Choctaw,
and more. Them Innians out west where we're goin'
cain't be no more fiercer than them I've fought
already."

"I suppose that's a fact." Barclay grinned. "It's
why I joined the army, for chrissakes. To fight Injins."

"Ain't gonna do much of that whilst ye're shackled for whuppin' up on folks who hold the power over
ye, boy," Greathouse said in not unfriendly tones.

"Ach!" Schellenberger said, speaking for the first
time. "Dot's the truth. If mein fruend here vould learn
to keep his mouth shut, he—und I—vouldn't be in
trouble so much."

"I'll tell ye boys somethin'," Greathouse offered.
"Was I ye, I'd take all the shit them boys can heap on
ye, and grin through it all. Then, soon's your enlist-
ments're up, ye hightail it outta here."

"To where?" Barclay asked, intrigued.

"Hell, the general can always use new men. He's an ambitious feller, he is. Got him all sorts of plans fer makin' money and sich. And even if he didn't want to hire ye on, there's a heap of other companies castin' their eyes to the west in search of their fortunes. Ain't no reason I can see why a couple eager young fellers like ye cain't join in."

Barclay nodded. That had certainly got his brain oiled, and he couldn't think of anything to say right now. But at least he had plenty to think about.

Greathouse took a look around. Most of the mountain men were gone, as were the soldiers. He grinned and eased a small bottle of whiskey out from under his blood- and grease-stained deerskin shirt. "Ye boys got a mite of a thirst?" he asked.

"Hell, yes," Barclay said, licking his lips.

"Yah vold," Schellenberger threw in.

Greathouse slipped Barclay the bottle. "Ye fellers enjoy that hooch now," he said as he turned and headed up the bank.

Barclay watched Greathouse in wonder for a few moments. He had never met anyone quite like the crusty old trapper.

"Vell, open dot bottle, mein freund," Schellenberger said impatiently, breaking Barclay's concentration.

Barclay grinned and jerked the cork out of the bottle. Looking around to make sure no one was watching, he took a healthy swallow and then handed the bottle to Schellenberger. Each got three drinks out of it before it was empty. Schellenberger, grinning, pitched the bottle into the rushing waters of the river, sailing it out over the top of the *Yellowstone Packet*. Then the two went back to work.

The trapping expedition stayed in camps outside the fort for three days, but then they shoved off. Barclay and Schellenberger were again toiling along the riverbank, covered with mud and mosquitoes.

Greathouse stopped by for a bit to say farewell to them.

Barclay had done some thinking since he and Greathouse had talked the other day, but he had made no decisions. He did, however, come up with a few questions. One of which he asked now: "Why're you takin' such an interest in us?" he asked.

Greathouse's face darkened a little, and Barclay could not tell if it was from sadness or anger, or maybe both. "I'm a feller don't take kindly to folks askin' me questions," he said evenly.

But Barclay was not to be put off. "That might be, but it's mighty queersome for an old feller like yourself to be kindly to a couple of boys he don't know, men who're doin' hard labor for crimes against the army." The last was exaggerated a little bit, but Barclay figured that was all right under the circumstances.

A smile twitched at the corners of Greathouse's thin lips. "Reckon it is at that," he said in a voice so soft Barclay was not sure he had actually heard him. Greathouse shook his head, as if trying to clear away an unwelcome memory. "Fer some reason, I saw ye two, and ye reminded me of my sons, though I cain't say why. Ye don't look like them or anything. Maybe it's jist an ol' coot comin' up lonely bein' so far from home and hearth."

"I didn't know a man like you would have a home," Barclay said. "No insult meant," he hastily added when he saw the old man's eyes darken. "It's just that I thought with you bein' a trapper and all that you'd never had time to settle down and have a real home."

Greathouse nodded. "That's a reasonable assumption, I reckon. But I did. Had me a fine wife, raised us seven chillens—five girls and two boys."

"And where are they now?" Barclay realized as soon as he asked it that it was probably the wrong thing to ask of any man.

"My Beth, she passed on twelve year ago, I reckon it were. Life's harder on a woman, ye know." His voice came from a far away, long ago place. "She caught the gallopin' consumption and was took from me. My daughters now, they're all married, to good men, though I still got some doubts about Sarah's feller. My boys, though, they're with their Ma. One of 'em was kilt by a Shawnee raidin' party a year or so afore his Ma was took from us. The other'n—Jethro Junior—he was kilt by the Limeys when we cleart them bastards out of N'Orleans back in 'fourteen."

"Und dot's vhy you showed me und Miles some kindness, isn't it?" Schellenberger asked in a quiet voice. It made sense. He was only twenty-four, and Barclay a year younger. He could see how someone like Greathouse, in a momentary flash of melancholy, might bestow a little friendship on a couple of suffering young men who were perhaps close to the ages of his sons when they died.

Greathouse nodded. "Yep." He spit out some tobacco juice, which seemed to shake him out of his reverie. "Anyway, ye boys mind what I told ye. If ye don't ye'll keep gittin' in dutch, and ye'll nary git out of here. But ye mind yer manners around the chiefs—big'ns and little'ns—ye'll come to the end of sich onerous duty and can git on with makin' somethin' of yer lives."

"It ain't gonna be easy, old-timer," Barclay said. "But I'll give it a try."

"Farewell, boys," Greathouse said, grinning. He had returned to his rightful self.

"Goot-bye, mein herr," Schellenberger said more solemnly than the situation called for.

"You watch yourself out there in them wilds, old man," Barclay said irreverently. It was his way. Despite having a favorable opinion of Greathouse, he had always found it difficult to express any kind of sentimentality. "I'd hate to hear you was killed out there before I had an opportunity to repay you for that little gift you give me and Klaus the other day."

Greathouse looked back and grinned. "I jist might hold ye to that pledge, there, sonny. When we come back this way next spring with our load of peltries." He waved and hurried off. Moments later he had jumped onto the deck of the *Rocky Mountains*, and then the two keelboats were pulled away from the bank by the straining cordellers.

3

Barclay had plenty of time to think about what Greathouse had said, and about his future. Especially when his good friend Klaus Schellenberger was released from his punishment about a week after the keelboats had pulled out. Now working alone, Barclay kept on with the project of repairing the wharf. Since he was by himself, he was now chained at one ankle. At the other end of the six-foot length of forged chain was a fifty-pound iron ball, ensuring that he would not make any attempt to escape.

While he liked Schellenberger considerably, Barclay began to enjoy his solitary labors. It made him attached to no one—in more senses than just the physical. He considered what the old trapper had said to him, and he vowed silently to make the effort to watch his tongue, especially around Pennington. He did have enough sense, however, to know that such a thing was far easier to promise than to actually put into practice.

He managed pretty well, swallowing the insults directed at him by both Captain Pennington and Sergeant Noordstrom. That surprised the NCO and the officer, and finally Pennington just had to ask about it. He waited until the day Barclay was to be released after completing his sentence, though.

When Barclay stepped outside the guardhouse

unshackled for the first time in a month and a half, he was feeling pretty good. He could feel the juices rising in him, and he wanted to shout and holler—and cause trouble. He had to fight the latter feeling.

Pennington was waiting for him outside the guardhouse. Arrayed behind him was most of the company he commanded. Barclay smiled and waved at the troops. A few of the men grinned back. Pennington was not amused. "You're a disgrace," Pennington snapped. "A filthy, high-smelling reprobate. An affront to every soldier who takes pride in himself and in his call to duty."

Barclay bit back—literally—the retort that was ready to burst forth, clamping his teeth on his lower lip until it bled.

"Nothing to say, Private?" Pennington said with a sneer.

"No, sir," Barclay said, mostly evenly.

Pennington's eyebrows arched high in surprise. "I can't believe it," he finally said.

"It's true, sir," Barclay said, now trying to keep from vomiting at his subservience.

"Well I'll be damned," Pennington said with a whistle.

"You sure will," Barclay said so low that no one but Private Watrous standing just behind him heard. Watrous stifled a chuckle.

"What's brought this on?" Pennington asked smugly. He had won, and that pleased him. It also opened the opportunity to heap more abuse on Barclay, only this time without being sassed in return. It had always annoyed him that Barclay had continually gotten the better of him in their verbal exchanges. Maybe now that wouldn't happen.

"I had a heap of time for reflectin' on my ways," Barclay said truthfully. Then he deviated from honesty a little bit. "And I realized I was only hurtin' myself with my poor behavior." He nearly gagged on the words.

Barclay caught Schellenberger's eyes, and the German nodded just a bit. He knew what Barclay was up to, and he approved of it. He also knew how difficult it was for his friend, and he was proud of Barclay for at least trying.

"My, my, my," Pennington said sarcastically, "even an idiot like you can make an intelligent decision now and again."

"Yessir." The word almost stuck in Barclay's craw, but he got it out.

"Of course, now I'm in something of a quandary as to what to do about you. Seeing as how your uniform is in such disarray, I should put you on report and toss you back in the guardhouse." Pennington was enjoying himself immensely. "However, since your previous punishment seems to have taught you a lesson or two, I'm inclined to be a bit kind-hearted. What do you say, Private?"

"The decision is all yours, sir, but I'm sure you'll make the right one." A few more sentences like that, Barclay thought, and I'll be back in the hoosegow, since I ain't gonna make many more of them. It's either that or I'll get sick to my stomach.

"Well," Pennington said pompously, as if he were making a great and beneficent decision, "I'll give you three hours to make yourself presentable and get back in the ranks."

"Yessir," Barclay said, almost relieved. He had figured that Pennington was going to continue his insulting statements and questions for a while. "Since time is short, may I be dismissed, sir?"

"Why, yes," Pennington said, a little befuddled. He had been certain that Barclay's new attitude was a ruse and that he was saving up some nasty comments for the end. It confused the officer when that did not happen.

Barclay hurried off, nearly running toward his barracks, before Pennington could think up something else to try to goad him into causing himself more trouble. Inside, he sat a moment on his cot, looking down at himself. Pennington had been right about at least one thing—he was a disgrace. His uniform pants and blouse were ripped—almost shredded—and covered with mud and spots of blood. There was no way he could get the uniform into serviceable shape, whether in three hours or three months. And he had no other uniform. He had lost his extra one in a card game over the winter. It had been a foolish thing to do, but that had never stopped him before and it most likely wouldn't stop him in the future.

"That son of a bitch!" he suddenly muttered, jerking his head up. He realized that Pennington knew he had no extra uniform and this was another torment. Barclay figured that either Sergeant Noordstrom or one of the few privates in the company that were of his ilk must have told the officer.

Once Barclay figured this out, he also knew that Pennington's magnanimous gesture was a double-edged sword. It would make the officer look good in front of the men, and it was guaranteed to get Barclay into trouble again.

"We'll just see about that, Numb Nuts," he muttered. With a determined look, he headed toward Private John Beecher's cot. Beecher was one of the few men he did not get along with, and he and Beecher were about the same size.

Barclay knelt at Beecher's padlocked wood storage locker. Pulling out a small folding knife, he opened it and then probed the lock's keyhole with the point of the blade. It took nearly fifteen minutes of patient work, but at last the lock popped open. With a nod, he folded the knife and put it away before lifting the top of the locker.

Barclay grinned when he saw the neatly folded uniform. Beecher also had an extra muslin shirt there, as well as a clean pair of socks. There was nothing Barclay could do about his boots, since no one seemed to have an extra pair, but the uniform and shirt would do. He picked them up, trying not to rub them against his own filthy uniform.

Closing the locker lid but leaving it unlocked, he headed out and down to the river. A small cove was the place where most of the soldiers came to wash off—on those infrequent times they did bathe. Here the water pooled up to four feet deep over a pebbled bottom. It would have made a much better place to moor the keelboats that came up and down the river, except that it was far too small to allow those ungainly craft in.

Barclay stripped down and plunged into the bitterly cold water. He scrubbed himself swiftly but vigorously with the cake of lye soap he had brought along, and then hurried out of the water. He was grateful that the trees around the cove kept out most of the wind. The warm sun soon dried him, and he dressed in his pilfered uniform. Since his old uniform was unsalvageable, he pitched it into the brush nearby, then he headed back toward the barracks.

He had planned to leave his filthy old uniform in Beecher's locker, which was why he had left the wood box unlocked. But he realized while performing his ablutions that such a thing would be foolish. If he did that, everyone would know for certain that he had done it. But if the uniform simply disappeared, that was another story. Everyone might suspect him, but they would have a hell of a time proving it.

Barclay lay down on his cot and napped for an hour before rising and going out to meet the rest of his company. The men were repairing a guard tower that had been blown over during the winter. Barclay marched up to Pennington and saluted smartly, reporting in.

Pennington's jaw almost hit the dusty ground, and then he gave Noordstrom a dirty look. Suddenly worried, Noordstrom shrugged, indicating that he didn't know how Barclay had managed to pull it off.

"All right, Private," Pennington said a little sullenly, "join the men."

"Yessir." Barclay saluted again and then turned. As he walked away, he thought, Got you again, Numb Nuts.

"Take your place alongside your friend Private Schellenberger," Lieutenant Doug Hodges said. Hodges was a young man—not much older than Barclay—but he seemed calm and reasoned far beyond his years. His face, reddened by the sun already, was long and narrow and his ears stuck out almost at right angles to his head.

Barclay had often felt sorry for Hodges. Captain Pennington treated the young officer almost as poorly as he treated the enlisted men. In an unusual arrangement, Sergeant Noordstrom wielded more power in D Company than did Hodges, who was, at least nominally, the second in command.

Yet Barclay had never known Hodges to complain or cause any trouble about it. Because of that, Barclay also admired the young officer, wishing he could handle himself like Hodges since the two endured basically the same circumstances. Barclay had finally come to decide that Hodges acted the way he did because Pennington held his military career in his hands. The wrong word or two in the right ears would ensure Hodges of a career as a lieutenant stationed on posts even more obscure than this one, if such a thing even existed. Barclay could not blame him.

"Vhere'd you get the clothes, Miles?" Schellenberger asked as Barclay fell into step alongside his friend, heading out the gate of the fort.

"I commandeered 'em," Barclay answered with a grin.

Schellenberger returned the smile. "Whose?"

Barclay took a quick look around. "Johnny Beecher."

"A goot choice," Schellenberger said in agreement.

"I thought so."

The two had easily fallen into a pattern of work, since they were long used to doing so. They walked side by side out of the fort to where the lumber crew had cut timber. They would each heft an end of the log and march back into the post. They did most of their talking on the trip out, since it would mean shouting when they were at opposite ends of a log on the return.

"Are you goink to keep up this beink-goot act?" Schellenberger asked as they began another trek.

"If I can," Barclay said with a grimace. "But I ain't so sure that's possible. Christ, I thought I'd puke my guts up before when I was doin' it."

"You did goot, though."

"I suppose. But I just know that bastard's going to ride me constantly, just tryin' to get a rise out of me."

"So?"

"So, Numb Nuts is going to say somethin' sooner or later that I just won't be able to ignore. Then I'm going to have to kill him."

"Hah!" Schellenberger said with a short laugh. "You haff kilt nobody in the first place, und you should save your thoughts of killink for the Indians."

"Fat chance we got of doin' that," Barclay grumbled. "We been here more than a year and the only Injins we've seen is some poor ol' Ioways, who couldn't hurt a bug even if they wanted to, and them Sioux. They were tough-lookin' boys, for sure, but they're at peace with us."

They grabbed a log and jerked it off the ground, each letting it settle on a shoulder. They walked at a good pace to the fort and set the log down.

"They vouldn't haff built this fort here if they didn't think there'd be some need to control the Indians," Schellenberger said on their way out again.

"Hell, Klaus, I think they put this shithole here just to get rid of misfits like me and you. And Numb Nuts."

"You think dot's true?" Schellenberger asked, face serious.

"I don't know what the hell I think any more, my friend. When I got sent out here, I thought I was goin' to some wild and woolly place where there was all kinds of ferocious animals and wild savages to fight. But we ain't done diddly since we got here except repair buildings and sit on our asses all the goddamn winter. Hell, the closest thing we come to an Injin fight was the time last summer when them Pawnees showed up, and that one boy got himself some rotgut and then tried to provoke the whole garrison into fightin' him."

"Dot vas funny," Schellenberger said with a grin.

"Come to think of it, it was, wasn't it?" Barclay smiled.

"Maybe us beink here has scared avay all the hostile Indians, Miles," Schellenberger mused.

"It's more like they all come downriver for a look-see, got an eyeful of what poor devils we are as a fightin' force and went back up the river where they're sittin' now laughin' at us."

Schellenberger looked around, taking in the laboring men. "Yah. I think maybe you're right about dot. This is a sorry lookink excuse for an army."

"That it is. I've come to think that the Sioux've been friendly toward us because they don't consider us worth fightin'."

"Dot could be. Und if it is, I hope they continue to have such thoughts toward us, mein freund. Because if they decide to be unfriendly, they could ride over this fort vithout a thought."

Barclay looked sharply at his friend. He had never

considered such a thing before, but now that he did, the thought gave him chills. "That'd be a hell of a lot more Injin fightin' than I'd want to see in my life, let alone at one time."

"Yah. For me, too. But, you see, Miles, dot maybe you don't vant to wish too much to do some Indian fighting. You might get a lot more of it than you bargained for."

Barclay laughed, not really worried about the possibility. Facing too many Indians was just too outlandish a thought to even consider. "At least that'd be better than wanderin' around here like this haulin' logs," he said with his usual bravado.

4

Barclay's subservience lasted eight days—longer than anyone, including himself, had expected it would. But by then he had had enough of such nonsense. Mainly because Captain Pennington and Sergeant Noordstrom had ridden him so hard, trying to make him crack. The insults, insinuations, and assignments to the worst duty were nearly constant.

It was a card game, though, that was the last straw. Barclay and several other men were playing euchre in a corner of their barracks one rainy evening. A sputtering candle spread a sparse light over the blanket that held the men's wagers—money, tobacco, whatever small personal items they thought they could afford to lose.

Barclay had just raked in a meager pot when Noordstrom lumbered up behind him. "Private Barclay," the sergeant rumbled, "report to Corporal Vanderplaas. The stables need mucking out."

"I'm busy," Barclay said tentatively, still trying to retain his calm and his reasonable demeanor.

"Too goddamn bad, boy. Now move it."

"Eat shit and die, Numb Nuts," Barclay snapped.

With an angry snort, Noordstrom grabbed Barclay by the collar and jerked him backward.

Barclay rolled and came up onto a knee, hands up in a defensive posture.

Noordstrom just stood there, though, making no move to attack. He laughed. "Think you're a tough one, do you, boy?" he said with a smirk.

Barclay rose slowly. "Tough enough to take you, Numb Nuts," he said with just a touch of his old arrogance in his voice.

"Let's say we just test that, eh, you little toad," Noordstrom said in challenge.

The smugness on the sergeant's face whisked away any remaining wisps of determination to stay on the straight and narrow that Barclay might've had left. "Best get some help," he retorted.

"Just what I wanted to hear," Noordstrom said, flexing his bull-like shoulders. "Damn, I'm going to enjoy this. First I get to kick your ass around the barracks for a while, then I get to punish you, too." He smiled, and then sighed in exaggerated pleasure. "What more could a sergeant ask for?"

"You could ask for some help, Numb Nuts," Barclay cracked.

Noordstrom laughed. "You're the one needs help, boy," he said easily.

"And he'll get it, too," Schellenberger said, rising.

The other soldiers followed the big German's lead, until all five of them were arrayed against Noordstrom, who was beginning to look just a little bit concerned.

"No," Barclay said a little urgently. "You boys sit back down. This here's between chicken dick and me. There's no call for you to get yourself in dutch because of me."

"Hell," Schellenberger said with a small laugh, "ve don't need you to get into trouble. Ve can do just fine by ourselves."

"All the same, this one ain't your fight."

"We'll decide what's our fight and what ain't," Watrous said, with his usual logic.

"Don't you try'n butter me up, my friend," Barclay

said a little sarcastically. "Numb Nuts here and his bug-gerin' boss're gonna do what they want to me, no matter what you all do. There's no reason you boys should get caught up in the crossfire."

"You going to do something, Barclay?" Noordstrom asked with a sneer. "Or are you just going to stand there and jaw with your friends all night?"

Barclay charged. His right shoulder hit Noordstrom in the midsection, and he drove the sergeant back until he slammed up against the wall. Then he straightened fast, and jerked Noordstrom forward, sweeping his feet out from underneath him.

Noordstrom fell. So surprised had he been by Barclay's strength, that he had found himself unable to react right away. The next thing he knew, he was on the floor, with Barclay looming over him. He finally managed to regain his fighting sense, and kicked the private in the stomach as Barclay moved to jump on top of him.

Barclay's breath burst out, and he staggered to the side a few steps, before stopping. He had his breath back, though, by the time Noordstrom was on his feet and moving toward him. Still he played possum, hop-ing to lull the sergeant. It worked, too, as Noordstrom, thinking he now had the upper hand, came toward him unwarily. Barclay suddenly snapped upward and swung a fist, with most of his body behind the punch.

Noordstrom's nose splattered, and he was stopped cold. He hung there in the air, eyes somewhat glazed.

Barclay stepped up, turned Noordstrom so he faced the door and walked him some steps toward it. "Somebody want to open the door?" he asked almost cheerily. When Watrous had done so, Barclay stepped back, place a boot sole on Noordstrom's buttocks, and then shoved as hard as he could.

Noordstrom stumbled forward, out the door and

then fell with a splat in a big, muddy puddle that had pooled just outside the building.

A moment later, a livid Captain Willard Pennington stormed into the barracks room. "Just what the hell is going on here?" he roared, trying to make up in volume and vehemence what he did not possess in command and authority.

"Nothing, sir," Barclay said pleasantly, looking as innocent as a choir boy.

"What the hell do you mean, nothing?" Pennington demanded. "My top sergeant is lying outside in a mud puddle with the door of this barracks open, and you say nothing is going on?"

"Oh, that," Barclay said off-handedly. "Nothing wrong, sir." His face looked perfectly innocent. "Sergeant Noordstrom and the rest of us were discussin' the unusual weather of the day, sir, when the Sergeant decided to step outside and see if the storm had worsened. He stumbled and fell. He must've hit his head on the ground."

Schellenberger, Watrous and the others were trying with limited success to suppress chuckles.

Pennington was acutely aware of the fact that the men were being amused at his and Noordstrom's expense, and that only served to anger him all the more. "You are a goddamn liar, Private Barclay," he said tightly. "And a damn poor one at that."

"That so, sir?" Barclay asked, still playing the innocent to the hilt.

"That is. I—" Pennington stopped and turned as Noordstrom, helped by two soldiers, entered the room.

The NCO was drenched, but much of the blood from his battered nose had been washed away in the puddle and rain. He still looked a little dazed.

"Ah, Sergeant," Pennington said with a nod. "Private Barclay was just telling me how you went outside to check the weather and fell, almost knocking yourself out in the process. Is that what happened?"

"Hell, no . . . sir," Noordstrom said adamantly.

"So I thought. Just what did happen, Sergeant?"

"I ordered Private Barclay to report to Corporal Vanderplaas, as you had told me to do, sir." He seemed to be regaining some of his strength. "Private Barclay argued the point. When I went to take corrective action, he sucker-punched me and shoved me outside."

Barclay smiled in self-deprecation. "Is there no limit to how far you'll sink, Numb Nuts?" he asked sarcastically.

Noordstrom looked as if he had been suddenly slapped. "A sucker-punch is the only way a pipsqueak like you could ever knock me down," he said stiffly. Even in his lingering daze he realized he had made a serious error in telling the story the way he had. Now he wanted to save face, and was fairly certain that it wouldn't work, not with the men anyway. But Pennington might buy into it, which was the more important matter.

"Well, Private?" Pennington asked.

"Well what, sir?" Barclay countered.

"What do you have to say about this?" Pennington asked, trying to rein in his annoyance.

"I think Numb Nuts there is makin' up a story so he doesn't have to explain how a little feller like me knocked the bejesus out of him," Barclay answered blandly. "Sir."

"If I didn't think you'd consider it a victory, I'd have you run out of the army, Private," Pennington said tightly. "You have been no end of trouble for me and the other good men of D Company."

"You wouldn't know a good man if one come up and bit you on the pecker," Barclay said evenly. Suddenly he grinned. "Then, again, you probably would," he added.

It took a moment—and the enlisted men's laughter—before Pennington caught on to what Barclay had said. "Why you scurrilous bastard," he breathed, nostrils flared in humiliation and anger. "You're under arrest, and will be kept in the guardhouse until I can decide whether to shoot you or hang you."

"Ah, the problems of rank and privilege," Barclay said scornfully.

"Make your little jokes now, Private," Pennington snapped, trying to regain control over his emotions. "You won't have long to enjoy them." He looked over the rest of the group. "As for you others, you won't escape punishment."

"They ain't done anything," Barclay said calmly.

"Then you accept full responsibility for what happened here?" Pennington demanded, pleased at having boxed Barclay in.

"For what? Kicking the crap out of Numb Nuts there?" Barclay smirked. "Sure, I take responsibility for that, sir. Hell, I don't need their help to dispose of the likes of him."

Pennington saw red, and he said nothing for a while as he both tried to get control of himself and figure out how Barclay could keep playing him for a fool like he did. It was infuriating. Finally he felt able to talk. "So they had no part in today's fracas?"

"No, sir, none whatsoever," Barclay lied without a qualm.

Pennington suspected Barclay was lying, but he wasn't sure it was worth quibbling over at the moment. Barclay was his nemesis anyway; the others were mere accomplices at best, followers led like sheep. "Sergeant, are you sufficiently recovered to see to Private Barclay's arrest?" he asked over his shoulder.

"Yessir," Noordstrom said eagerly. It gave him a boost of strength and energy.

"Then see to it."

"Yessir." Noordstrom shrugged off the two men who had been helping him. "What about the others, sir?"

Pennington shrugged. "Did they have any part in today's events?"

Noordstrom was about to launch into the story of how they had threatened him, lining up with Barclay against him. But before he could open his mouth, he wisely realized that making such a statement would do nothing to advance his cause in Pennington's eyes. Even with his aching nose and head he knew it was better to keep this one to himself, lest he look like a bigger fool than he already did. "No, sir," he said evenly, but his eyes burned in the direction of Schellenberger, Watrous and the others.

"Fine. Well, Sergeant, go about your duty." He glared at the enlisted men for some moments before turning and heading for the door.

"Private Watrous," Noordstrom ordered, feeling as if he were back in command again, "go get me some shackles."

"What for?" Watrous asked astutely. "So you can beat the crap out of Miles on the way over to the guardhouse when he has no chance to defend himself?"

Pennington stopped at the doorway and turned back. He had not thought of such a thing, but it sounded like a good idea to him. From the eager tension he could see in Noordstrom's back, he figured the notion was not lost on the Sergeant either. Now all they needed was a reasonable response for Watrous, and then he could allow Noordstrom to take care of things.

Barclay could see the thought taking hold inside Noordstrom, but he was not too worried. "Even you can't be that damned stupid, can you, Numb Nuts?" he inquired. He expected no response to that, so he just continued. "The only place you'll be able to do that is outside between here and the guardhouse, or in the guardhouse itself. Either place, there'll be plenty of witnesses, not all of them from D Company. And that won't sit real well in some quarters. It could hurt your career, you know, and the Captain's, too."

As soon as Pennington heard it, he knew Barclay was right. Shaking his head in annoyance, he headed outside into the rain. He would leave this decision with Noordstrom. If the Sergeant was stupid enough not to realize the truth in it, too, then Pennington didn't want him around.

Noordstrom might not have been brilliant, but he was cunning enough to see the trap here. "The hell with the shackles," he growled. He grinned maliciously. "Of course, it won't make any difference. If I wanted to pound you, I wouldn't need you chained to do it."

"Shit, Numb Nuts, you'd need me chained and have four other toads just like you to help."

Noordstrom shrugged, but his grin grew. "Besides, boy, you ain't going to be a bother to me and the Captain much longer. He'll make good on his promise to see you meet your Maker. And the sooner the better, I say."

"I think I'll wait till it happens before I start worryin' about it."

"I await the day. Now move. And, asshole, don't try running."

"Where the hell could I run even if I was so inclined?" Barclay snorted. "You think I'm gonna try to run to the guardhouse to beat you there?"

"Who knows what a fool like you'd think to do," Noordstrom said. "Now, let's go."

With a shrug—and a grin toward his friends— Barclay headed out into the rain and the gloom.

5

Barclay languished in his cell for several days, wondering just how long Pennington would let him rot here before letting him go. He did not—could not—believe the officer was serious when he had talked of having Barclay hanged or shot. Still, he could not be absolutely sure where Captain Willard Pennington was concerned.

He was, in some ways, grateful to be locked up. Spring was well advanced now, it being almost June, and so the heat and humidity could be mighty oppressive. While it wasn't exactly cool inside the guardhouse, he at least wasn't outside drilling on the parade ground or working at any one of the many jobs that needed doing around the fort. He was a little surprised that Pennington hadn't put him on hard labor again, but he accepted it with relief and he planned to enjoy it however long it lasted.

Since he was friendly with most of the enlisted men on the post, he was rarely without a little company. He and the guards, or whoever was in the cell next to him, would spend the day playing cards or talking, mainly trying to one-up each other with their tales of adventure. Most of those tales were made up of whole cloth, since the men were young yet and had not really had the time nor the opportunity for much real adventure.

But numbing boredom soon became the dominant factor in his stay in the guardhouse. There were only so many card games a man could play, only so many lies a man could make up before he started repeating himself. Within three days of being confined in the guardhouse, Barclay was beginning to wish that he was on hard labor. At least that would get him outside some, and keep him from this stultifying tedium.

It was another three days, though, before Barclay got any relief. Pennington, Noordstrom and a troop of six men arrived at the guardhouse and ordered the soldier on duty to unlock Barclay's cell.

"Well?" Barclay asked cockily, "Are you gonna hang me or shoot me?"

"I haven't decided yet. Until I do, I'm going to work you like a dog. Within a week you'll be begging me to end your misery." Pennington had regained his humor, and with the prospect of further humiliating and debasing Barclay, he actually was in a fine mood.

Noordstrom wasn't quite so cheerful. His nose was still swollen and the skin around it puffy and discolored. The area just under his eyes was the most mottled, showing a variety of sickly hues.

Barclay laughed. "The only thing I'd ever beg you for, Numb Nuts," he said, "is to have you keep that hideous sot of a wife of yours away from me."

Pennington blanched, and raised his hand as if to strike Barclay. Then he thought better of it. Humor soured, he growled, "Shackle his ankles."

Over the next three days, Barclay dug pit trenches for latrines, while filling in others that were filled almost to overflowing. He also mucked out the stalls, and cleaned more areas along the river. All the jobs were filthy and hard; they stank and were accompanied by hordes of insects.

No matter how bad the tasks were, though,
Barclay was determined right from the beginning that
he would not complain. He did well with it, too, past-
ing on a smile and allowing his natural arrogance to
shine through whenever Pennington or Noordstrom
was around.

He worked steadily, but took his time. He knew
that the quicker he finished each job, the sooner he
would be assigned another. So he worked, slowly
enough to annoy Pennington, but not so ploddingly
that Pennington could really say much about it.

The boredom of his labors was broken on the second day by the arrival in the area of several thousand
Sioux, who had come to trade. They camped a mile or
so off, so that the Indians and soldiers would not be
able to mingle too much. As the Indians moved in and
out of the fort, Barclay would sometimes stop and
watch them for a few minutes now and again, fascinated by the proud, arrogant warriors, and struck by
the attractiveness of the women.

He often wondered what it would be like to be
with one of those women. Unlike most of his army
comrades, he did not look down on Indians. Well,
Indian women, anyway. He had heard that they were
mighty solicitous of men, which would be a pleasur-
able thing, he thought. He dreamed of the hot embrace
of such a woman.

The thing that really made him wonder, though,
was how one went about meeting Indian women. There
were many Indian females down around St. Louis and
other frontier towns, and they were available for a pit-
tance. But they had never impressed Barclay. They were
dumpy and dirty, worn and miserable. He wondered
how any man could say an Indian woman was something special. It was only after he had gotten out here
and actually saw some of the Sioux that he began to
harbor thoughts of bedding an Indian woman.

He still hoped to meet an Indian woman one day and maybe have a fling with her. It would be unthinkable to have been stationed out in Indian country like this and go home without having had that experience. He sighed. The work he was doing was not very conducive to dreaming of the carnal pleasures a Sioux woman might afford.

By the fourth day of his sickening labors, he was beginning to think that perhaps he might be condemned to these menial, rancid, humiliating jobs for the rest of his life. And so he began to consider doing something really heinous. If he did, then perhaps Pennington would make good on his promise to shoot or hang him. That was starting to look like a better alternative than a life spent under Pennington's infernal command, assigned until his dying day to the job of cleaning up other men's waste.

It was while he was having these morose, disgust-inspired thoughts that he spotted a keelboat coming down the river toward him. It seemed odd that it would be heading downriver at this time of year. It occasionally happened, but not often. Usually they came upriver, like the one that had pulled in just this morning. That one belonged to the Missouri Fur Company, and a group of maybe eighty men was led by Joshua Pilcher.

Something else bothered him about the keelboat, too, as he watched it. There seemed something odd about the craft. Moments later, he realized what that was: the keelboat seemed to be a little bit out of control, enough so that to Barclay it appeared that the craft, and thus the men on it, were fleeing from something.

He continued watching, leaning on the long-handled spade he had been using. The keelboat stopped at the small wharf, and a number of men tumbled off it. Most appeared to be boatmen, and even from fifty yards away, Barclay thought they looked mighty frightened. But a couple of the men were fur traders who had gone upriver with Ashley not long ago. They didn't appear to be scared at all; they seemed quite angry.

When the men from the boat had hurried into the fort, Barclay returned to his work. He still wondered what was going on, especially when noise inside the fort began to grow. "Somethin' must be goin' on," Barclay muttered, silently cursing himself for his misdeeds. He figured he was going to miss out on whatever was causing the excitement.

He was wrong about that, however. Less than an hour after the keelboat had put in at the fort's dock, Corporal Mac Dunnigan and two privates hurried down to where Barclay was working.

"What's going on, Mac?" Barclay asked.

"The Rees've attacked General Ashley and his lads," Dunnigan said as one of the privates unlocked Barclay's shackles. "Up the river, at their village."

"I thought the Rees were mostly peaceable," Barclay said, surprised.

Dunnigan shrugged. "I dunna know anythin' more aboot them than ye, lad. I've heard they're generally friendly but not all the time. And I suppose it does nae matter now, does it?"

"Reckon not," Barclay said, shaking his legs one at a time, grateful to be free.

"Let's go, laddies," Dunnigan ordered. "There's work to be done."

"What's going to happen, Mac?" Barclay asked, as the four men headed toward the fort.

"Colonel Leavenworth's plannin' to lead a punitive expedition against the Rees. He wants every man available, either for heading upriver or for watching the fort while the others're gone," Dunnigan said. "That's why they sent us for ye, laddie."

Barclay nodded. He was never quite sure what to

make of Corporal Mac Dunnigan. The flame-haired giant with the huge, bright mustache was a decent enough man, and a good NCO. But Barclay was never sure the Scot was his friend or not. He wasn't overly friendly with anyone. On the other hand, he wasn't antagonistic to anyone either. He seemed to get along with everyone, including Noordstrom and Pennington, which bothered Barclay. Yet he treated Barclay respectfully despite the pair's obvious loathing of the Private.

Then they were in the fort, and Barclay gave up wondering about Dunnigan. He split off from the Corporal and two privates and headed for a water barrel just outside his barracks. He hurriedly washed up, removing but little of the dirt and stink of his work off him. Then he rejoined the men of his company in preparing for the expedition.

The Missouri Legion, as the expedition was called, didn't leave until the next morning, however. When it did, it was an impressive sight. There were three keelboats: the one sent downriver by Ashley, Pilcher's, and one that had come upriver more than a week ago with supplies for the fort. Accompanying the three craft were two hundred and twenty men of the Sixth Infantry, and eighty fur men under Pilcher's leadership. Riding along on painted ponies were nearly a thousand Sioux warriors looking for a chance to wreak some havoc on their long-time enemies. The keelboats were loaded with arms, including two six-pound cannon, and ammunition, as well as enough supplies for the army for two months.

Barclay had been as excited as anyone when he learned about the impending punitive expedition. He figured that he was finally going to see some fighting. He lost a huge dose of his enthusiasm, though, when he found out that his punishment would continue, in the form of being one of the men poling or cordelling the three keelboats up the river.

The long, heavy keelboats often were poled upriver. A line of men would work on each side of the small, flat-topped cabin of the keelboat, each jamming a long pole into the river bottom, pressing down with the butt of the pole to his shoulder and walking forward. Then he would return to the stern along the inside of the walkway and take his place again.

But poling was not always possible, and so the captains had to resort to cordelling. A rope was tied to the keelboat's bow and a line of men would tow the craft upstream. The men would walk along the shore, if possible, but that was rare. Usually they were forced to walk in the water along the bank.

Those jobs were every bit as difficult as Barclay had thought they would be, particularly the latter. It stretched and wrenched every part of his body. Within ten minutes, he was in agony, his overworked muscles aflame with pain. Before much longer, his hands were ripped, raw and bleeding, and his feet and ankles ached from the rocky, uneven river bottom.

Stopping for a meal was the biggest relief Barclay had ever felt. He plopped himself down on the riverbank, his limbs quivering. He was so much in pain that he felt like crying, but he would not let himself do that in front of the other men.

Schellenberger eased himself down next to Barclay, letting out a small, involuntary groan. "So eine schiebe," he mumbled. "Oh, shit."

"I can agree with that, my friend," Barclay said, afraid to nod lest he find another sore spot. "Jesus Christ, I ain't ever had this much painin'."

"Ach, I know vhat you mean."

"How'd you get roped into this goddamn duty?"

Schellenberger shrugged, which he realized right off had been a stupid thing to do. "I am your friend," he said casually. "So Captain Prahlhas—Blowhard— punishes me, too."

"I'm sorry, Klaus," Barclay said sadly. The pain had made him somewhat depressed. "It might be better if you were to become my enemy instead of stayin' my friend."

"Ach! I pick mein freunds. I don't let some dummkopf make those choices for me."

"You'd feel a hell of a lot better right now if you wasn't my friend."

"Yah, dot is true. But then I vouldn't have ein freund."

Barclay smiled weakly. "There is somethin' to be said about friendship, ain't there?"

"Yah."

A mess line was forming, and the two men watched for a few moments. Then Schellenberger asked, "You think you can get your ass up?"

"I expect. Why? Are you that hungry?"

"Nein. I need you to help me up vhen ve do go to eat."

"Indolent bastard, aren't you?" Barclay said with a small laugh.

"Yah!" Schellenberger agreed heartily. He did get up by himself, and ended up helping Barclay just a bit. They went and got their ration of hardtack, boiled salt pork and coffee. Shuffling, they went back and reclaimed their seats on the ground, leaning back against rocks. They ate gingerly, trying not to hurt their raw, rope-burned hands. When they were done eating, each pulled his cap down over his eyes and nodded off.

It was with deep dissatisfaction that they awoke to the calling of sergeants and corporals.

"Damn," Barclay commented. "I wonder if they'd miss us if we just kind of kept sittin' here, not makin' any sounds."

"They vould. How could they not miss somevon like me, as big as I am?"

"I suppose you're right." Barclay painfully pushed himself to his feet, using the rock on which he had been resting for a lot of support. A few minutes later, the two split up, Barclay heading for the lead keelboat, Schellenberger for the next one.

Barclay took his place at the rope with a new respect for the regular boatmen. They seemed to do this with such ease. They might be frightened of Indians and come running downriver as soon as trouble showed up, but he could not fault them for their work habits or abilities. He felt he would be lucky to last another half an hour splashing through the water or walking along the muddy bank doing his part to tow the heavy, ungainly boat against the Big Muddy's powerful, never-ending current. He could not begin to understand how these men did this—or wielded the long poles—day after day all day long.

With a sigh, he bent and grabbed the rope, wincing when it touched the oozing flesh on his hands. Suddenly the rope tensed. He sucked in deep breath and let it out. Then he strained against the rope.

6

The one thing Barclay was grateful for was that for two days he saw nothing of Captain Pennington and very little of Sergeant Noordstrom. He figured it could not last forever, and it didn't. On the second night out, Noordstrom stomped over to where Barclay was sitting, aching legs stretched out before him, his back resting against a log. Schellenberger was on Barclay's left, Watrous on his right.

"Get up, Barclay," Noordstrom ordered.

"Why?" Barclay was in no mood to play games with the Sergeant.

"I've got a job for you," Noordstrom said, growing angry.

"Piss off, you infernal idiot," Barclay snapped.

"Get up!" Noordstrom said, voice hissing out like steam from a tea kettle.

"Or what, Numb Nuts?" Barclay countered.

"Maybe he vill put you in chains, Miles," Schellenberger said with a laugh.

"That'd be a terrible burden," Barclay said with a nod. "Yes, indeed, a punishment that'd cut me to the quick." He looked up at Noordstrom. "Now go away."

"Just remember, boy," the Sergeant growled, "that if you don't get killed by the Rees, you'll have to come back to the fort. Then you'll be at my mercy."

"I'll worry about that some other day," Barclay said reasonably. "But on this expedition, I ain't gonna take no shit from you. You and Captain Numb Nuts wanted to keep on punishin' me, and you've done a hell of a job at it, havin' me on the cordelle line. That's enough."

"I'm keepin' track of all this, Private," Noordstrom said tightly. "And the sum's not going to be to our liking."

"Dammit, Numb Nuts, go away."

Noordstrom turned and stomped away, fuming. Barclay sat there and shook his head. "What an idiot," he muttered. "Damn."

"Things ought to be real interesting when we get back to the fort, Miles," Watrous said. Unlike Barclay and Schellenberger, he was on one of the keelboats, not pulling it along. Though he, too, was a friend of Barclay's, he was not considered of the same ilk, for some reason. He couldn't explain it, but he accepted it, and even enjoyed the freedom from automatic suspicion. Neither Barclay nor Schellenberger held it against him.

"Shit, it's always interesting there. I've had nothin' but interestin' things to do since I got to that shithole."

"That's because you're such an obedient feller," Watrous said with a laugh.

"Yah," Schellenberger added, "und he is so curious that he is alvays lookink for new thinks to try."

"You boys're just green-eyed since I get to do all the interestin' things," Barclay said, affecting a hurt look.

"Oh?" Watrous countered, raising his eyebrows. "I didn't know diggin' shit trenches for the rest of us boys was so interesting."

"See, that's just one of the many things you don't know, Jay," Barclay said. He put on a warm smile. "Now, if you were to get on Captain Pennington's 'good' side, you might enjoy such knowledge."

Watrous laughed. "I'd rather stay in the dark about such things, Miles."

"You don't know what you're missin'," Barclay prodded. But then he laughed, too.

Barclay learned a few things as the days passed. There wasn't much he could do about his aching muscles, except perhaps rub some horse liniment on them at night. But he had quickly realized that he could wrap buckskin or leather around his hands to protect them from the rope. That was some relief, as was the fact that his body was ever so slowly getting used to the huge demands being placed on it. He still did not like this job, and faced it with loathing each morning, but he began to think he might survive it.

It took almost a month of cordelling, poling, rowing and infrequently sailing for the Missouri Legion to make its way up the river to where the Cheyenne River entered it. There General William Ashley waited with his other keelboat and the bulk of his men. Ashley was eager to get back upriver the several miles to the Arikara villages and get some revenge.

Since it was midafternoon, they would spend the night there. After Barclay and the small unit he was assigned to set up their camp along the bank of the river, he slipped off alone. He had not seen Schellenberger since they had arrived here. He wanted to look around and see what he could see. But he also wanted to avoid Noordstrom, who would be certain to find something menial for him to do if he were hanging around his camp.

He moseyed over to the Sioux camp but kept a respectful distance. He knew none of the warriors, and so was not really sure how he would be received if he went any closer. Just because the Sioux were the army's allies in this venture did not mean they would be all that friendly to individual soldiers.

Barclay stood a while, just looking toward the camp. There were no tipis, and he assumed that was because there were no women along. Then he ambled on, heading toward Pilcher's camp, but no one there seemed interested in talking with a solitary soldier. It was when he was meandering through Ashley's main camp that he spotted Jethro Greathouse.

"Mind if I set with you a spell, Mister Greathouse?" he asked politely.

"Mister Greathouse!" one of the other men at the fire said with a laugh. He looked up at Barclay. "You're callin' that goddamn ol' reprobate 'Mister'?"

"Well," Barclay said, deciding that he might as well start off trying to hold his own with these men, "I figure that when a man reaches such an advanced age, he deserves a little politeness." He paused ever so slightly. "Since that might be all the old buzzard's got."

The men laughed.

"Damn, the shit I have to put up with from troublesome infants," Greathouse griped good-naturedly. "Pull up a pew, boy. There's meat and coffee, if you're of a mind."

Barclay knelt, grabbed a battered tin mug, filled it with coffee and then sat on a rotting log a little to Greathouse's left. He sipped the foul coffee, and ate some meat, keeping his mouth shut, preferring to listen to the other men. He might be cocky, but he had enough sense to know that he could learn a lot from these men.

Eventually, though, he decided he could—maybe even should—inject himself into the conversation. It had grown desultory anyway. "I thought I'd heard that the Rees were generally peaceful to whites," he said. "Seems that wasn't true. Or was it, and maybe somethin' just went wrong?"

"Shit," Jim Boggs drawled, spitting through the gap between his two front teeth. He was a tall, hatchet-faced man with bright gray eyes, a long thin nose, and a scraggly mustache. His ears were extraordinarily long. "Ain't an Injun I know of isn't a flibbertigibbet. Goddamn critters can't seem to make up their minds and then stick with it."

"That's a fact," Greathouse added. "The Rees've been peaceable far as we knowed, but this year somethin's set their tails on fire. Damn, we didn't hardly have time to pull up to the bank when they come agin us. Goddamn craptious buggers."

"Now we aim to pay them corrupt sons of bitches back. See if we ain't," Boggs said harshly.

"Is it really that important to get revenge?" Barclay asked, not really surprised. He just wanted to know if there was any reasoning other than just plain old revenge.

"Hell yes, boy," Boggs said, as if Barclay had lost his mind. "You don't nary let red serpents attack you and git away with it. Nary! Ye understand that, boy?"

Barclay nodded, worried that Boggs was about to attack him.

"You let Injins git away with such crap once, and you'll nary see the end of it," another trapper—Charlie Mahoney—said more calmly.

Barclay nodded again. That made sense to him.

"And it's not jist us we're thinkin' about," Greathouse added. "It's ary trapper or trader comes after us. These Rees git away with this goddamn fracas, and they'll hit every company comin' up and down the river. And they might be able to convince some other fractious redmen to join in their evilness. It ain't a prospect none of us wants to have to think about."

"That would make life a little difficult, wouldn't it?" Barclay said dryly.

"Boy catches on quick, Jethro," Mahoney said.

"He's an all right critter—for a goddamn soldier," Greathouse said evenly.

"You plannin' to fight, boy?" Boggs asked. He was a standoffish man, one who placed little trust in others. Nor did he find much to like about them. He was suspicious to the point of paranoia.

"It's why I joined the army in the first goddamn place," Barclay responded flatly. "But I ain't done shit but set on my ass and get in trouble down to Fort Atkinson."

"You best be ready to fight, boy," Boggs said, as if he hadn't heard Barclay.

"I just said I was ready for it." He paused, then shrugged. He didn't like Boggs's attitude, nor the annoyance with which Boggs was looking at him. His natural streak of rashness began to assert itself. "I hope you can say the same for yourself, Numb Nuts."

"You might not live long enough to face them Rees, sonny," Boggs was only a year or so older than Barclay, but he felt he was much older and more experienced.

"Oh?" Barclay countered. "What're you gonna do, breathe on me? That'd do it, I suppose, leavin' me layin' here gaspin' for air."

"Mouthy little bastard, ain't you?"

"Goddamn right I am. And I'm tired of numb-nut bastards like you thinkin' you're the cock of the walk just because you been out in the mountains a year."

There was no warning. Boggs was sitting there one second, and the next he was half on top of Barclay, one grimy hand reaching for Barclay's throat, the other drawing his knife.

Barclay was surprised, but he recovered quickly. While the past month had left him sore, it had also strengthened him. With a deft—well, lucky—move, he knocked Boggs's hand away from his throat, and then managed to sink his teeth into the trapper's chin.

Boggs howled and jerked his head away. His right hand came up with the knife in it, and he immediately plunged it forward.

Barclay darted his head to the side, and the knife blade dug into the dirt less than an inch from his ear. Before Boggs could get himself ready for another try with the blade, Barclay reached out and grabbed the trapper's nuts and squeezed as hard as he could in his awkward position. It was enough to get Boggs to jump up and back away from him.

Barclay rose slowly, warily watching Boggs. He felt sure that someone would put a stop to this now. They had each done a little damage to the other, but not too much. He risked a quick look around, and he realized with some dread that no one was going to interfere. They sat, looking interested, making small wagers. A few other trappers had gathered around and stood watching.

"Ain't nobody gonna help your yeller ass now, boy," Boggs said.

"Come on at me again, then, chicken dick," Barclay said a lot more bravely than he felt. He was quaking inside. It was one thing to want to make war on Indians, who were only savages anyway. It was entirely another to fight a white man, face to face, to the death. He wasn't sure he was prepared for that.

He had no more time for such thoughts, though, since Boggs was charging him. The trapper slammed a shoulder into his midsection, wrapped his arms around Barclay just below his buttocks, and then lifted the soldier a little off the ground. Boggs growled as he threw Barclay up and back.

Barclay landed hard on his seat, and went backward, hitting his head on a small, sharp stone. Though groggy, he was aware of Boggs coming at him again. Stunned by the feral look in the trapper's eyes, Barclay still managed—barely—to roll out of Boggs's way. He got a momentary breather when Boggs's landing knocked the breath out of him for a few precious seconds.

Getting to his feet, Barclay turned to face Boggs,

who had also gotten up. His head ached, as did most of
the rest of his body. He was still a little dazed, though
his head was rapidly clearing. When Boggs charged
him again, Barclay jumped to the side, and then dove
over the fire. He hit a lot harder than he had expected,
and rolled in a sprawling somersault. But as he came
up, he grabbed a large stick of firewood. He swung it
just as Boggs jumped over the fire.

The wood caught Boggs on the left temple, and he
crumpled. Barclay edged warily up on him and knelt.
Boggs was not dead; wasn't even fully unconscious,
but he was plenty dazed. The soldier tossed the stick
aside. Before he could push himself up, a knife suddenly appeared in the dirt several inches toward his
right.

"Finish him, boy," someone shouted.

Barclay took the knife in his hand and held it to
Boggs's throat. He was flooded with feelings he had
never encountered before. He wondered if he really
could kill another person. That had never been a question before; he had always just assumed that when the
time came, he would do what he had to. Now he was
not so sure.

More than that, though, he questioned whether he
wanted to kill Boggs. He could see no reason to do so,
even though he was certain the trapper would kill him
without a qualm if the situation were reversed.

Voices filtered in to him, almost all calling for him
to kill Boggs. With the rush of adrenaline and the prodding encouragement of the small crowd, he felt he had
made up his mind. Besides, he wanted to see if he had
it in him to kill someone. Now was a good time to test
himself.

Suddenly, though, he shook his head. Life
shouldn't be taken so lightly, he thought. Boggs was
helpless here, and slaying him would not be much of a
manly or heroic thing. Anyone would be able to do it

under the circumstances. He decided that he could kill Boggs if he wanted to; it was just that he didn't want to. He stood, knife still in hand. "Who's this belong to?" he asked, eyes scanning the sea of hard faces around him.

"Mine," a man said.

Barclay flipped him the knife. "You want him dead, Numb Nuts, you kill him. I ain't gonna do your dirty work for you." He turned and began walking off, feeling the aches start up again. He hadn't gone ten feet when he heard a piercing, angry bellow behind him. He turned just as Boggs plowed into him, slamming him to the ground.

"Ungrateful son of a bitch," Barclay mumbled, as he fought to keep Boggs from getting a grip on his throat, and tried to throw the trapper off. Having little success, Barclay suddenly pounded the side of his fist against the wound in Boggs's temple. He didn't get too much leverage, but the wound was still so new that he figured it must have hurt like hell.

Barclay shoved, pushing Boggs off him. He rolled until he was on hands and knees looming over Boggs. He grabbed the trapper's throat and squeezed, ignoring the fresh bleeding that had started from his palms under the buckskin protecting his hands. "I gave you a chance, you dumb bastard," he said softly, more to himself, really, than to Boggs. "You should've took it.

The light dimmed in Boggs's eyes, and then went out. With a sinking feeling, Barclay rose. He stumbled away, feeling his gorge beginning to rise. He made it into some brush along the river before he vomited. Despite the sickness, he was still grateful that no one could see him.

He didn't know how long he stayed there, but it was almost dark by the time he stumbled back toward his camp. He felt weak and shaken.

7

"Vhat the hell hoppened to you?" Schellenberger asked as Barclay plopped himself down across the fire from the German.

"What makes you think somethin' happened?" Barclay countered. He still felt shaky and he was grateful to have a log to lean against.

"You're all pale, like you've been sick."

"I was." Barclay sighed, and then he told the story. It didn't take long, but it held the attention of his fellow soldiers.

"Vell, Verdammt noch mal," Schellenberger said. "Goddamn, you vent und kilt your first man." He sounded proud of his friend.

"Well, it don't feel as good as I thought it would, Klaus," Barclay said truthfully. "In fact, it don't feel good at all."

"You poor boy," Sergeant Noordstrom said from behind Barclay. His tone was mocking.

"You hear somethin', Klaus?" Barclay said, winking at his friend. "Like maybe some putrefyin' cow releasin' a week's worth of flatulence."

"Yah, I heard· dot," Schellenberger agreed. "I thought it vas the vind blowink through a dead tree."

"Very funny, boys," Noordstrom snapped, not amused. "The captain'll be interested in hearin' that

you're now a blooded soldier, Barclay. He might even
let you lead the first charge against those red hostiles
tomorrow. That'll really let you show your mettle."

"Leaf him alone, Sergeant," Schellenberger said
quietly.

"Since when did you become his nursemaid?"
Noordstrom asked with a sneer.

Schellenberger ignored the insult. "Haff you ever
kilt a man?"

"Of course I have," the Sergeant said haughtily.

"Yah, of course," Schellenberger responded sarcastically. "Und you never felt bad about any of them?
Maybe the first?" He paused, then answered himself.
"Nein, you never haff, I suppose. Dot vould mean you
had a heart und a brain to haff feelinks vith."

"You're gettin' to be as smart-mouthed as your pal
there."

"Yah," Schellenberger agreed. "Und I vill kick
your ass like mein freund did to you if you don't go
avay now und leaf us alone."

Schellenberger looked at the German's hard face,
and realized he might be outmanned. "You'll pay for
this, Schellenberger," he snapped. "Both of you will."

Schellenberger shrugged. He would worry about
the threat if and when it ever came to pass. He didn't
really think Noordstrom would make good on it anyway. He sat back at the fire, across from Barclay and
grinned.

"That wasn't necessary, you know, Klaus,"
Barclay said. Then he weakly grinned back. "But I'm
glad you did it, my friend. I don't know as if I could've
put up with his crap right now."

"I don't know vhy anyvon should haff to put
up vith his shit at any time," Schellenberger said
fatalistically.

"You put yourself up for more trouble with this,
though."

"Ach, dot schweinhund vould find some reason for creating me trouble no matter vhat I did or didn't do. Don't you vorry about it."

Barclay nodded. He ate his supper without much appetite, and kept mostly to himself for the rest of the evening. He was horrified at how easy it had been to kill. At how easy it had been for him to turn from a decent human being—even if he was something of a smart-alec—into a killer in the mere blink of an eye. At how easy it had been to snuff out a life. In his daydreams of becoming a warrior, things had never been like this. There was no realization of what had happened for real just a few hours ago, of how he had rendered a man blank for all of eternity. He wondered if he could carry that burden.

He felt a little better in the morning, almost as if he had dreamed the fight with Boggs. But he was still a little rocky as he ate his bacon and beans, and drank coffee.

Watrous, always the intelligent, astute one, could see what Barclay was going through. "Somethin' you have to remember, Miles," he said softly, "is that you aren't to blame for what happened yesterday."

Barclay shrugged, not really interested right now in being perked up.

"He would've killed you, Miles," Watrous said. "Sure as hell."

"Don't mean it was right."

"I suppose not, in some ways. I suppose you could've just let him kill you instead."

"Maybe that would've been better," Barclay mumbled.

"Hogwash! From what you said this Boggs feller was a pretty accursed reprobate anyway, and won't be missed much nor by many."

"I don't know, Jay," Barclay said sadly. "I—"

"Listen to that feller, boy," Greathouse said,

marching up to the fire and squatting next to it. "He's talkin' true."

Barclay looked at Greathouse, brows raised.

Greathouse spit into the fire and grinned. "Jim Boggs was a despicable man; a festerin', inflamed boil on the ass of mankind. His demise ain't no great loss to no one."

Barclay nodded, knowing in his head that what Greathouse and Watrous had said was true, but his heart could not accept that.

"Besides," Greathouse added, "it was that craptious wart who started the fracas, boy. Ye give him ary chance to git out of it with his life. He warn't wise enough to take that gift ye give him, and he paid for his foolishness."

Barclay nodded again, spirits lifted minutely. Some of what Greathouse and Watrous had been saying was beginning to sink in. "Why'd he have to go and make that last move against me?" Barclay asked, almost plaintively.

"'Cause if he had any brains at all, they was up his ass pipe is why," Greathouse said with a snort.

Barclay sat in silence a bit, digesting all he had heard. It all made sense, yet it was still hard for him to accept. Still, his innate senses of self-preservation and cockiness were beginning to resurface. And that, he knew, was a good sign. With that fractionally rising humor came an increasing ability to think once again. And so a question arose. "Why didn't you or the others try to stop that fight, Jethro?" he asked. "Instead of just settin' there watchin'?"

Greathouse sort of grinned as he lit a long, thin-stemmed pipe. "General Ashley might like to think he runs these expeditions like an army, but it ain't that way in actuality. Can't be. Not when he went and hired a herd of the most fractious, bickerin' coots ary stepped on a keelboat. Ain't too many of the men with this group'd lift a finger to help another 'less he saw somethin' in it for himself."

"That don't ring true," Barclay said. "Hell, you've been mighty friendly to me, both back downriver, and now settin' right here."

Greathouse shrugged. "Ye ain't with Ashley's men," he said lamely.

"Then why didn't you help me against Boggs?" Barclay asked logically.

"'Cause it wouldn't've been the right thing—" Greathouse said, clearly embarrassed.

Watrous suddenly laughed. "He took a liking to you back at the fort, my friend," he said. "But he couldn't let himself show that to the others."

Schellenberger joined in the laughter. "Yah. Dot must be it."

"I hope the Rees kill all of you malignant serpents," Greathouse growled. He did not like the idea that these men had hit the mark with their joking suppositions. He almost regretted that he had made any overtures of friendship to Barclay, but not quite. He had spent many years prowling the woods east of the Mississippi, and most of that had been solitary, at least since his partner—Caleb Harris—had died at the Shawnees' hands twenty-some years ago now. When he had first spotted Barclay, it had taken but a moment to realize that the young man reminded him of Harris—more so than his sons. It was why he had stopped and talked with Barclay. He harbored no illusions that Barclay could take Harris's place at this late date, nor even that Barclay might somehow go along with him on the Ashley expedition. It was just a bit of friendly conversation with a man who brought to mind a favorable time in his life. He was beginning to wonder now if perhaps more might come of this new friendship. He wasn't about to let that out in the open though.

"Come on, old man, admit it," Watrous said, still chuckling.

"You boys're plumb deranged," Greathouse offered. He pushed himself up, silently cursing the advancing years that had robbed his joints of their fluidity and his muscles of some of their vitality. His face betrayed nothing of this, though. "I jist come by to see how sonny boy was doin'. Seems he's in fine fettle, so I'll take my leave of ye bickerin' young fools now." He took several steps, then turned to look back. "A word of warnin' for ye, boys—all of ye best be prepared to kill today."

Tensions rose among the men as the boats moved slowly up the Missouri River. Few of them had any battle experience, and even fewer had fought Indians. No one knew what to expect. They had heard some stories about how ferocious the Rees were; they had also heard the Sioux denigrating the Rees as poor fighters, men who lived in dirt houses and grew things in little gardens instead of living free. So the men were left to wonder whether they were about to face a horde of painted savages or a group of frightened dirt-dwellers.

The work of cordelling, while physically still incredibly strenuous, was so monotonous that it did nothing to keep Barclay's mind off of his concerns about having killed Boggs the evening before. Worrying about what was ahead of him did, though.

Within a mile of the Arikara villages, they moored the keelboats. Units were formed, and then the march toward the villages began. It was already well into the afternoon, and they hoped to be within sight of the nearest village before darkness came. Then Colonel Leavenworth would develop a plan of attack.

They were not far from the towns—as some of the

trappers had been calling them—when they heard war cries and a bit of gunfire.

Orders suddenly were shouted, and the soldiers broke off in squads, running toward the villages. The sound of battle increased in intensity, as Barclay pounded along in a squad led by Corporal Dunnigan.

They broke over a bluff and stopped on the top, looking down onto the flat that spread out for a few hundred yards. It was the first view Barclay had of a real Indian town, and he was not impressed. Not that he could actually see much, just a walled-in village of earthen houses. It appeared to be nothing more than a big, brown splotch in the middle of some flatness.

Many Arikaras were fleeing toward the sandhills to the north, while others did battle with the Sioux who had accompanied the Missouri Legion.

Barclay was not, of course, privy to the planning circles of the army command, but he could not help but think that Colonel Leavenworth was not pleased with this. The army was not prepared to join the fight, and it seemed as if the Sioux had attacked far sooner than might be wise. It appeared to Barclay that this premature attack by the Sioux would seriously harm Leavenworth's ability to plan a proper attack to adequately punish the Arikaras.

Barclay didn't care all that much that Leavenworth's plans might have been subverted. It did bother him a little that it now seemed unlikely that he would get to see any Indian fighting. However, that didn't seem to mean as much to him today as it would have at this time yesterday. Having just killed a man went a long way toward tempering his desire to join a battle where death would be almost certain.

Orders came down for several units—including the one Barclay was with—to head down the bluff toward town and lend what support they could to the attacking Sioux. The rest of the troops would wait in reserve, in case the Arikaras decided to turn back and join the battle in full force.

With a combination of trepidation and exhilaration, Barclay followed Dunnigan and the others down the steep slope of the bluff, until he hit flat ground. The land here was not as barren as it had looked from up above. There was a lot of sage, with other brush, and even some small trees here and there. Small cactus had to be avoided, since their sharp thorns would pierce even shoe leather.

Barclay wasn't sure what to do as he approached the battling Indians. The Sioux obviously had the better of the Rees at this point, and indeed were coming close to perpetrating a massacre on the nearly helpless Arikaras.

He slackened his pace and took a look around. No one else seemed to know what to do either, and they were all slowing to a walk. Corporals and sergeants were issuing orders, forming men into firing lines. But they were reluctant to have their men shoot, lest they end up killing their allies. Kneeling there, rifle at the ready, Barclay had an opportunity to look over the battling Indians. One Sioux in particular caught his attention.

He was tall and broad-shouldered, dressed in flowing buckskin war shirt, leggings, breechcloth, and moccasins. A feathered war bonnet was tied under his chin. Long fringes on his shirt and leggings flapped wildly as the man fought with an air of arrogant assurance. The warrior wielded a stone-headed war club in one hand, while he protected himself with a bullhide shield on his other arm. All in all, he was mighty impressive, and Barclay assumed the Sioux was some kind of chief.

Barclay turned his attention away when Dunnigan gave the order to prepare to fire. They sent a volley toward a group of Rees trying to get away, having some effect. Barclay wasn't sure if he had hit anyone.

As he was reloading, Barclay glanced back toward the one warrior who had so impressed him. The Sioux remained in the midst of a still-swirling battle, yet he was somehow solitary; none of his comrades being within a dozen yards of him. And two Arikaras were creeping up behind him as he fought two others in front of him.

Barclay watched in stunned fascination, thinking he should shout a warning or something. Then he realized that no one would hear him with all the noise of the fighting, so he wondered if he should try to help the warrior somehow.

All the while, he was reloading, making the moves automatically. He considered firing at one of the Rees, but Dunnigan had just given the order to fire again in the other direction. Along with his fellows, he did so.

Then, making his decision, he dropped his empty rifle, jumped up and sprinted toward the two Arikaras who were about to attack the Sioux from behind.

8

Barclay felt right off that perhaps he had made an error. Not that he minded trying to help the Sioux. It was just that the running was a godawful mistake after more than five weeks of towing keelboats up the fast-moving river. Within two steps his legs were on fire and he didn't think he could continue.

But press on he did, ignoring both the agony that roared up his legs and jarred the rest of his body, and Dunnigan's shouts, which he assumed were orders for him to return. He noticed that several other Sioux warriors were racing toward the chief from the other direction, but they were a lot farther from helping him than Barclay was.

As he neared the battling Sioux, he was surprised to realize that neither Arikara was aware of him. That would help, since he was quite certain by now that he was in no physical shape to really fight two battle-hardened warriors. Throwing caution to the winds, Barclay finally barreled into the two Arikaras.

All three men sprawled across the ground, stirring up a little dust amid the new grass. Barclay groaned a little as his aching body hit first bone and flesh, and then the hard earth. Adding to his pain were the cactus thorns he picked up when he rolled over a prickly pear.

Getting to his feet, Barclay felt as if he had been the floor for a barn dance—dented and gouged and bruised from the stomping of too many feet. He couldn't help but wince.

He actually yelled with pain when one of the Arikaras slammed into him, flattening him again. He was able to get his arms up, though, as the Ree straddled his knees and reached out to stab Barclay. He managed to fend off the warrior's blade, though it clipped a piece of flesh out of his left forearm.

Suddenly Barclay remembered the single-shot pistol in his belt, and had a fleeting moment of wonder that he hadn't thought of it before. He tugged it out as he tried to ward off several punches and stabbing attempts by the wild-eyed Arikara.

Barclay got the pistol out, and thumbed back the hammer with one hand, no mean feat under the circumstances. Then he shoved the pistol's muzzle against the Ree's stomach and pulled the trigger.

A cloud of smoke, partly trapped between the two bodies, obscured Barclay's view for a moment, but then he could see the Indian's dark eyes dimming. He didn't have the strength, however, to hold the Arikara's body up with one arm, and the upper half of the bloody corpse fell onto Barclay's chest.

Barclay lay there, feeling each ache in his suffering body and wondering just how he was going to get the body off him. He was certain he would be unable to move the dead warrior by himself. On the other hand, he figured, he could just lie there and rest for a day or a week. His muscles certainly could use the indolence to recover a little.

The problem was resolved for him when one of the Sioux pulled the Arikara off and dropped the corpse next to him. The Sioux grinned and held out a hand. With trepidation, knowing it was going to hurt, Barclay took the warrior's hand and allowed himself to be pulled up. He winced involuntarily as the old pains found renewed vigor inside him, before settling back to a dull, constant throb.

The warrior—Barclay noticed he was the one he had come to help in the first place—was still grinning. The Sioux was a few inches taller than Barclay, which surprised the soldier a little. The man was in his late thirties, Barclay figured, and looked in the prime of manhood. He appeared to have all his teeth, which was more than Barclay could say for a good many white men of the same age. His face and body were fleshy without being fat. The warrior's high, unlined forehead was covered with white paint speckled with red dots. The paint went down to the warrior's rather prominent, wide nose. The bottom half of his face was unpainted, though sweat had carried some of the color down there. Barclay decided that all in all, this man was as impressive up close as he had been from a distance.

"You one good sumbitch," the Sioux said, his words thickly accented but quite understandable. He clapped Barclay on the shoulder.

"Thanks," Barclay said, not sure of himself.

"No. I thank you," the warrior said. His voice was a deep, pleasant rumble, like comfortable thunder in the distance.

"Wasn't much," Barclay mumbled, feeling quite discomfited by the situation.

"Hell, was much," the Sioux said, adding a nod to his wide grin.

Barclay shrugged, but he grinned back.

"I'm Walking Thunder," the warrior said. "Who're you?"

"Private Miles Barclay."

Growing serious, Walking Thunder said, struggling with the English words, "I am much thanks for you save me."

"Like I said, it wasn't much."

"Goddamn, was much. Goddamn much," Walking Thunder insisted solemnly.

"Glad I could be of help."

Walking Thunder nodded, then cocked his eyebrows quizzically. "You good?" he asked. "You look hurt."

"I'm painin' all over," Barclay said with a rueful grin. He wondered if Walking Thunder understood all this. "But it ain't from the fightin'. It all comes from haulin' them goddamn keelboats up the goddamn river."

"Bad work," Walking Thunder said with an understanding nod. "No real man would do that."

"I don't have much choice."

"Army bad, too," Walking Thunder said firmly. "It not right a man should live so. Men should live like the Lakota."

"I'll have to check that out sometime, Walkin' Thunder," Barclay said seriously. "But right now I expect I better get back to my squad before I get in even more trouble." He grinned again.

"You cause army trouble?"

Barclay nodded.

"Goddamn, I like you," Walking Thunder said with a laugh. "Good sumbitch make trouble for long knives."

"I'll remember that next time I'm in the guard-house," Barclay said with a laugh before lurching off toward his squad. He stopped along the way to retrieve his rifle, knowing that the soldiers were watching him.

"Looks like ye made yersel' some friends there, laddie," Dunnigan said when Barclay reported back to his squad.

"Reckon so," Barclay admitted. Once again he was uncomfortable in the role of hero, if that's what he was being considered. "Better than havin' those Indians as enemies, I suppose."

"Aye, that it'd be."

"I suppose you're gonna report me for havin' done it, though?" Barclay asked more than said.

"Why would I do that, laddie?"

"Disobeyin' orders," Barclay responded, somewhat surprised.

"I dinna hear ye disobeyin' none of my orders," Dunnigan said firmly. "Any of ye other lads hear Private Barclay go against my orders?"

The men of the squad—all friends of Barclay—shook their heads.

"Ye did, however, follow my orders to the letter, when I sent ye off to help our poor savage ally. Aye, exceeded my orders from what I could see."

"Thanks, Mac," Barclay said gratefully.

"Aye," Dunnigan growled. "Now get your ass back in line, laddie, before I have to do somethin' awful to ye." But he winked.

Captain Pennington and Sergeant Noordstrom were not happy with Barclay's newly acquired status as savior to the Sioux. But what really made them angry was the fact that they could do absolutely nothing about it. Oh, they had planned to, for sure, and had even begun taking steps to have both Barclay and Dunnigan court-martialed for disobeying their orders.

Barclay had thought about Dunnigan's taking "credit" for him helping Walking Thunder after the squad had reported back, and had wondered about it. Claiming he had issued the orders for it would certainly make Dunnigan look good in some eyes. Barclay just wasn't sure if he resented it or not.

He changed his tune, however, when Pennington started plotting court-martials. Barclay realized that Dunnigan was taking a considerable amount of the heat that would otherwise have fallen on his own already overburdened shoulders.

Pennington's anger really soared, however, once word got to Colonel Leavenworth of what Barclay had done. Barclay hadn't realized until then just who he had aided. Dunnigan gave him the news.

"That red savage ye saved was a big chief, laddie," Dunnigan said as he squatted by the fire next to Barclay. "The way Ashley's men explain it, he's not the big chief—they say the red men have no overall chief, which dunna make sense to me—but is one of their most important war chiefs."

"That's interesting."

"Interesting hell, laddie. It's saved our bacon."

"How so?"

Dunnigan grinned. "Since Colonel Leavenworth learned just who it was ye saved, laddie, Captain Pennington and his nefarious partner canna touch the neither of us two."

A slow, satisfied smile spread across Barclay's face. "That would cramp their plans, wouldn't it?" he said.

"Aye."

"Well, I don't know how long my bein' in the colonel's good graces is gonna last," Barclay said, "but I aim to enjoy it while it does."

"That'd be wise," Dunnigan said thoughtfully, "since when ye—and I—fall out of favor, things might go hard on ye."

"Won't be no different from normal, then, will it?" Barclay said with a crooked grin.

"I suppose not, lad." Dunnigan put his hands on his knees and pushed himself up. With a nod at Barclay, he walked off.

"Gott in Himmel, if you ain't the hero," Schellenberger said with a straight face. He had kept quiet all the while Dunnigan was there.

"Jealous?" Barclay was a little surprised. He did not think his good friend would be so, but he certainly didn't seem pleased. That only added to Barclay's confusion of emotions.

"Of you savink a redskin's neck? Nein."

"You sure as hell seem like it." Barclay was getting irritated. He wanted to be left alone for a while to try to sort things out. He didn't need his best friend riding him about his so-called heroics.

"Gettink sensitive, are you?" Schellenberger countered. Then he burst out laughing. "I vas only joshink vith you, mein freund."

"Well don't," Barclay said in irritation. "Not for a while anyway."

Schellenberger was taken aback, but not too much. He thought he understood why. "Are you still bothered by the incident vith Boggs?"

Barclay nodded. "I hadn't figured that out yet when I went and killed another man. Jesus, I'm a little worried that I might be turnin' into nothin' but a cold-blooded killer."

"Nein, nein, nein," Sergeant growled. "Both those men vere tryink to kill you, und vould haff done so vithout a thought if you hadn't kilt them first."

"I suppose. But it still ain't easy takin' a man's life." Barclay had kept up a good face since his brief, bloody fight with the Arikaras, but now that he was basically with just a few friends, it was filtering back into his consciousness again.

"No, it's not," Schellenberger said quietly.

Barclay's eyebrows rose. "You know?"

"Yah. It vas back in the east, several years ago."

"You never said anything about that, Klaus."

"It's not somethink a man likes to talk about. It vas like you und Boggs—self-defense. But it vas different."

"How could it be different?"

"Ve are soldiers now."

"Boggs wasn't an enemy, as far as me bein' a soldier goes. That Ree today, yeah, he was, and maybe that's why it's a little easier to accept that than it was for Boggs. But maybe it's easier to accept because I'm gettin' used to killin' folks."

"No, you vere just doink your duty today. Vith Boggs," Schellenberger shrugged, "some men just act like dot. Und you have to deal vith them the best vay you can."

"It still don't seem right somehow," Barclay said with a sigh. "But I reckon I better get over it if I'm gonna stay out here fightin' Indians."

"Yah."

Barclay stalled before saying anything else, but then he ventured, "You think I maybe didn't feel so bad about killin' that Ree today because he was an Injun?"

"Nein," Schellenberger said without hesitation. "After all, you saved another Indian. The von you kilt vas the enemy. Dot is all."

Barclay considered that for a bit, then decided that perhaps his friend was right. He had held no particular disliking for the Arikara he had killed, other than the natural loathing any man would feel for another who was trying to jam a knife blade into his vital organs.

That made him feel a little better, though he was still bothered by knowing that he had killed two men in two days—and had done so with relative ease.

He ate his evening meal hungrily, though he didn't taste much of it. Then he turned in as soon as he could. Sleep did not come easily, though, as he found it hard to erase the visions of Boggs's body, and of the Ree's face as the light of life drained from it.

Sleep did come at last, and though Barclay's dreams were troubled, they served to ease his mind somewhat. When he lined up with his squad in the morning, he felt considerably better, and was beginning to think he could get on with life, and do whatever he was called upon to do.

9

Frustrated that the early attack by the Sioux had ruined what plans he had had for punishing the Arikaras, Colonel Leavenworth ordered the two six-pound cannon to the top of the bluff. There, with whatever soldiers were not on duty—watching the supplies, keeping a lookout in case the Arikaras returned, guarding the keelboats and such—the Colonel sat and watched as the cannon pounded the Ree village.

The allure of this quickly waned, and the soldiers began drifting off. They formed small groups and played cards or took care of personal equipment until they were called upon to relieve other troopers on official duties.

Throughout the day, the pounding of the two cannon continued, and the men occasionally wandered back up the bluff to see if the bombardment was having any effect. No one could see that it was, though.

By midafternoon, Barclay and the squad he was assigned to had just come off duty guarding the perimeter of the camp, when they saw a council of war between Leavenworth, Ashley and Pilcher.

Interested, Barclay and his companions took seats near where the military and civilian leaders were meeting. They were out of the way, but close enough so that they could hear.

It was obvious right from the start that Ashley and Pilcher were angry, arguing that the Rees had not been sufficiently punished. It was also clearly evident that Leavenworth was having second thoughts about having formed the Missouri Legion and leading it out here. He had done so without getting the approval of his commanders, and now he was worried that perhaps he had endangered his career with such a rash decision.

Ashley and Pilcher argued that the army, along with the trappers, should simply attack the town, root out the Rees and butcher those who could not get away. "After what they did to my boys, and the way they did it," Ashley thundered, "they don't deserve no better."

"Calm down, General," Leavenworth said soothingly, using Ashley's honorific. "I don't think an assault on that protected village would do much more than get a bunch of our men killed. We've been shelling it all day, but we haven't done a damned thing to it except throw some dirt around. Besides, it's too late now that all the Sioux have pulled out."

Barclay was surprised at hearing that. "Wonder when the hell they did that," he whispered to Schellenberger on his right.

"Yah," Schellenberger answered in kind. "But even more to vonder about is vhy they left."

Then the two shut up and listened again.

"It was your foolishness that's cost us such a great advantage, Colonel," Ashley snapped. "If you had attacked that damn village this mornin' like Josh and I told you we should, they would've stuck around. The Rees would've been chastised proper and we would've been on our way upriver again by now."

"I would not risk the lives of my men so carelessly," Leavenworth said stiffly. "I figured that softening the Arikaras up with a day-long bombardment would make our attack that much safer. I didn't know the Sioux would take off without notice."

"You've been out here long enough to know the way the Sioux behave. Hell they were bored half to death sittin' out there waitin' for you to stop fartin' around with those cannon and join the battle."

"You should know patience about fightin' isn't the red man's way," Pilcher tossed in. "That's why they attacked right off yesterday. And that's why they left. They just got plumb tired of waitin' for you to do something. Now you're out of powder and ball for the cannon, and your allies have gone home."

"We should not have to rely on the services of savages anyway," Leavenworth said, growing angry himself.

"Fine," Ashley countered. "But are you ready to send your men against the Rees? Josh and I are. And our men look forward to exacting some revenge for the depredations those savages've brought on us."

"I don't think that's wise," Leavenworth said. His misgivings about this entire expedition were growing by the moment.

"You have another plan?" Ashley asked skeptically.

"Offer the Rees an olive branch," Leavenworth said flatly. "With the understanding that they not molest any other keelboat expeditions up or down the river."

Pilcher was livid. "Why you lyin', chicken-livered son of a bitch," he roared, loud enough for just about all the camp to hear. "You told me back at Fort Atkinson that the Rees should be beaten into submission and that you were bound on makin' sure that they were."

"Situations change," Leavenworth said evenly. He had said those words, and had meant them at the time. But that was before he had had time to think about what this expedition might mean to his career. Now that he had done so, he thought he would be far better

off making peace with the Arikaras, and then reporting
back to his superiors that he had beaten the Rees into
suing for peace. Everyone would be happy then—
except perhaps these volatile trappers and traders, who
were more than half savage anyway and nothing but
trouble.

"You're a blight on the name of all good men who
make their way out in these wilds, Colonel," Ashley
said harshly. He was nearly as angry as Pilcher was.
Though his group had been the one attacked, he had
not been lied to by Leavenworth right to his face. That
was enough for him to keep his reason, at least for
now.

"Another insult from you, sir," Leavenworth said
sternly, "and I'll have you shot."

"You ain't going to do any such thing, and you
damn well know it, Colonel," Pilcher said. He was still
enraged, but he had gotten himself under control.

"Don't wager against it, gentlemen. Now, is there
anyone among either of your parties who can converse
with these savages?"

"I suppose old Jules LaSalle can make do, in signs
if not in the Ree lingo," Ashley said after some thought.
"He's been around the Sioux and other tribes in these
parts for some time."

Leavenworth nodded. "Get him. I'll send him and
two other of your men, and two of mine as a peace
commission."

Ashley and Pilcher considered more arguments,
but both were astute enough to know that such
entreaties would fall on deaf ears. They could go along
with Leavenworth's plan, or they could make their
own plans to attack the Arikara village with just their
own men. The latter, they knew, was far too risky.
They were businessmen, out to make money; dealing
with recalcitrant Indians was not their primary purpose. Both nodded and left.

Less than half an hour later, the peace "commission" was making its way across the seemingly endless sweep of emptiness from the foot of the bluff to the town.

Barclay, who was one of the two soldiers along, felt exposed out here in the open like this, and he cursed Captain Pennington for having "volunteered" him—and Schellenberger—for this mission. It was, he knew, another way for the officer to get back at him, even though it would seem to others as if this were a plum assignment.

Barclay wasn't sure how he felt about all this. He had joined the army to fight Indians, and in some ways he still wanted to do that. However, having just fought—and killed—an Arikara, he wasn't certain he was in any humor for fighting any others at the moment. The other side of it was that he did not much like marching toward an Arikara village under a white flag to see if they wanted to make peace. It somehow cut to the bone.

He could see on the other men's faces that they, too, took little liking to this peace business. At least not under these circumstances. Here their allies the Sioux had beaten the Rees in open battle, and the army had pounded the village for most of the day with cannon fire, and yet it seemed like they were the ones suing the Arikaras for peace, rather than the other way around. It was enough to turn a man's stomach.

Barclay turned his attention to the five Rees tentatively heading their way. The two groups stopped a few feet apart. All the men sat, except for LaSalle and a Ree chief. The two talked, mostly using sign, though with occasional words in English, Arikara, Sioux, and Mandan.

The conference didn't last long. Mostly LaSalle told the Rees that, if they attacked any more keelboats, the army and all the trappers they could round up would descend on the Arikara villages and would leave them in ruins and all the Arikara men dead.

The Rees had little choice but to agree to leave the trappers and their keelboats alone. They had seen how many men could be amassed against them in a very short time, especially when the white men brought along hordes of fierce Sioux. If those forces put their minds to it, the Arikaras would not stand a chance.

Finally LaSalle and the Arikara chief sat, and a long pipestone pipe was produced. It was filled with tobacco and lit. All the men smoked from it a little. Barclay didn't know why, but he went along with it. Then each group began the march back to his own side.

Though the whole thing had taken less than ten minutes, Barclay had had trouble staying awake through it, and he was glad to be back with the troops.

LaSalle reported to Leavenworth, Ashley and Pilcher: "It's done," he said with a shrug. "Wasn't much to it."

"They promised to leave the keelboats alone?" Leavenworth asked.

"Well, goddamn right dey did," LaSalle snorted. "What de hell do you t'ink, eh?" He shook his head, wondering how someone with such limited intelligence could become a colonel in the army.

"They might've been recalcitrant."

"Bah," LaSalle spit. He waved his hand in disgust at Leavenworth, turned and walked away.

Barclay and Schellenberger tried to stifle their chuckles with limited success. The two other trappers made no such effort. They simply laughed and followed LaSalle off toward their own camp.

With relief, Barclay and Schellenberger returned to their squads. Barclay was grateful that Pennington and Noordstrom were still mostly leaving him alone. He knew it wouldn't last, since moments after getting back

to his squad he had learned that they would be depart-
ing in the morning.

The trip downriver was a breeze, comparatively speaking, though Barclay didn't really know it. Since there
was only one keelboat going downriver—neither
Pilcher nor Ashley could, or would, afford not to keep
their craft—the majority of the soldiers had to march
back on foot.

Barclay wasn't sure whether he was lucky or not
being among that legion. While it was a long, hard trek
back, he did not have to deal with Pennington. The
captain was going back on the keelboat. He did have to
contend with Sergeant Noordstrom, but his authority
was tempered by the presence of Lieutenant Hodges,
and the baleful glare of Corporal Dunnigan.

It was the first time Hodges had ever really been
allowed out of Pennington's sight, and Barclay wondered why. It didn't matter much to him; he was just
surprised was all.

The march was uneventful, except for a chance
encounter with a small group of Pawnees, who tried to
put on a show of bravado but were rather cowed by
the vastly larger force of soldiers.

The only other excitement, such as it was, came in
Noordstrom's attempts to bully Barclay a bit. The
sergeant had little heart for it, though, since he was not
under the direct protection, as it were, of Pennington.

The long march gave Barclay time to think, however. On the last night near the Arikara villages, he had
spent time with Greathouse, LaSalle, and some of the
other trappers. The mountain men had filled his mind
with stories of the adventures they had had. While a
number of Ashley's men were still new to this profes-
sion, the same could not be said of many of Pilcher's
men. Some of the latter had gone west to the moun-

tains back with Manuel Lisa before the second war with the British.

Barclay had suppressed his natural cockiness and kept his mouth shut. Instead he just listened, fascinated by the stories of encounters with wild animals and wilder Indians; of the pleasures of Indian women and the silky plushness of prime beaver fur; of the terrors of starvin' times and brutal mountain winters. The first excited him, the middle thrilled him and the last worried him more than a little.

He even ignored Schellenberger's asides to him as he listened to the tales, which served to instill in him the flames of desire. He wanted to join these buckskin-clad men going west, to see the high peaks of the Stony Mountains, to meet and treat with Indians, peaceful and otherwise, to feel the bitterness of cold mountain streams.

What had really stoked the flames for Barclay, though, was when Ashley himself had drifted over to the fire where Barclay was a guest and chatted for a bit. When he learned that Barclay had been the one to risk his life to save Walking Thunder's, he congratulated the young man.

"And I'll tell you, son," Ashley added, "if you ever get tired of this soldierin' nonsense, I'd be more than happy to have a young man of your grit and determination along with me."

Barclay flushed. "I'm obliged for those kind words, General," he said in an awestruck tone. "But I'm afraid I've got me a spell left to go before my time's up servin' the Sixth Infantry."

Ashley nodded. "I figured. But you keep it to mind when that day comes."

So Barclay had plenty to consider as he marched step after weary, pain-racked step alongside the Missouri River. He wanted nothing more than to simply slip away from the soldiers one night at camp and head back upriver. On his own, he figured he could catch up to Ashley's and Pilcher's keelboats in a few days. It might be a little tricky getting past the Arikara villages, but he thought he could do it.

Such thoughts were mighty enticing, especially on those days when Noordstrom was annoying him again. But he was uncertain. While the desire was there—and his inherent rashness egged him on—the reasoning part of him told him it would be foolish. At least right now. He had less than a year to go before his enlistment was up. He had made it this long despite the constant sniping by Pennington and Noordstrom. He figured he could make it the rest of the way. Especially if he renewed his vow of trying to become a good soldier and stay out of trouble. If he could do that, the last year would be relatively easy. Then he could sign on with Ashley, or anyone else heading west.

There were plenty of times on the trek when he wavered in his resolve; times when the thought of the freedom represented by the fur men was almost more than he could bear. The farther along he got, though, the less he wavered and the more firm he became in his thoughts of getting through the rest of his enlistment without trouble.

10

For the most part, Barclay managed to put aside his new-found longing to be out west, at least for a short while. But he did catch himself now and again staring upriver, dreaming and wondering what it would really be like out there, bedding Indian women, fighting warriors, trapping and trading beaver. He was aware of the dangers, but in his mind they were minuscule compared with the glories and adventures he imagined he would have.

The protection he had acquired by saving Walking Thunder had pretty well expired by the time the army column reached Fort Atkinson, much to his regret, though not to his surprise. However, when Pennington and Noordstrom picked up abusing him, they seemed to still be treading lightly around him. It was almost as if they had been warned against being too harsh on him. That made it a little easier for him to keep his calm. Like the last time he had done that, it infuriated his nemeses all the more. But with his sights set on the Rocky Mountains a year hence, he was able to endure.

Not that his life was ideal. Far from it. Pennington and Noordstrom continued to make sure that Barclay—and quite often Schellenberger because of his association with Barclay—got the worst duties available. For his part, Barclay performed those tasks stoically, no matter how onerous, to the increasing chagrin and annoyance of the Captain and the Sergeant.

It was a strain for Barclay, though, and it began to show on him after a little while. It was mostly in small ways—temper at friends when he lost at euchre, anger at the poor food, standoffishness with almost everyone except Schellenberger and Watrous.

What turned out to be the last straw was one of the most odious tasks at the post: the removal of the piles of manure from the stables, which had to be taken and dumped outside of the fort somewhere. Though all the soldiers at the fort were infantrymen, and the river was used for the majority of travel, they still stabled quite a few horses and mules. Barclay was required to handle this repulsive chore far more often than others, and he did it with no outward sign of distaste, though he abhorred it and he loathed Noordstrom for seeing that he was assigned to it so frequently.

The selected site for the dumping was about a quarter of a mile downriver from the fort. The spot was at a steep slope down to the river itself. The slope was free of brush and larger stones, making it an almost easy job for Barclay to back the wagon up to the slope and shovel the manure and old hay off the back of the wagon. It would slide down the slope and into the rushing waters of the river.

Barclay was hot and bored when he set out one afternoon with a load of manure. It had rained all day yesterday, and the storm had left lingering clouds and the threat of more rain. The high humidity, combined with the heat, made the day oppressive.

He got to the dump site and backed the wagon up. Wearily he hopped down and chocked all four wheels with rocks, then climbed into the stinking bed of the wagon. Grabbing his shovel, he began shoving loads of fly-infested waste off the slick bottom of the wagon.

He was about halfway through when he saw a

patrol marching toward him from the fort. He ignored it, since it was a common thing these days. Patrols were always marching hither and yon for no particular purpose other than to give the men something to do, as far as Barclay could see. This one was of only slightly more interest than usual simply because Sergeant Noordstrom was leading it. He generally assigned that to someone else while he stayed inside the fort, not exerting himself more than necessary. Barclay shrugged; it meant nothing to him.

Barclay bent back to his work as rain began falling. "Damn," he muttered. All rain would do was make the manure smell worse than it already did. He was not paying as much mind to the job as he should have—well, he never really did; after all, it didn't require an abundance of intelligence.

So, as he gave a shovelful of manure a good, strong push, his foot hit an extra-slick spot near the rear of the wagon bed. He had no chance to regain his balance, and he fell, hitting his buttocks and back against the rear of the wagon. Then his rump hit the ground with a hard thud, and he started sliding down the slick slope, scraping over small protruding stones, the back of his head bouncing semi-rhythmically on the mud and manure.

Just before he hit the water, he heard hysterical laughter, and for some reason he thought it was Noordstrom. Then he was in the river, eyes and mouth scrunched up so as not to encounter the floating globules of waste that had not yet been swept away. He has so much momentum built up that he sank fairly deep, and the current immediately grabbed him and slammed him up against a sunken boulder.

Most of his air popped out, but Barclay managed to keep himself from trying to draw in a breath. But hitting the stone had kept him from being dragged downriver. He kicked his feet and clawed at the boulder, attempting to get to the surface.

His head finally broke above the water and he desperately sucked in a lungful of air. Gasping, he latched onto a partly submerged log and hung there for some moments, thankful that he could breathe. Then he gingerly turned in the water and began pulling himself toward the bank.

Hearing the laughter again—or was it still? he wondered—he looked up the tall bank. Standing there with arms akimbo, laughing wildly, was Sergeant Sven Noordstrom.

"Hell of a show you put on there, Barclay," Noordstrom called down. "But I'm waitin' to see how you get back up here."

Barclay knew now that he could expect no help from Noordstrom, nor from the other troopers, since none of them would buck the Sergeant in such an instance. He also knew that he was going to have a hell of a time getting back up the slick slope. He hung there on the log, the lower half of his body being buffeted by the current as he considered his options. They were few, and none pleasant.

He could stay where he was, waiting until Noordstrom and the troopers left, and then hope that someone else would come along to help him. That seemed foolish. He was sore from hitting his rear end and back on the wagon, his head hurt from bouncing and the current was doing little to ease his aches. More to the point, though, he suspected that Noordstrom was in no hurry to leave. Barclay figured the sergeant would want to watch him try to crawl up the slime-coated incline.

Another option was to let himself be swept downriver from this miserable little haven, and hope that he could reach the bank under his own power at a place that offered an easier way out. That was, however, quite risky, since he was in pain and was not the best swimmer. He was not at all sure he would be able to control his movements enough to get safely out of the water at some more accommodating spot.

His third alternative was to simply suck in his gut, grit his teeth, ignore Noordstrom, and begin the long, treacherous climb toward the wagon. There was danger in that, too, however. There was little to help him. Even on the sides of the slide area there was little that he could grasp onto. There was an occasional boulder and a bush here and there, but none looked very stable, and they were infinite distances apart. Slick, sheer cliffs lined the slope at spots, offering no handholds. If he tried making it up the slope and slipped back down, there was a good chance of him being in a worse pickle than he was now.

The longer he stayed where he was, the more difficult any of his choices would be. He would begin to weaken sooner or later, limiting what he could do. He didn't think that would happen for a while, but still, it was another risk, and one that he did not really have to take. Besides, the longer he was here, the angrier he got. Not only at having gotten into this untenable situation in the first place, but at Noordstrom's mocking laughter and words from so far up the bank.

After another five minutes or so in the cold, foul water, Barclay made up his mind. There was no way Noordstrom was going to leave soon, and he was not comfortable being in the water for long, so it had to be a long arduous climb. Barclay did take another minute or two to stay where he was, looking up the incline, trying to plot a course that might bring success. It looked mighty hopeless from his position, though.

The first order of business was getting up onto the beginning of the bank from the log without slipping back into the water. Sucking in a deep breath, Barclay forced himself under the water again, keeping a firm, somewhat frightened grip on the log. Then he jerked himself up with his arms as hard as he could. He flew out of the water about waist high, managed to complete a tottery half turn, and then landed with his rump mostly on the log.

As he sat there for a few seconds catching his breath, he felt quite proud of this minor success.

Finally he squiggled over on the log to where its end rested against a small, almost flat, muddy spot. Wavering as he tried to keep his balance, Barclay tried to stand up on the log. It took three tries but he made it, and then stepped onto the tiny flat spot. It was, he figured, the only haven he was going to find.

Cursing himself and Noordstrom relentlessly in a low mutter, he lay on his stomach and reached up the slope as far as he could. He felt a rock and with his fingernails clawed at the mud on the up-slope side of it until he had a handhold of sorts.

He pulled himself up with his left arm. With his right, he scrabbled in the slick mud above and slightly to the right of his first hold. It took repeated attempts, but he finally had another handhold.

He alternated arms, always reaching out to carve himself another handhold a little farther up than the last. It was exhausting work, made worse by the steady rain, and within minutes his arms and legs were trembling from the effort. Noordstrom's laughter faded into the background, lost amid Barclay's concentration and the sound of the river below.

After what seemed like hours to Barclay, he stopped for a breather. He held a precarious perch, but one that was more certain than any of the others he had managed to find—a small, almost dead bush growing at the base of the cliff.

With trepidation, he looked up the incline. As he had feared, he had made little progress, and still had a mighty long way to go. He wanted to scream in frustration, but did not.

After a too-brief rest, Barclay began clawing his way up the muddy slope again. His breaks became more frequent, as he was tiring rapidly, but he continued to press on.

He was about halfway there when Noordstrom called his name. He looked up just in time to see at least one shovelful of manure hurtling toward him. He buried his face almost in the mud as the waste material splattered over him, accompanied by another burst of laughter from Noordstrom.

Barclay looked up to see Private Jamie Mulholland pushing another load of manure off the wagon and down the slope. Mulholland was one of the few enlisted men at Fort Atkinson whom Barclay did not get along with, and seeing what Mulholland was doing now—at Noordstrom's instigation, he assumed—sent another burst of rage through him. He would not forget this, and he vowed then and there that Mulholland would pay for it.

Barclay buried his head again and three more times to weather the flood of animal waste that cascaded over him. Then it seemed to stop. With the slight rest and the new flames of rage pushing him on, he resumed his long, tedious, gut-wrenching trek.

He hissed and swore when he slid a quarter of the way down again after having made some good progress. But once again Noordstrom's laughter gave him the impetus to continue.

When he was about three-quarters of the way to the top, he began to think that he would not be able to make it. He was certain he did not have the strength to scrabble out any more handholds in the slick mud, or the power to pull himself up by them even if he could claw them out. Only hate and a desire for revenge kept him going.

It helped him a little when Noordstrom called down to him shortly after, "Well, Private, it's time we went about our business. But you've given us a hell of a day's worth of amusement, boy." Then he was gone from the lip of the steep slope.

Moments later, Barclay could hear Noordstrom ordering the men on their way.

Barclay sighed in some relief. He didn't need Noordstrom right there to keep his anger up. No, the flames of his rage would not be so easily extinguished.

With renewed hope, Barclay resumed his ascent, and finally he reached the top. As he crawled onto the flat next to the wagon, he flopped onto his back. The rain splashing on his face did not faze him as he lay there, chest heaving.

He didn't know how long he lay there, since he dozed off, but it was just about dark when he managed to creakily climb onto the wagon and head back to the fort.

"Where the hell've you been, Private Barclay?" Corporal Vanderplaas asked angrily.

"None of your goddamn business." Vanderplaas was another of the few men here who rubbed Barclay the wrong way.

Despite his anger, Vanderplaas chuckled a little and pointed to Barclay's uniform. "Goddamn, boy, what've you been up to?"

"That ain't none of your affair either," Barclay said stiffly. "The wagon's yours to deal with."

"Like hell, Private," Vanderplaas snapped. "Now clean that up and tend the horses," he commanded.

"You can order me all you want, Corporal," Barclay answered in a harsh voice, "but I ain't doin' it. I'm going over to the infirmary "

"Cap'n Pennington don't cotton to malingerers," Vanderplaas warned. "You should know that."

"I know it," Barclay said stiffly. "And I ain't malingerin'." He turned and walked out of the stable, cutting off any possible continuation of the argument by Vanderplaas.

Captain Paul Stringham, the post surgeon, patched up Barclay's cuts and gave him some horse liniment for his aching muscles. There was nothing much else he could do for him, other than give him some laudanum for the pain. Barclay gladly accepted the bottle, figuring it was the closest thing to whiskey he was going to get for a while.

The doctor also gave Barclay written orders for him to spend the next three days in bed while he gave his body time to recover. Barclay could find no reason to quibble with such an order, particularly when he knew it would annoy the hell out of Pennington and Noordstrom.

Barclay went back to his barracks, where Schellenberger, Watrous and several other friends asked what had happened. Barclay stripped off his torn, muddy uniform, washed up as best he could from a small basin, and put on a clean uniform someone gave him. Then, as he shared his bottle of laudanum with the others, Barclay explained what had happened.

He went through it again—though in a much abbreviated version—when Pennington stormed into the barracks demanding to know why Barclay had disobeyed Vanderplaas's orders. Barclay had trouble fighting back a laugh when he handed Pennington the written orders he had received from the surgeon.

In a huff, knowing there was nothing he could really do to counter the physician's orders, Pennington stomped out, as the enlisted men laughed at the officer's annoyance.

11

Barclay wasn't back to full strength at the end of the three days, but he was close to it. And he was feeling his old self again—cocky, irrepressible, full of deviltry. He also continued to nurse an unwavering hatred for Sergeant Sven Noordstrom. Doing something about that, though, was pretty much out of the question, at least for now. During his three days off, Barclay had done some thinking about Noordstrom. What he had decided was that he would do everything in his power to take what Noordstrom dished out. For now. But when his enlistment ended, and he was no longer under Noordstrom's sway, the Sergeant would pay.

He did not have to be quite so concerned about Private Jamie Mulholland, however, and as soon as he had recovered, Barclay paid a visit to the barracks next to his own. Spotting Mulholland back in one corner, Barclay headed that way. The other men, knowing what had happened, got out of the way. Most were friendly with Barclay, but they were not, as a rule, against Mulholland. Still, they wanted to see how the two men handled themselves in such a situation.

"Hey, Barclay," Mulholland said in a comradely way. "What're you doin' here?"

"Lookin' for you," Barclay said calmly.

"What fer?" Mulholland asked, feigning surprise. He knew why as well as everyone else did. He was, however, a little surprised at Barclay's calm demeanor. He had expected Barclay, but had figured the man would come storming at him one day. Barclay had a reputation of rash behavior. Mulholland had sort of counted on that, figuring he could handle a man who wasn't thinking so well because of his rage.

"Wanted to bring to your attention some of your ill-mannered ways," Barclay said evenly as he stopped at Mulholland's bunk.

"Oh?" Mulholland tried to pretend as if he were still surprised, but even he knew he wasn't fooling anyone. He dropped the grin. "I suppose this is about that little bit of foolishment from the other day."

Barclay nodded. "You got to answer for that bit of foul behavior, Numb Nuts."

"Shoot, I don't got to do no such thing," Mulholland drawled. "Leastways not to some pukish snot like you."

Barclay nodded. "I see," he said evenly. "Don't have the stones to stand up for yourself, eh? Got to hide behind Noordstrom's skirts?"

The other men laughed a little.

Mulholland did a good job of masking the sudden flush of anger that burst inside him. "A man's got to follow orders," he said flatly.

"That's odd. Nobody else on that detail thought it necessary to follow that particular order."

"You need to take that up with Sergeant Noordstrom," Mulholland said stiffly. He was angry and irritated, but he didn't want to get into a fight if he could help it. If he could stay out of trouble, he figured he would be a corporal before long. Noordstrom would see to that.

"You best watch yourself, boy," Barclay said with a smirk. "If Noordstrom ever stops suddenly, your head's gonna go straight up his ass all the way to your shoulder blades."

The laughter among the men was greater this time, and it carried a more cutting edge to it.

Mulholland flushed. "You're treadin' thin ground here, Barclay," he said tightly. "And could be settin' yourself up for some big trouble."

Barclay snorted in derision. "There ain't no amount of trouble I can get into that'll stop me from makin' you pay for what you did to me, Numb Nuts."

Mulholland decided that he had nothing left to lose. He was not going to get much help—or even sympathy—from the other soldiers. And, he thought, by taking care of Barclay, he should gain even more favor in Noordstrom's eyes. He bolted up off the cot.

Mulholland slammed into Barclay and drove him back two or three yards before the back of Barclay's knees hit another cot and he fell across it with Mulholland on top of him. Barclay's head almost hit the floor on the other side of the primitive cot.

Though at an awkward angle, Barclay managed to get his right arm up and jammed the ball of his thumb against Mulholland's Adam's apple. It had little effect, and slid off right away, but Barclay kept pushing the thumb up, hoping to shut off the carotid artery. All the while, he was trying to fend off Mulholland, who was trying to do the same thing.

Barclay got his left arm up and clamped it on Mulholland's hand at the base of the thumb, and then twisted with as much strength as he could generate from his position.

Mulholland yelped as the ligament in his thumb got twisted almost to the point of tearing.

Then Barclay yanked hard on the thumb, twisting Mulholland's wrist. Trying to keep from having his wrist or thumb snapped, Mulholland rolled up a little. Barclay kneed him on the side, knocking Mulholland off him. Mulholland could not catch his balance on the edge of the cot, and he fell off with a low thud.

Barclay jerked upright and then hurriedly got to his feet. He whirled and kicked Mulholland in the rump, sending him sprawling on his face. "How'd that feel, you pus-eatin' son of a bitch?"

Mulholland reached out with his right hand and grabbed the end of a cot. He partly pulled himself up, shaking his head. Droplets of blood dripped to the floor.

Barclay stepped up and grabbed the arm Mulholland had on the cot. He twisted it up and around his foe's back. Keeping the pressure on the arm, Barclay also grabbed Mulholland's collar. Then he tugged Mulholland up and shoved him forward hard and fast, until Mulholland's face smashed into the log wall.

"You still think it's funny shovelin' horseshit on someone?" Barclay asked.

In response, Mulholland stomped on Barclay's instep.

Barclay shucked air through his teeth with the pain, and jerked his foot out of the way so Mulholland could not do it again. But he did not release his grip. Instead he twisted Mulholland's arm even higher along his back, forcing a hiss out of him.

Barclay held Mulholland there, face against the rough log wall, while he thought of what to do. He was in something of a quandary. He didn't want to kill Mulholland, but he did want to make sure the soldier was as humiliated as he had been. Then it came to him.

Just to make sure Mulholland was going to be amenable to moving, Barclay pulled him back a foot or so and then slammed him nose-first into the wall again. Then he released Mulholland and turned him so they were face to face. "You and I're going for a little walk, Numb Nuts," Barclay said evenly.

"Eat shit," Mulholland said, his sibilance spraying Barclay with blood.

Barclay punched Mulholland on his already battered nose, knocking his head back against the wall.

Mulholland was not done fighting, though,
despite the pain in his face. As he bounced back off the
wall, he tried to knee Barclay in the groin.

Barclay grabbed Mulholland's leg at the knee and
punched him in the face again. Mulholland lost his balance and fell, Barclay making no effort to prevent it.
Then Barclay jumped up and came down hard with
both boots on Mulholland's left tibia. The shinbone
snapped, and Mulholland screamed.

Barclay bent and hauled Mulholland up by the
shirtfront. "Like I said, Numb Nuts, we're going for a
little walk."

"I can't," Mulholland said through gritted teeth.
"My leg."

Barclay shrugged. "Have it your way," he said
evenly. He shoved Mulholland toward the door. When
Mulholland fell face down, Barclay stepped between
his spraddled legs, squatted and grabbed an ankle in
each hand before rising. He moved off, dragging a
squawking, clawing Mulholland out.

A group of soldiers followed, some quiet, some
worried, some laughing, all interested in seeing what
Barclay had in mind. The crowd of onlookers grew as
men, hearing the commotion, joined the parade, asking
others what was going on.

Barclay headed directly for the pit trenches used
as toilets by the men. Barclay had dug—and filled
in—many of them during his frequent punishments.
At the edge of one stinking trench, he stopped and
dropped Mulholland's legs, eliciting another yelp of
pain.

Tired of Mulholland's hollering, Barclay whirled
and kicked the wounded man square in the testicles.
Then he reached down and grabbed the gasping
Mulholland by the shirt and pulled him up. "Still

amused, Numb Nuts," Barclay commented. Then he shoved Mulholland forward.

Mulholland lurched ahead two hops, then tried to put weight on his broken leg. It would not hold him, and he toppled. He hung on the edge of the foul pit for a second before tumbling over it. He landed with a soggy plop in the raw excrement and urine-made mud.

To complete the insult, Barclay stood on the edge of the shallow pit, took out his penis and urinated all over the howling Mulholland. "Next time you think to debase someone for your amusement," Barclay said after he had buttoned himself back up, "you best cogitate on it a hell of a lot longer than you did this past time, Numb Nuts."

Then he walked away, heading for his barracks, ignoring the men who watched him with varying expressions.

Schellenberger and Watrous, along with several other soldiers, followed him into the barracks by a few seconds. Schellenberger and Watrous sat on each side of Barclay on his cot. The former lit a pipe, the latter picked at his teeth with a sliver of wood. Barclay sat silently, drumming the fingers of his right hand on his right thigh.

"You haff really bought yourself a heap of trouble this time, mein freund," Schellenberger said quietly.

"I expect you're right, Klaus," Barclay responded noncommittally.

"Are you prepared to accept the consequences, Miles?" Watrous asked.

"I suppose."

"There's a good chance you'll get hanged over this one, you goddamn fool," Watrous said. He had been somewhat amused by the spectacle, considering what Barclay had been through, but now that he sat and thought about it, he realized how stupid Barclay had been.

"Might be," Barclay agreed.

"Vhy couldn't you haff been satisfied vith thumpink that schweinhund?" Schellenberger asked. "Or vaitink until dark some night to do somethink to him? Vhy did you haff to do such a think in public like dot?"

"You boys just don't understand," Barclay said evenly. "You can't understand. You weren't out there, trying to crawl up the shit-slick hill in the rain while some numb-nut bastard poured horseshit down on your head in front of all kinds of other folks. Men you have to work and live with. Sure, I could've waited till I caught him alone in the dark. Hell, I could've killed him like that and most likely gotten away with it. But he had to be debased in public—the way he did to me."

Neither Schellenberger nor Watrous could argue with that. They had never experienced such a thing, but each thought he would react just as Barclay had if they were ever put in such a situation. Besides, both knew their hotheaded friend well enough to know that Barclay had really had no other course to take.

"You vant to leaf here?" Schellenberger suddenly asked.

"Leave here?" Barclay countered, looking blankly at his friend.

"Yah. Get away before they come for you."

"That'd be desertion," Barclay said stupidly. He was surprised Schellenberger would mention such a thing, since he, like Barclay himself, was a man of his word. They had agreed to serve for a specified length of time, and they would do so. But here was Schellenberger suggesting he desert to avoid punishment.

"Yah, dot it vould." He tried to grin but was unable to pull it off. "But you vould still be alive."

That was a consideration Barclay hadn't figured on. He wasn't sure that he would be hanged or set before a firing squad—after all, he had not killed

anyone—but he could not be sure. As much as
Noordstrom and Pennington hated him, they could
easily persuade each other that an execution was
called for.

"What the hell would I do?" he asked as he
warmed to the idea a little.

Schellenberger shrugged. "Who knows. You could
vorry about dot vhen you get back to the settlements.
Or," he added pointedly, "you could maybe go vest
und look up those trapper folks you vere so taken
vith."

Barclay's interest was suddenly piqued for real.
That was something he wanted to do—was planning to
do—anyway. Now might be the time to do it.

Watrous, ever the practical, put a damper on the
plan. "That'd be foolish, too," he said. "You have no
idea where they are, and there are thousands upon
thousands of miles of uncharted lands out there.
Besides, there's always the matter of the Arikaras and
Pawnees and who knows how many other hostile
tribes."

"So you're sayin' I should stay put here?" Barclay
asked, disappointed.

"Not at all. The decision to take off is all yours. All
I'm sayin' to you, Miles, is that you'd be better off goin'
east. You can always sign on with one of those trapping expeditions next year."

Barclay nodded. That made a lot of sense. There
were other factors to consider, too, such as the sheer
distances out here, as well as the fact that winter was
not all that far off. He could never make it to the mountains and find Ashley's party before winter set in.

"Reckon I can do that," he said calmly. Then he
added, "But I can't ask you boys for help."

"I can offer to help mein freund if I vant,"
Schellenberger said.

"I have to agree with Klaus," Watrous noted.

"Horseshit. You boys're in trouble often enough just for bein' my friends. There's no need to stick your neck out for me."

"Ach!" Schellenberger growled. "They vill say ve helped you anyvay. So, if ve're goink to be in trouble, ve might as vell giff you some help so they haff reason to giff us trouble."

"Well, when you put it that way . . ." Barclay said with a slight grin.

The three began making plans, continuing to speak quietly, not wanting the other men to overhear. They were fairly certain that none of the others would say anything, but they decided they should be as careful as possible. They knew they had to act fast, since someone would be around to arrest Barclay very soon.

12

Even as the three tried to make fevered plans, Barclay suspected that it would be in vain. And he was right. Within ten minutes of him dumping Mulholland in the waste trench, a livid Pennington stormed into the barracks. He was followed by an equally enraged Sergeant Noordstrom, a cowed Lieutenant Hodges and ten troopers of G Company, none of whom looked like he wanted to be there. They stopped in front of Barclay's cot.

"Of all the despicable things one soldier's ever done to another," Pennington fumed, "this is far and away the worst I've ever encountered. It was a loathsome act that only a man with a degenerate mind could come up with."

Barclay shrugged. "I got the idea from somewhere else," he said, glaring at Noordstrom for a moment before looking back at Pennington.

"You've sealed your fate with this depraved act, Private," Pennington said. His rage was slowly giving way to a gloating feeling. He had always despised men like Miles Barclay, ones who were arrogant with no reason for it, who thought they were better than others when they were really inferior, who flouted the rules and dared those in authority to do something about them, who thought they were above the law.

Pennington had always considered Barclay one of the worst he had ever encountered, and he had tried his damnedest to get rid of the thorn in his side. It appeared now as if he were going to get his wish. Yet he could not be too elated, since he considered it merely the way things should be. Willard Pennington was an arrogant man of aristocratic birth, or so he would like everyone to believe. He had built himself up in his own mind until he felt he was better than any man alive. To have such a mosquito as Private Miles Barclay annoying him so constantly was unbelievable to him, and so it was only right, at least in his mind, that Barclay should come to a bad end, and he would be relieved of this annoyance. So caught up in himself was he that he would not—actually could not, by now—see that he had as many of the same character faults as Barclay did, and then some.

Barclay could see in Pennington's eyes how the officer felt about him, and he regretted not having killed Pennington before now. He was almost shocked at the thought, since he had never before wanted to kill a man. But it was no matter now.

Barclay shrugged. "If you execute me, I'll be dead, but you'll still be a lily-livered toad with no stones."

"Chain him and drag him to the guardhouse," Pennington snapped. "Limit his rations to once a day. And make sure that these two—" he pointed to Schellenberger and Watrous, "do not have guard duty. And I warn you two that if you give me even the slightest reason to, I will have you in jail with your reprehensible friend here. Is that understood?"

Schellenberger and Watrous saluted with a decided lack of enthusiasm, and echoed, "Yessir."

"Carry on," Pennington commanded.

In moments, Barclay was shackled hand and foot. Under the guard of ten men led by Noordstrom, Barclay shuffled out the door and across the compound to the wood guardhouse. He was placed in the cell, and two soldiers unhooked his chains. As he did so, one whispered, "Keep your spirits up, Miles. Maybe things'll work out."

Barclay nodded and sat back against one wall. Alone, in the barren cell, Barclay had time to think, and he didn't like that, since he had to examine his faults, foremost among them being his stupidity. Others might call it rashness; hell, he had done so all his life, but when looked at objectively, it was plain old stupidity. Barclay knew he had a good head on his shoulders. He just wished now that he had used it.

The extent of his foolishness was large, and could all be laid to his pride. If he could have swallowed the early insults; if he could have tempered his impetuousness; if he could have gotten off to a better start with Pennington. There were so many ifs, and none of them made a damn bit of difference now.

Barclay spent the next two days in the corner of his cell, hardly moving except to take his one poor meal per day or to stretch out on the single spare blanket he had for sleeping.

The solitary existence wore on him quite quickly, since his thoughts were all a-jumble. He alternated from regret that he had not killed Pennington and Noordstrom, to ruing the way he had handled Mulholland, to despair for wasting a life so full of promise, to rage for having been locked up for something that any man with any self-respect would have done.

He considered it somewhat fortunate that the court-martial was scheduled only two days after his arrest. He was not surprised at its brevity; he and everyone else knew what had been done, and that he had done it. He also knew that no one was really interested in hearing his version of events, so he kept his own testimony brief.

If was, of course, no shock either as to what the verdict was. The panel of officers didn't even have to leave the room to deliberate. He was guilty, and that was that.

What did surprise Barclay—and everyone else at the fort—was the punishment. Everyone, from Captain Pennington to Lieutenant Hodges to Sergeant Noordstrom to every enlisted man on the post, including Barclay himself, had expected the death penalty to be ordered. But the punishment that was handed down was thirty lashes, to be administered by Noordstrom on Barclay's bare back.

Barclay was stunned, and it was only when he was back in the guardhouse that it really hit him, and then he wondered about it. He was not sure at all that he liked the idea of being whipped, especially by a man who hated him. The pain he would experience would be nearly intolerable, and he was not sure he could take it without breaking down, which to him would be the ultimate insult. It would be less traumatic, he thought, to just face hanging or the firing squad.

Fortunately, he did not have long to sit and worry about it. The lashing was scheduled for the next morning, just after dawn. It was that much less time for him to let the horror of what he faced build up in him to the point where he would burst from it.

There was one small benefit to all this: he was given a decent meal that night, and a fairly decent breakfast. They didn't want to overfeed him with the latter, however, since they didn't want him vomiting midway through his punishment.

The squad that came in the morning to escort him did not find it necessary to shackle or bind him. With the entire garrison gathered to watch, there was no way for him to escape.

Barclay found it rather difficult to joke with his companions as he was marched out toward a post that had been sunk into the earth in the middle of the parade ground, but he made a stab at it.

"I kind of feel like a goose just before Christmas dinner," he said. "And you're the farmer here, Corporal Dunnigan."

"Aye, laddie, I can see how ye might have that feelin'. But I'll tell ye, I'd rather have it that way than the other."

"You're losin' your sense of adventure, Mac."

"I've had enough adventure in my life, laddie." Then Dunnigan grew serious. "Ye think ye can stand up to this, lad?"

"Damned if I know. But I got my doubts."

"I dunna know if I could take it either. All I can say to ye, Private, is to keep strength in yer mind. The more doubts ye have there, the less ye'll be able to handle the actual lashin'."

Barclay nodded, not sure if he could do that, but grateful for the advice anyway. "Thanks, Mac. I'll try to keep it in mind."

They stopped at the pole. "Take off your blouse and shirt, Private Barclay," Dunnigan ordered, his voice commanding, officious.

Barclay did as he was told, tossing the garments to one of the soldiers. Then two other troopers tied Barclay's wrists together and then tied the rope to an iron ring through the post, high up, stretching Barclay almost onto his toes. His naked back gleamed whitely in the pale shimmer of the early morning sun.

Suddenly Noordstrom appeared on the other side of the pole. He was grinning evilly. "I'm gonna enjoy this, Barclay," he said. "Yes, indeed, I am."

"Get on with it, Numb Nuts," Barclay said, spitting in Noordstrom's face.

Noordstrom sneered as he wiped the spittle off his

face. "You'll be a whimperin' little shit by the time I'm done with you, boy."

"It's gonna be dark before you get done if you don't get started sometime today."

"Eager little bastard, aren't you?"

Barclay shrugged as best as he could in his awkward position. "It's got to be done, might's well get it over with."

"Sergeant Noordstrom!" Pennington bellowed from somewhere behind Barclay. "Proceed with your duty before we all grow roots here."

"Yessir," Noordstrom said. He smirked once more before moving out of Barclay's sight.

Barclay braced himself, saying what few prayers he knew, and trying to focus his mind on something, anything, other than what was about to happen. He wasn't sure how successful he was until the first hissing sting of the lash on his back. It hurt like all hellfire, and he knew he had not been successful at all in trying to blank his mind to his punishment.

His mind was still on the first lash, and the burning it had brought when the pain was joined by another, even sharper one. "Oh, shit," he whispered.

The whip strokes continued, each worse than the last, until Barclay felt as if his entire back was a sea of flames, and he was groaning continuously. But then, somewhere amid the shock of the sheer, intense pain, Barclay found a little spot of peace.

He had a sudden picture of a rushing stream, and a small camp next to it. Snow-covered mountains reared their stony heights skyward beyond the camp. Horses grazed nearby, tied to a rope strung between two cottonwood trees. And he sat in that camp, near a fire. Next to him was a woman. She was a dim form, her face not really distinguishable. He was sure she was an Indian woman, though, and that she was young and attractive.

The pain seemed to fade away, as long as he kept that picture in his mind. It was a picture entirely of his mind's making, since he had never seen a place like that. It was a dream, implanted in his brain by trappers sitting around a fire not far from an Arikara village. He did not know why he held it so strongly, and even if he could've considered it at the moment, it wouldn't have mattered to him.

He was unconsciously still moaning with each stroke of the whip, but otherwise he gave little outward indication that he was being flayed. He was even unaware of when it ended for sure. As he clung to that pastoral image in his mind, he only slowly became conscious of being carried, and he figured the beating must have been completed. Then he realized he was on a bed of sorts. After that, there was only darkness—no pain, no mountain scenery.

He awoke in the fort's infirmary, lying face down. He could not remember why he was here, until he shifted his shoulders thinking he would roll over. He yelled as fire roared across his back, the flames licking conflicting trails through his flesh. His head sank back on the cheap, straw pillow.

"How're you feeling, Private?" Dr. Stringham asked.

"How the hell do you think I'm feelin', Numb Nuts?" Barclay countered, his voice a hiss of anger and agony.

"Since I assume you're still in considerable pain, Private, I'll not report you for speaking to an officer in such tones and with such language," Stringham said.

"Thanks," Barclay said sarcastically. He didn't know whether the post surgeon was serious or not, nor did he really care right now. "How long've I been here, sir?"

"It's the afternoon of the day after you were lashed."

"I know how I'm feelin', Captain," Barclay said, thinking there would be nothing wrong in being polite if he could. "But how'm I doin'?"

"You'll survive," Stringham said dryly.

"Will there be lasting troubles?"

"You'll be scarred, have no doubt of that. Possibly badly. But I don't think there'll be any permanent affect as far as your activities go."

"How long will I be laid up?"

"A week, two. Maybe more. I can't tell. Each man heals at his own pace. With healing salves and good food, you should be back on your feet fairly quickly."

"I hate to ask this, Captain, but do you have somethin' to ease the painin' any?"

"Laudanum's about all. I'll see that you get some."

"Obliged, sir. Not to seem ungrateful, but I'd appreciate some of that laudanum now, and then a little peace."

"Of course." Stringham was glad Barclay couldn't see the annoyance on his face. He hated being dismissed so abruptly, though it happened all the time with men who were sick or wounded.

It was a week before Barclay was really up and about, and two more after that before he was feeling mostly healthy again. It was then that he finally returned to his barracks.

The time in the infirmary had given him more time to think; time to nurse the hatred that dwelled in his chest like one of his vital organs. And he was something of a changed man when he returned to the barracks. Not so much that casual friends would see it, but certainly enough to be noticed by men such as Schellenberger and Watrous. He was quieter, more circumspect. He was not as rash, but his two close friends were certain that Barclay would be just as wild as before, if need be. He just wouldn't let it be seen in his face beforehand.

He was also more determined, but he kept that to himself, too. He was determined to head west as soon as he could—to find that spot of his imagination, and the woman who had been there with him. He hoped to get to that point without getting in more trouble, but he would do whatever he thought necessary along the way.

In addition, he vowed that Captain Pennington and Sergeant Noordstrom would pay for what they had done to him. He knew he would carry the scars of his whipping for the rest of his life, and he planned to make sure his two enemies also had something to carry with them for all their days. But that, he decided, would wait until he was no longer a soldier, and therefore out of the grasp of the army.

Though he still joked and made light of things, Barclay was bitter and resentful, and he brooded as winter began to move its ungraceful presence into the fort. Though he had fully recovered his vigor by Christmas, his sullenness did not leave him.

Noordstrom took it easy on him until after the year turned, but then he began tormenting Barclay again, giving him the worst duty, taunting him, trying to goad him into doing something that would bring another harsh punishment. Noordstrom had been rather disappointed that the whipping had not broken Barclay, and he was determined to break the soldier somehow.

But Noordstrom's bullying had little outward effect on Barclay. The private kept his face blank, his demeanor even tempered. Inside he seethed, but one could not tell it from looking at him. He did derive a small amount of pleasure, however, in knowing that his new persona was all the more irritating to both Noordstrom and Pennington. That helped him keep his focus on his plans.

13

For Barclay, the winter took a lifetime and a half to pass, but somehow he managed to keep out of trouble for its duration. He sulked and brooded through the long, cold, snow-filled months, though, keeping a cap on his anger only by dint of knowing that this troublesome chapter in his life would be over soon.

When spring—well, actually just March—arrived, Barclay's spirits began to rise. It would not be long now before he would be a free man, and that knowledge allowed him to slough off the problems Pennington and Noordstrom tried to create for him. He waited and waited for either of those two to say something to him about his imminent release from army service. But neither did, and he finally went to Dunnigan about it.

"My enlistment ought to be up in a month or so, Mac," he said, a little nervously. He was worried that something might have gone wrong.

"Aye, so?"

"I'd be obliged if you was to find out for me exactly when I can leave here. I figure Captain Pennington or Sergeant Noordstrom ain't going to do so."

"Aye, it'd be unlike either of them to go out of their way for any of the men," Dunnigan allowed.

"That's the gospel truth," Barclay said with a bit of regret and anger. "So, Mac, will you do that for me?"

"I'll do what I can, lad, but I canna make ye no promises."

"I know." Barclay's anger and annoyance grew.

It was three days before Dunnigan got back to Barclay, since he didn't get on all that well with Pennington or Noordstrom either. "I dunna know how to tell ye this, lad," Dunnigan said quietly. He and Barclay were alone in the barracks; Dunnigan didn't think the other men needed to hear this. "But the captain says he dunna know where your papers are. He says he canna find 'em anywhere, and that until he does, ye'll have to stay put right here."

"That lyin' son of a—"

"Aye, he's likely that all right," Dunnigan agreed. "But I canna see that there's much ye can do aboot it."

"Like hell there ain't. I'll just . . . just . . ." He stopped, knowing there was nothing he could do. Not yet anyway. He was too enraged right now to think straight, and until he could, coming up with a workable plan was impossible. With considerable effort, he brought himself under control. "Did he say how long that might be?"

"Nae. But I'd figure it'll be a time. He dinna seem to place a high priority on it."

Barclay nodded. "Somehow that don't surprise me," he said dryly. With a sigh, he added, "Well, Mac, I'm obliged to you for doin' what you could."

"T'weren't nothing, lad," Dunnigan responded with a shrug. He cocked an eyebrow at Barclay. "Ye aren't gonna do nothin' strange now, are ye, lad?" he asked.

"Strange?" Barclay countered innocently. "Like what?"

"Like tryin' to cause harm to yon Lieutenant or the Sergeant." His golden-red mustache twitched a little. "Ye remember what happened to ye the last time ye did something like that."

A twinge of phantom pain ran across the scars on Barclay's back, and he shuddered involuntarily. "Yeah, I remember," he said bitterly.

"Then I hope ye'll refrain from such things," Dunnigan warned.

Barclay nodded. "I did so all winter. I expect I can do so awhile more." He paused, then added, "But I ain't sure how much longer I can keep myself under rein."

"I understand, lad. But ye hold on as best ye can. I'll see if I can dig around some and find those papers for ye."

"I'd be in your debt forever was you to find 'em, Mac," Barclay said.

Dunnigan nodded. "Now, lad, better be gettin' back to your duties."

Those duties for Barclay still consisted of some of the worst tasks in the fort. Barclay did them with no enthusiasm, though with enough dispatch to keep himself out of trouble. He nursed a growing anger and resentment again, nurturing it like a child. The hatred spiked at times, such as when Ashley's two keelboats came downriver, heading for St. Louis. And again several weeks later when the *Yellowstone Packet* and the *Rocky Mountains* stopped by the fort on their way back up the mighty Missouri carrying supplies for Ashley's brigades.

This finally was more than Barclay could stand, and he began making plans. He knew damned well when his enlistment was up, and he had even factored in some extra time to make up for the days he had spent in the guardhouse and such, figuring the army would expect him to make at least some of that up. But since Pennington had said nothing to him about any of this—and gave no indication that he intended to look for the papers to make things official—Barclay decided it was time to act. He knew Dunnigan was doing what he could, but he also knew the corporal was rather limited in what he could accomplish, partly because of his rank, and partly because of the captain's distrust of him.

Barclay said nothing to anyone once he had devised a plan, such as it was. There wasn't much to it, really. He didn't even mention it to Schellenberger. He figured it would be better if no one knew, even though there was always the risk that Pennington would believe Schellenberger—and Watrous, too—were in on it, even if they weren't.

In each of the next several days, he snuck into the mess area and filched some hardtack, buffalo jerky, parched corn, coffee, sugar, and salt. He took only a little at a time, stashing it in a canvas sack and then shoving the bag under a pile of old, unused gear in a corner of the barracks. In addition, he snatched a small coffeepot, small fry pan, and a small boiling pot, plus a spoon, a crude two-tine fork, a tin mug, and a canteen. Those went into the bag with the foodstuffs.

He also pilfered a rifle and two pistols from the armory, as well as powder, ball, a few flints, patch material, and the other accoutrements needed for shooting. On one of his little forays into the armory, he also stole a shooting bag of good leather. It had several compartments inside for the various items.

He secreted everything but the three guns with the food in the forgotten corner of the barracks room. The single-shot, flintlock rifle and two pistols were under the lumpy, straw-filled tick on his hard-wood cot.

He bided his time with it all. Since he had made his decision, a strange, welcome calm had come over him, and so he was not rushed. He still wanted to

get out of the fort as early as possible, but haste, he
knew, would only cause him trouble, and that would
never do.

So he made arrangements carefully, giving no outward sign of his desire to be away from the place. He
did his onerous chores without complaint, keeping
Pennington and Noordstrom off guard. So they did not
suspect anything and therefore paid little attention to
him above the normal.

Then the time came, he decided. When everyone
was busy, he slipped back into the barracks and dug
out his pilfered supplies. He stuck them in his foot-
locker, under some clothing and other things, and then
went back to his duty.

He went to bed that evening when everyone else
did, but he could not have slept even if he had wanted
to. When he was sure everyone else was asleep, he
arose silently and pulled on his pants and boots. He
pulled the stolen weapons out from under the foul
straw mattress and leaned the rifle against the cot.
Tossing the pistols on the bed, he got out his shooting
bag and the other supplies. The shooting bag went over
his shoulder, and he made sure the small, sharp patch
knife was in place in the sheath stitched to the strap of
the shooting bag. It was.

He hung his full powder flask on his belt and
stuck the loaded pistols into the leather band. Leaving
the rifle where it was and the canvas sack of supplies
on the floor, he made his way silently to where
Schellenberger slept loudly. In an urgent whisper, he
called Schellenberger's name.

It took three times before Schellenberger came
awake, and then stiffened as he tried to figure out what
had woken him.

"It's me. Miles," Barclay whispered.

"Vhat's wrong?" Schellenberger responded in the
same tone.

"Nothin'. I just wanted to tell you I'm leavin'."

"Now?" Schellenberger pushed up onto one elbow and looked at the pale blob of face next to his bed. "They playink a joke on you und just giff you your papers?"

"Shit," Barclay scoffed quietly. "Captain Numb Nuts ain't ever gonna find my papers, so I'm just takin' my leave of this infernal place."

"Alone?"

"Yep."

"Vhy didn't you ask me if I vanted to go?" Schellenberger asked. He sounded hurt.

"Didn't think you'd want to. And I never said anything to you 'cause I didn't want to get you involved in my schemes."

"But—"

"Look, Klaus," Barclay said, "if I'm gonna make any distance before mornin', I got to get movin'. I can't stand here arguin' with you. I just wanted to tell you I was leavin'."

"Yah, I understand." He was sad to see his good friend go, especially under such circumstances, but he could understand the need for it. "Vhere vill you go?"

"I'm headin' upriver, hopin' to find General Ashley, or even some of Mister Pilcher's men, if they're out there somewhere."

"You'll never find them out there in dot vilderness."

"Maybe not, but I got to try it. Besides, the keelboats just went upriver from here a few days ago. As slow as they are, I ought to be able to catch up to 'em before long, even if I am on foot."

Schellenberger thought his friend was crazy, but he was not about to say that. "Vell, goot luck, mein freund," he said, reaching out to shake Barclay's hand. "Think of this fellow vonce in a vhile."

"I will, Klaus. Bye." Barclay rose and went to his bunk, grabbed his rifle in one hand and the canvas bag

in the other and slipped outside. He kept his back
against the rough logs of the barracks and slid along it,
around the corner until he was at the back, where the
rear of the cabin formed part of the fort's outer wall.

He slung the rifle over his back with the leather
strap, and then managed to loop the canvas bag over
his shoulder. Taking a deep breath, he began climbing
up the side of the cabin in the pitch dark corner. It was
hard work, trying to find hand and foot holds in the
chinks of the wall and on places where the edges of
logs stuck out a bit.

Fifteen minutes later, he was sitting on the roof,
taking a few seconds to catch his breath. Finally he
eased himself over the pointed logs of the fort wall,
hung there for a moment, and then dropped to the
ground. So far, so good, he thought. He kept close to
the wall until he was on the same side as the river, then
he darted toward the brush. He didn't think the guards
would be able to see him, since the moon had not really
risen yet, but he didn't want to take any chances.

From there, he kept right to the edge of the brush
that lined the riverbank anywhere from a few feet to
several yards back from it. He had to watch his step,
too, lest he go tumbling off the steep bank at spots. A
quarter of a mile from the fort, he moved away from
the river some, to where he was out on the plain. That
made the walking go a lot easier.

He was all right for the first four hours, but then
he began to flag. He had spent too many days on hard,
onerous duty, and had gotten too little sleep to be very
fresh. But he persevered, moving ever onward, though
at a reduced pace. He stopped occasionally, giving
himself a little rest. That made him cold, though, even
with the coat he wore, so he never halted for long.

By dawn, he was moving very slowly, but he figured he had made a fair number of miles. He spotted a
large cottontail not far away, and he stopped. Kneeling,

he brought his rifle up and fired. He had been one of the finest shots at Fort Atkinson, so the shot was easy. Still, the gunfire rang out loudly in the emptiness of this land; only the river's muted roar, a few hundred yards to his right, kept it from being too eerie.

He walked on, angling back toward the river, looking for shade and shelter. It was not hard to find along the mighty river, and he quickly chose a spot. He was exhausted and considered skipping a meal, since that would mean a lot of work, and just going to sleep. But he decided that he needed food if the rest was to really help him recover.

Dragging slowly, he gathered up wood and tinder. Not wanting to waste any time at all, he sprinkled a pinch of gunpowder on the tinder, and with a few smooth strokes of steel on flint, it ignited. It was only minutes before he had a decent fire going. He put a little river water in the coffee pot, smashed some coffee beans and added them to it, and then placed the pot near the flames. With the coffee started, he swiftly gutted and skinned the rabbit. He dangled the carcass over the flames from a crude tripod made of stout sticks lashed together with a rawhide thong. At last he sat back to wait.

He almost fell asleep a couple of times, but he managed to jerk himself awake at the last moment both times. The aroma of the sizzling meat and boiling coffee aided him. He pulled the coffee away from the fire first, deciding there was no real reason to wait before having some. He poured a mug full and relaxed a little, sipping the hot brew doused with sugar.

Before long the meat was done, and he hacked off a chunk with the same big, wood-handled knife with which he had butchered the rabbit. He ate the piece and kept going back for more, until he had eaten about half the rabbit. He was tempted to finish it off and hope he could catch something else in the evening for his next meal, but then decided that would be foolish. He settled for one piece of jerky instead—he wanted to husband his pilfered supplies as long as he could, since he did not know what he was facing out here in the wilderness.

He drained his coffee, and then stretched out on the ground, pulling his coat over him as a blanket. He felt fortunate that some new grass was sprouting; it gave him something a little better than the stony ground as a mattress.

14

The going got a little easier after that, as the days began passing in almost blissful boredom. For the first couple of days after he fled the fort, he moved as fast as he could, as he had visions of an army pursuing him with reckless speed. But as that became less and less likely, he slowed his pace some, evening it out.

He hunted daily as he walked along, grateful that he had pilfered and brought along an ample supply of powder and shot for his .54-caliber "common rifle" made at the Harper's Ferry plant in Virginia. With the abundance of game of all kinds, Barclay could keep himself well supplied with meat. He dined nightly on deer, rabbit, raccoon, possum, even buffalo now and again. He supplemented the meat with a little parched corn sometimes or with berries, turnips, wild onions, and other edible vegetation he found along his route.

His only concern, as he passed his seventh day on the trail, was finding Ashley's keelboats. He figured he should have caught up to them by this point, but he wasn't too worried yet. He figured they weren't much farther ahead, and with him making steady progress now, he should be able to overtake them in a few more days. He figured they were just pushing as hard as they could to get upriver to where the trapping parties were waiting.

Other than that minor consideration, he actually felt quite good. His body had quickly become used to the walking, and the regular, filling meals strengthened him and lifted his spirits considerably. He had not had decent food—even if he could not cook this meat as well as it deserved—since he had signed up with the army. Rations at Fort Atkinson, as well as every other post he had been at, were poor, both in quality and the way they were cooked. He sometimes had thought that the only saving grace of army meals was the small portions the men received.

The weather was pleasant enough, with the days not too hot yet and the nights still fairly cool. He was rather surprised that he had seen no rain, though the afternoon sky had been cloudy a few times, and thick mist clung to the trees and brush along the river just about every morning. He knew the sublime weather could not last forever, but he did not quite expect the frog-strangler of a storm that swept across the prairies, following the Missouri's course straight into his face.

Enjoying the daydream he was having, Barclay never even saw the storm coming. The first he knew about it was when he suddenly became aware of a deathly stillness in the air. He stopped short and looked up at the sky, which was a threatening, blackish gray. Thick, mottled clouds hung overhead like ripe melons about to burst.

As he had every day, he was walking a quarter of a mile or more away from the river so as not to contend with brush and mud and the Missouri's sharp bends, ox bows, high slick banks, and the cliffs that lined it in places. Out here on the flats, he could make much better time. Of course, now he wished he were along the river itself, so that he might find some protection from the storm brewing over his head.

"Well, good goddamn," he muttered, knowing he would never reach cover before the downpour began.

The wind was picking up again already, and the clouds moving faster, as if eager to release their cargo. Still, he turned and walked at a swift pace at a diagonal that would bring him to the river fairly soon. He was not sure that he would find shelter there immediately, but he figured that he would eventually. And it was better than trying to weather the storm out here in the open, especially if there was lightning.

He glanced up again when he heard a deep growl of thunder swell over the land. A few moments later came an ear-piercing crack of thunder that seemed to almost slap him across the side of the head, it was nearly that painful.

Seconds later, the skies split and the rain fell in a blinding, pounding cascade that soaked him through to the bone almost immediately. He grumbled and groused, and then finally shouted in impotent fury at the rampaging of the storm. The wind, though, tore the words from his lips and threw them away with a vengeance.

Between the heavy rain and the darkness of the clouds, he could barely see, and so he slowed his pace so that he didn't wind up hurting himself somehow. He finally neared the river, but found that he was on a sandstone cliff looking down on the water an estimated hundred feet below him.

"Goddamn, God, don't you ever give up tormentin' me?" he spat through the rain. Then he sighed and turned upriver, following the cliff. After half an hour of walking, he finally reached an area where trees and brush were growing, and he could feel that he was walking downward somewhat.

Then he slipped on a patch of mud and slid down a slope straight toward the river. It was a rocky bumpy ride, with the prospect of him drowning when he hit the water at the bottom. Scrambling wildly, he managed to stop himself before he got quite that far. He lay

there on his back for a bit, breathing heavily, letting the
rain pound him in the face. He didn't care. He was just
glad to be alive.

Finally he rolled over and pushed himself up. It
was then that he spotted the cave. It was about halfway
up the steep, rocky bank—almost a cliff. It looked
mighty inviting, even if Barclay didn't know how big it
really was. He stood there a while, trying to determine
if there was any way to get to it without killing himself.
Then he shrugged. About the only way was to just go
ahead and do it however he could.

It took a hell of an effort, but he made it to the
cave, having scrambled and clawed and slid backward
and climbed and wheezed. But he was there. He sat on
the edge of the cave, protected from some of the rain
by a slight overhanging chunk of rock, and tried to
catch his breath. The boiling brown Missouri was
partly obscured well below him. It carried an enlarged
cargo of its usual freight of logs, brush, dead animals
and tons of silt.

Barclay stood and turned, edging into the cave. It
was pitch black inside, partly because of the storm. He
didn't go too far in, just enough to realize that it was
big enough for his needs. He took off his pack and rifle
and set them down, grateful that he had shot two rabbits before the storm had hit. With those in his bag, and
the supplies he still had from the fort, he could survive
for several days here if that became necessary, but he
didn't think it would. He would need a fire, though,
and that meant having to go out to gather some wood,
which meant risking the treacherous climb back to the
cave at least once if not several times. But it would
have to be done. So he headed out.

He gathered up an armful of wood after a precarious climb down to the bottom of the cliff and then back
up to the top on what was the only thing that passed
for a trail here. Going back to the cave, though, he

dropped quite a bit of the wood in the venturesome trip. He got smart the next time, and wrapped up his load of fuel in his coat, which he then tied up and slung across a shoulder. With his hands and arms free, the climb went much easier this time. He made two more excursions before he decided he had enough wood, at least for a while. And the last time he also grabbed what tinder and kindling he could find.

It took some doing to get a fire going, but he finally managed. By then he was shivering. The temperature had plummeted and Barclay was soaked. He needed the fire and some hot food and coffee—and some dry clothes.

Once the fire was burning to his satisfaction, Barclay put the coffeepot on, then stripped himself down to nothing. He tossed his clothing aside, not caring right now where it landed, and squatted close to the flames. His temperature eventually rose, and the shivering stopped. By then, the coffee was ready, and Barclay eagerly drank some. The hot liquid helped warm him even more, and he was beginning to feel relatively good. He was a little uncomfortable sitting here in the nude, but he tried to ignore the feeling.

He finally rose and saw to his clothes. There was no place to hang them, and really no place to even drape them. He finally resorted to puffing up his sack of supplies as much as he could—after taking one of the rabbits out—and then laying one piece of clothing at a time over it near the fire, starting with his long flannel underwear.

He at last got around to skinning and gutting the rabbit. With nothing else at hand, Barclay used the ramrod from his stolen rifle as a spit for the carcass. There were more than enough rocks around to prop the hickory stick up so the meat hung in the flames.

Restless, he rose and walked toward the back of the cave. It wasn't as deep as he had thought it might be—perhaps only fifteen feet, by about the same wide. It would, however, do just fine for him for a while. He didn't plan to stay here long anyway. He was even a little glad the cave was rather small. While trying to warm up at the fire, he had finally had a chance to think, and when he did that, he suddenly began harboring thoughts that perhaps somewhere in the deep recesses of this cave there might be a bear hunkering down.

Too hungry to wait any longer, Barclay squatted by the fire again and sliced off some meat. He ate swiftly and then cut off more. Before long, he had whittled the rabbit carcass down to a few stringy pieces of meat dangling from some charred bones.

He put on his underwear, which were mostly dry, and relaxed a little now that his naked flesh was covered. He placed his pants on the sack of supplies, and laid his socks on rocks right next to the fire.

Finally he sat back with another mug of coffee. Outside the rain still pounded down, the wind still roared and thunder still boomed. But Barclay felt just fine sitting in his warm little haven.

"Piss on you, Ma Nature," Barclay said in mocking tones, raising his tin mug in a false toast.

Once he finished his coffee, Barclay considered just turning in, but duty won out over sleep. He painstakingly cleaned his two pistols and his rifle. First, the lead balls had to be pulled, and the drenched powder emptied. Then the mud and dirt had to be cleaned off, touch holes freed of muck, and then everything had to be oiled. Finally he reloaded all three weapons and set them aside, proud of himself for having done what was right.

He checked his pants, and found that they were pretty well dried. He pulled them on, and then his socks. As he placed his shirt on the canvas sack so it would dry, he silently cursed himself and his vain discomfiture. He should have dried his coat first, so that he would have some sort of covering for sleeping. He sighed. It was too late to worry about that now.

Barclay built up the fire so it would last, and then he stretched out near it, trying to avail himself of as much of its heat as he could. He was asleep almost instantly, having worn himself out with all his climbing and the chills he had received.

The storm showed no sign of letting up the next morning. At least Barclay thought it was the next morning—it seemed a be a slightly lighter shade of gray outside. Not that he cared. He simply held his coffeepot outside to catch some of the still drenching rain, then put it on the fire. He still had a fair amount of fuel, the other rabbit, some of his original supplies, and all his clothes were dry. He didn't want to sit here more than today and at most one more day, but for now he was content enough to stay put, relax, and watch the storm blow itself out. If it ever did.

Barclay ate only about a third of the rabbit in the morning, wanting to conserve a little. He was beginning to wonder if perhaps the storm might last several days. If so, he wanted to be at least somewhat prepared. After eating, he sat back, wondering what to do with himself. But there was no real answer.

He was dreadfully bored by what he estimated was midafternoon, yet the rain had not slackened, so he had no desire to go outside. So he just sat, trying not to curse his bad luck and attempting to keep his mind focused on his dream of becoming a trapper in the Rocky Mountains. He could still conjure up the picture of the vision he had had back at the fort—the one with him at the campfire with the young Indian woman. He found he was even able to begin to form a face on the woman, though he knew that if he thought about that too much, he would realize that the face was purely his imagination. No woman—red or white—could be that lovely.

Even those daydreams began to wear thin after a while, and he found it more and more difficult to keep the thought of what he had done out of his mind. He was beginning to feel guilty about having deserted—which is how the army would look at it. He didn't see it as running away so much as having shirked a duty he said he would do. That galled him, especially when he realized that that was how he would be remembered.

He tried to convince himself that none of those things mattered now. Or at least they wouldn't matter once he joined up with the trappers. Then he would be one of them, and this sordid episode in his life would be long forgotten.

It was not easy to forget about it, however. He had left behind the only real friends he had in Schellenberger and Watrous; he had ruined his reputation, and he had pretty much severed all ties with his family. He was certain he would never be able to go back east now.

He wondered if there were men in the mountains who had a more stained past than he did. He had heard stories about some of the men who had headed west, but he had not believed most of them. He tried to assuage his conscience now by telling himself that at least a few of those stories had to be true. And his, he argued silently and firmly, could not be the worst. Or could it?

15

The rain finally began to let up the next afternoon, and by then Barclay was pacing the cave like a snared animal. He had had far too much time to think, too much time to worry, to let his conscience and guilt gain the upper hand on his rational side. Running low on food, sick of the rain, and disgusted with himself, he was irritated as all hell, at least until the rain began to dwindle. Once it did, he began to think he might have a chance of getting out of here soon. That cheered him a little. But only a little.

Still, it was another long, dull day for Barclay, a day of more rancid thoughts and self-recriminations. He finally shouted in irritation, more annoyed with himself for his poor thoughts than anything else. He was sick of feeling disgusted with himself, and angry that he felt so guilty about having done something that was, when one looked at it, forced on him. If Pennington had not tried to keep control over him the way he had, Barclay would not be feeling like this. Or so he tried to tell himself.

Barclay had a restless night, and awoke groggy. His spirits rose a little, however, when he realized that he did not hear the rain, and despite the mist that drifted past the mouth of the cave, he could see that the day was brighter, and held the prospect of abundant sunshine.

Encouraged, he ate some jerky and a bit of hard-tack and had two cups of coffee. Then, without further delay, Barclay slung his rifle and pack over his shoulder. With something approaching boyish joy, he scrambled down from the cave, and then back up the slick path to the cliff top. With an eager step, he marched out, angling away from the river, slogging through the mud that splashed around the new growth of prairie grass and wildflowers.

Barclay tramped on, feeling better all the time. The sun did come out after a bit, burning away the morning's haze. The heat rose, but after the cold rains of the past couple of days, Barclay didn't mind at all. The only thing that did concern him now—as it had before the storm came—was not having caught up with the keelboats. That was now worsened by the fact that he had lost two and a half days in sitting out the storm. He did not think the keelboats would have done the same, which meant that he had fallen even farther behind.

With that concern in mind, he moved a little faster, but still kept a smooth pace. He needed to make up a fair amount of time and distance, but he didn't need to wear himself into the ground right away. Still, with determination planted firmly in his mind, he found that he was stronger than he had thought. His pace was sure, steady and rather swift, and he walked until past dark, having stopped only once every two hours for five minutes to rest. And he halted for a bit to butcher a deer he shot. He could not carry the entire thing, so he just carved out some of the better portions, wrapped them in some of the deer hide, which he stuffed in his canvas sack before marching on.

He kept up that tempo, as well as the long hours, for four days before he had to slow down some. That didn't bother him so much per se, but he was becoming increasingly worried about ever catching up to the keelboats. That was beginning to seem more and more like a dream—one that went along with the one about becoming a trapper, and having the beautiful young

Indian woman at his side. He began to believe that all these things were illusions, and that all he was going to find out here was more empty space and loneliness. He thought that he might wander forever, following the course of the Missouri River for the rest of his days. That was a depressing concept to him, and one he did not want to linger on.

Barclay tried as best as he could to keep such disheartening thoughts in check and he was more successful at some times than others, of course. At times when he was able to do it, he felt pretty good about life, and he would tramp on with his head high and a lively step. When those poisonous thoughts came unbidden into his head, and he could not banish them, he tended to plod along, waiting for a disaster to happen.

The weather held pretty well after the big storm. He got rained on a little, two days after leaving the cave, but the shower didn't last long and it never got above a hard, persistent drizzle.

He was having one of his less than perfect days, when nothing seemed to be real to him, when devils and imaginings flooded his weary mind, when he thought he saw something in the distance. He stopped and stared, unsure if something was really out there or if he was conjuring it up. He caught movement again, and knew now he had seen something. What it was, however, he wasn't sure.

He walked on some more, senses fully alert for the first time that he could remember. He kept his eyes on the horizon, but saw nothing for a while, and he was beginning to doubt his sanity again, when finally he spotted something: three slowly moving figures.

"Damn fool," Barclay muttered, smiling a little at his silliness. "Nothin' but a couple goddamn buffalo." He relaxed a little and pushed onward. Though he felt foolish about having become unnerved by the sight of the bison wandering along, heading toward the river, he could laugh at himself. It was a good feeling for a change.

The next time he saw the three figures—about half an hour later—he found out they were not buffalo at all. And by the time he learned that, it was too late to take cover, even if any were available.

"Lord almighty," Barclay breathed as he saw that the three warriors had spotted him. He didn't know what kind of Indians they were, but when they kicked their horses into a gallop heading straight for him, he was sure they were not friendly.

He began to panic. While he might have joined the army way back when with the idea of fighting Indians, facing three warriors on his own was not what he had had in mind. Right now he wanted Corporal Dunnigan standing nearby giving orders in his calm, reasoned Scot's burr. And he wanted to be surrounded by men he knew and trusted; men like Privates Klaus Schellenberger and Jay Watrous.

But they weren't here. He was on his own, and he had three screaming devils thundering at him with every intention of splitting his head open and leaving his carcass to rot in the spring sun.

Barclay looked around, his anxiety growing, as he tried to spot a place where he could find some cover. If he could, he figured he might be able to stand off the Indians, maybe even discourage them, enough so that they would leave him alone and ride off back to wherever they had come from. But this far from the river there was nothing to hide behind; no brush or large bushes, and certainly no trees.

His breathing was ragged as he felt deep fear ice his guts and rivet him to the spot where he stood. And that both disgusted and irritated him. He had been trained by the army to handle trouble, and while he had never actually been in a real battle, he should be trained enough to be able to stand and face the enemy.

Just before the panic overtook him completely, he had a flash of insight that changed the situation for him. He had indeed fought Indians. Only once, maybe, but it was close up and deadly. He hadn't worried, hadn't thought of the consequences when he had charged into action to save Walking Thunder, an Indian he did not know. If he could do it then, well, by God, he could do it now, too—if only to save himself.

He swung his rifle on its sling in a smooth move as he dropped to one knee. By the time the kneecap hit the ground, the long, full-stock rifle was at his shoulder. Cocking it, he aimed carefully, no longer worried about the time or the warriors' headlong charge. He fired.

Barclay wasn't sure who was more surprised, him or the Indian who was knocked from his horse when Barclay's bullet hit him. But he had no time to ponder it, since the other two warriors were closing in on him fast. He dropped and rolled when one of the charging Indians fired a couple of arrows in his direction.

As he came up on both knees, pulling out one of his pistols, Barclay got a fairly good look at the two warriors. They were Pawnees, he thought, judging by the partially shaved heads topped by tall, greased roaches, and the glinting, dangling earrings.

Barclay fired the pistol, and a horse went down. Barclay was feeling pretty proud of himself—until he saw the warrior get to his feet while his pony lay there kicking in its death throes. "You stupid ass," Barclay muttered at himself.

He blanched as he dropped to the side. With his attention distracted by the dying horse and the Indian he had thought he had shot, he was unprepared for the attack by the other Pawnee. He just managed to get out of the way of the warrior's lance, which pinned his coat to the ground.

Barclay fell flat onto his back and jerked out his other flintlock pistol. He fired just as the Pawnee was turning his pony around to make another charge at him. He was sure this time that he had hit the warrior, since he fell off his horse. The pony trotted off while the warrior stayed on the ground. The Pawnee wasn't dead, but to Barclay he looked out of commission. Barclay refocused his attention on the warrior whose pony he had killed.

That Pawnee was almost on him already, though the warrior was limping. Barclay frantically jerked at the lance and managed to work it out of the ground. He tossed it aside and jumped up. "Keep on comin', Numb Nuts," he said with bravado. He certainly didn't feel brave. Not when he saw the nasty looking war club the Pawnee was carrying: a large stone, narrowed at opposite ends almost to a point; it was held on a stout stick with several thick wrappings of rawhide that had tightened into an ironlike bond; it was sparsely bedecked with a little paint and a couple of small feathers.

Barclay suddenly bent and scooped up the wounded Pawnee's lance. He had no idea of what to really do with it. All he knew is that it gave him a lot longer reach than he had without it, and that might be just enough to discourage this tough-looking warrior.

One glance at the Pawnee's face told Barclay that the Indian was not about to be put off by one skinny white man with a lance he didn't know how to use. Barclay took a tentative grip in two places on the lance, and then jabbed it in the warrior's direction, not really trying to hurt the Pawnee, just trying to keep him at bay.

Displaying little emotion beyond mild annoyance, the Pawnee smacked the lance out of the way with his war club. Barclay backed off a little, still keeping the spear out ahead of him, trying to retain his grip on it as the Pawnee continually whacked at it with his stone club.

The steady jarring was beginning to hurt Barclay's hands, and it was starting to irritate him, too. He seemed to be helpless to do anything with the lance despite its giving him a greater reach. He was unversed in its use, so all he could do was hold on and retreat. He was soon drenched in sweat, which stung as it seeped into his eyes.

"Dammit, dammit, dammit," Barclay muttered as the Pawnee gave the lance a particularly hard shot. The soldier decided he had had just about enough of this. He was tiring and knew he could not win a prolonged battle with the Pawnee, at least not while using these weapons, with which he was so unfamiliar. He decided he would have to try some trick. The only problem was in thinking one up.

Actually it was more like fate that gave him the answer. As he saw the now-smirking Pawnee set himself ever so slightly for another swipe at the lance, Barclay timed it, more or less. The timing, and the Indian's arrogance, might help him, Barclay thought.

The next time the warrior made his move, Barclay suddenly jerked the lance out of the way. The Pawnee's club hit nothing but air, and threw him off balance a little bit. Sweating and worried, Barclay lurched forward with the spear. The weapon's iron tip slid easily into the Pawnee's chest just over the heart and suddenly poked out the back, startling Barclay, who did not think he had pushed so hard.

With a roar of outrage, the Pawnee jerked his stone-headed war club around and slammed it against the spear again. The shaft of the lance snapped, leaving a portion of it through the Pawnee's torso.

Barclay looked at the piece of stick in his hands for a moment as if it were some sort of strange apparition. Then he shrugged and swung it for all he was worth. The stick snapped again when it encountered the Pawnee's head, and the Indian fell.

Barclay stood, breath coming hard as he looked down at the warrior. The Pawnee didn't look like he was going to go anywhere or do anything, which was a relief to Barclay. He tossed the last part of the lance shaft down. "Numb-nut bastard," he muttered, as the Pawnee tried to rise, but to no avail.

Shaking with reaction now that the battle was over, Barclay walked toward the Pawnee he had shot with his pistol. The warrior was dead. So was the first one—the one he had dropped with his rifle shot. By the time he returned from checking those two, he found that the Pawnee he had lanced was also dead.

Barclay was ashamed for the relief he felt now that the three warriors were dead. Still, he couldn't feel too much guilt; after all, they had been hellbent on killing him, and now that they had been rubbed out, he did not have to worry about fighting them again. So he was relieved. Still, he did not feel right about getting any pleasure at all from the deaths of three men, especially when he had caused them.

He tried to shake off the gloomy thoughts and turned his attention instead to the two surviving Pawnee ponies. If he could manage to catch one of them, he would be in fine shape. He could catch up to the keelboats in no time at all. And he would not have to walk any longer. That alone would be worth some risk, as well as the expenditure of some time and energy. Trouble was, how to catch one of them. From what he had heard, Indian ponies did not like the smell of white men. If true, that would make it very difficult for him, being on foot, to catch one.

He shrugged. He certainly was not going to get one of the horses by standing here thinking about it. He took a deep breath and then walked off, heading toward where the nearest pony grazed, seemingly unconcerned about what had just occurred here.

"Lord," Barclay mumbled as he drew close to the pony, "you ain't ever smiled much on me, so I think maybe it's time you did. At least this once. I really could use one of these here horses."

16

Barclay didn't know what he had done, but he apparently was in God's favor this day. First he had withstood an attack by experienced, even if quite young, Pawnee warriors, killing all three, and he had done so with little more than a scratch from where the lance that had pinned his coat to the ground had nicked his side. It had scared him when he first looked down and saw the blood on his shirt, until he realized just how minor the wound was.

His luck continued, too, as he easily caught one of the Pawnee ponies. The animal apparently had no fear of him and was not put off by his white man's smell. Barclay figured he had been lied to by whoever had told him that tale. He simply eased up on the pinto and gently took the hackamore in hand. With a light tug on that rope rein, the pony followed him back to where Barclay had dropped his supplies in the fight.

Figuring he was on a winning streak, Barclay swiftly hobbled the pony with rawhide thongs taken from one of the dead Indians. Then he headed for the other horse. He thought that if he could get that pony, too, he would not only have a spare in case of an emergency, but he would also have a pack animal. That would allow him to hunt once every two or three days—depending on how hot it got, and thus how

quickly the meat spoiled—instead of every day. With
the speed he would gain by riding, he could make up a
lot of time.

The other Pawnee pony, however, did not see fit
to cooperate. Every time Barclay drew close, the
horse's ears would flick nervously, and then he would
shuffle a few feet off, big brown eyes rolling as he
watched this strange creature.

Barclay "chased" the pony for almost half an hour.
Then, out of frustration and the sudden realization that
there could be more Pawnees in the vicinity who might
wonder where their companions had gotten off to, he
gave it up. Hoping there were no more Indians around,
he hurried back to his supplies and the captured pony.
He cursed himself softly at having followed the other
horse more than a quarter of a mile. It wasn't the distance that bothered him; just the thought that he had
not thought of the possibilities. Had he realized from
the start that there might be other Pawnees roaming
the area, he would not have even attempted to get the
other horse. He would simply have mounted the one
he had caught and ridden on his way.

Which is what he did now, after taking just a few
moments to swab some tow flax through his three guns
to clean them a little and then reload them. He slung
his rifle and pack on his back, unhobbled the pony,
hopped aboard and left in a fair good hurry.

It was a joyful Miles Barclay who made a small
camp along the river that night. He had fresh deer
meat, some coffee left, a horse, and he had come
through a hand-to-hand battle with the Pawnees. Life
was pretty good, he figured. It could, of course, get better. He could have that Indian woman of his vision;
and he could be settled in with a group of trappers,
providing companionship and safety. But all in all, he
didn't think he could complain. Compared with his situation yesterday, he was in fine shape.

The miles began to slide by starting the next morning. He never pushed the Indian pony too hard—the one thing he did not want was to be left on foot again. He had done more than enough walking for one lifetime, so he would care for the horse as well as he could to ensure its continued service.

Still, even plodding along on horseback he covered a lot more territory than he ever would have on foot. And he was a lot more comfortable, too. He realized soon that he had a better view of the countryside while on the back of the horse. Not that the country he was riding through was scenic, but he should have more warning of impending trouble than he had the last time. That was a somewhat comforting thought.

The next several days passed uneventfully, except for the time the rattler reared back just ahead of him. The pony panicked and bolted, with Barclay clinging to the animal's neck, hoping to not get dashed to the ground. After a couple of miles, he managed to rein in the pony, and finally got it to stop. The horse stood, sides bellowing in and out.

Barclay slid off the animal, though he kept a very tight grip on the hackamore, just in case the horse decided to bolt again. But the pony seemed to have exhausted itself and made no effort to go anywhere.

After a while, Barclay hobbled the horse, and sat nearby, chewing on a piece of jerked buffalo. There was little left, but he was not concerned; hunting was still going well. He was annoyed, though, at being just about out of coffee. He had not taken much from the fort—nor much of the other foodstuffs—since he had not really thought he was going to be out here this long before finding the keelboats.

Finally he figured the horse had had enough time to rest. He packed up his few supplies, mounted the and rode off. He decided after a short while that

the pony was none the worse for its headlong race.
Barclay breathed a sigh of relief.

Each morning, Barclay would stand on the bank
of the Missouri, peering through the mist, if any was
there, and stare up the river, hoping to catch a sight of
the keelboats. He grew more irritated as the days
passed. He was sure the boats could not have traveled
this fast, and he wondered if perhaps he hadn't passed
them while he was walking along away from the river.
He didn't think that likely, since he felt sure he would
have had some sign of them. The men were often
noisy, as orders were shouted or as the boatmen sang
to pass the time; and the men from the boats would
have to come ashore to hunt. He should have seen or
heard something of the men's presence.

As he rode, he gave the matter some thought. It
took a couple of days, but he finally convinced himself
that the men propelling the craft up the Missouri did
that for their livelihood. Barclay had been judging the
rate at which the keelboats would be proceeding
upriver on the slowness with which the Missouri
Legion had traveled on the expedition against the
Arikaras. It took Barclay till now to figure out that with
mostly soldiers towing the keelboats up the river, the
pace would be far slower than if done by men who did
such work for a living.

With that thought cheering him, he rode on with a
better disposition, again picking up the speed at which
he traveled. But in the darker moments that still arose
now and again in his mind, he decided he would give
it only another week. Then? He didn't really know. He
would contemplate that when the time came. It was
just that he could not spend the rest of his life worrying
about where the keelboats were and whether he could
catch up to them.

He never got to that point, however. Three days
after making that decision, he spotted figures in the

distance. From his vantage point on the back of the pony, he could see right off that these were not buffalo. They were Indians; that was clear. And on this side of the river, they would almost certainly be hostile. After another moment's thought, he realized that any who were on the other side of the river probably would be hostile, too, except perhaps the Mandans. Especially to a lone white man.

Worrying that they might be Pawnees out for his blood for having killed their friends—as foolish as he knew that was; no one would know who it was who had killed those Pawnees—he stopped and sat, trying to keep the horse from moving. In some way, he hoped that the Indians out there would not see him if he stayed still enough. That would be the best thing, since it would avoid bloodshed. And there were precious few places for him to go.

One of the Indians pointed in Barclay's direction, and they all stopped. So much for not being discovered, Barclay thought. As he watched the warrior suddenly turn and start riding hard toward him, real fear crept into his chest and settled in for the long haul. Barclay figured he had every right to be afraid at this point. He spun and raced for the river, hoping he could find some defensible position there.

But luck seemed to be avoiding him again. As he neared the river, he could see no cover. He realized belatedly that he was on a cliff again, and he yanked on the rein almost hard enough to pull the pony over. The horse managed to stop.

He looked down at the strong-flowing river, and then back over his left shoulder. The Indians were closing in fast, heading from his left—upriver. He took one more look at the water that was perhaps thirty feet below, and made his decision. He backed the pony up a little, turned it and trotted off a ways. He suddenly whirled, facing the river again. "I hope you like flyin', horse, followed by a good swim," he muttered. Then he slapped the pony's rump with the palm of his hand.

A few seconds later, he and the horse were sailing through the air. Barclay had the fleeting thought, as he and the horse separated, that if there were boulders close to the bank here, this might not have been the smartest thing for him to have done. On the other hand, the alternative was a certainty—death at the hands of the pursuing warriors.

The pony hit with a loud splash an eye blink before Barclay did the same. The horse bumped into him, filling Barclay with relief. He didn't think he could swim across the river under his own power. He latched onto the animal's mane and let the rushing water help him onto its back.

"Swim, damn you. Swim," Barclay said urgently.

Man and animal made it a far better distance downriver than they did across, but they were making some progress in getting across the too-damn-wide river. They finally made it, with the blowing, exhausted horse lurching and bucking up a shallow, slick bank. Barclay stopped and dismounted. The animal needed to catch its breath, and would do a lot better without him still on its back.

As he stood there dripping, holding the rein, Barclay wondered how far downriver he had come. He had no clue, though he guessed it was a mile or more. That wouldn't set him back too far, and just might have taken him out of the hands of those warriors. That was a relief, and being on this side of the river was no worse than being on the other, he figured.

Then he wondered if he should stay where he was for a while. If he had truly left those Indians behind, they would be ahead of him now, and even being on this side of the river was no guarantee that they would still be on the opposite bank. There was a little cover here in the unlikely possibility that they had crossed over and were looking for him. That meant he would also have fuel for a fire. It might be wiser to just sit here for the rest of the day and leave in the morning, giving the Indians time to move on. He wasn't sure really how many of them there had been, but he had noted at least six. He harbored no illusions that he could stand them all off by himself, despite his success against the Pawnees not so many days ago.

He nodded. Staying put was the right—hell, only, he admitted—thing to do. He tended the pony as best as he could, though it was perfunctory, before hobbling the animal, allowing it to crop the rich, green grass. Then he sat and took out his three guns, cleaned and dried them before reloading them all, saying a quiet prayer that the powder in his flask had not gotten wet.

Still feeling some of the effects of his fright and the hellish river crossing, Barclay took his time gathering wood for a fire. He moved slowly, as if fearing that swift movement would make something bad happen. Kind of like tiptoeing through a graveyard.

He got a fire going, though it took quite a bit of effort. Then he set the deer meat he had taken the day before yesterday to cook, after he had given it a tentative sniff. He figured this would be about the last meal he would get out of the meat before it was too rotten to eat. He did, however, let it cook a lot longer than usual, until the outside was blackened and the inside well done. He didn't much care for the taste of it that way, but it was better than eating half-rancid meat, he figured. He did miss having coffee, though. He had run out three days ago.

Just after eating, he lay back, using his coat for a pillow. It was hot, and the sun plus all the exertion made him sleepy. He figured he might as well use the time to catch up on sleep. He didn't know when he might have another chance.

Something woke him some time later, but he was

groggy. He wasn't sure what woke him and had no idea of how long he had been asleep. He finally realized that the horse was shuffling and sneezing nervously. He shoved his hat back and opened his eyes. "Oh, sweet Jesus," he muttered when he saw the hard-faced warriors. He swiveled his head around, checking out behind him. More Indians were there, too. He was surrounded by Arikaras. And they did not look happy.

One Arikara came up close and squatted right next to him. The Indian reached out and fingered Barclay's tattered uniform blouse. "You long knife," he said, voice thick, guttural, heavily accented. "You bad goddamn sumbitch."

Barclay's eyebrows hiked upward in surprise. He didn't think any of these Indians would speak any English at all. He tried to cover it, though. "Yeah, I'm a long knife," he said, making sure his tone conveyed an arrogance he no longer felt. "And I'm good, goddammit. You're an Arikara—a goddamn Ree. You're the bad son of a bitch."

It was the warrior's turn to be surprised. "Why you say that?" he asked evenly.

"Why'd you say it about me?" Barclay countered. He was scared right down to his socks, but the bizarreness of the situation allowed him to keep up a conversation. It was all too surreal to take too seriously right at the moment.

"Goddamn long knives fired big guns at our village."

"How do you know I was one of 'em?"

The Arikara shrugged. "All goddamn long knives same. One bad, all goddamn bad."

"That's a stupid goddamn notion," Barclay said without conviction. There were far too many white men who felt that way about Indians. He could not blame Indians for reciprocating. Still, it was rather shocking to hear it coming from this red man's lips.

"Like hell it is," the warrior growled.

Barclay was not surprised this time. "But the Rees attacked the keelboats first," he argued. "There wasn't no call for you to do that. You'd always been friendly with the trappers."

The Indian shrugged, unconcerned.

"So," Barclay said slowly, fear nudging back into a stronger position inside him, "since I'm a long knife, you're gonna kill me?" He licked his lips nervously.

"Yep."

Barclay sighed. For some reason a strange calm had descended on him all of a sudden. Now that it appeared assured, and he was just as certain that he could do nothing to prevent it, death did not frighten him. Not that he looked forward to it. No, not at all. He had just seemed to instantaneously resign himself to it.

"Well, hell," Barclay said calmly, "let's get it over with. No reason to put off unpleasant business."

"We kill you, yes," the Arikara said. "But not now. Later. We take you to our village, long knife. There we'll kill you—slowly. You'll have much pain. All can see what a coward the long knife is. And all will see how the long knives pay for what they did."

It took but a moment for the horror of it to hit Barclay, and he blanched. He had heard tales of Indians torturing prisoners, and he was certain he could not deal with it if it happened to him. "How far away's your village?" he asked, hoping he had kept the fear out of his voice. He had also heard that most Indians respected men who did not show fear.

"Seven suns. Little more. Maybe not so much."

Barclay nodded. The thought of being dragged along to an Arikara village and tortured was the most frightening thing he could ever contemplate, but with a trip that would take a week to make, there was always a possibility that he could escape somehow. That was what he had to focus on now. That and nothing else.

17

The Arikaras bound Barclay hand and foot so he couldn't annoy them by trying to escape; they were not worried about that, nor were they concerned about him attacking one of them. They just didn't need the irritation. That done, they checked his stolen pony, went through his almost empty sack of supplies, and argued over his pistols. The leader—whom Barclay had finally figured out was called Rattling Hooves—took the rifle, shooting pouch and powder flask without debate. Barclay assumed it was because he was a chief. Not that it mattered.

Two of the Indians rode off soon after and each returned within half an hour with a freshly killed deer slung over his pony in front of him. It was a matter of only minutes before the meat was sizzling over the fire that another warrior had built up to accommodate it.

Barclay licked his lips as the aroma of the meat—and the coffee the Arikaras had begun to make—wafted over him. He hoped he would get a share, though he realized in his mind that such a thing was highly unlikely. There was no real reason for the warriors to treat him well. Sure, they might want to take him to their infernal village and torture him for everyone's enjoyment, but that didn't mean he had to be in good shape when he got there. He would wait and see, though. They just might be perverse enough to feed him.

It quickly became apparent that this was not the case. Barclay watched the Indians wolfing down baits of meat for a while before he decided he had to make an effort to get some. Trying to rekindle some of his natural cockiness, he called, "Hey, Rattling Hooves, how's about you let me have some of that meat." He tried to make it sound more like an order than a question.

The war chief ignored him, not even deigning to glance in his direction.

That annoyed Barclay, and helped temper his fear a little. He decided it was time to test the theory he had heard that all Indians respected arrogance and a lack of fear. He realized that some of the other tales he had heard about Indians were false, and this one could very well be, too, but if it was, then the worst they could do was kill him now.

"Why in hell're you so afraid of me?" Barclay demanded.

Rattling Hooves cast a baleful look at him. "Hah," he said sharply, though there was no humor to be seen in his dark eyes or on his chubby, broad face.

"Don't you scorn me, Numb Nuts," Barclay growled. He was sure he sounded tough, though he was quaking inside. "You're a chicken-livered dog, afraid of feedin' one long knife." He spat to the side to show his contempt.

Some of the other Arikaras were beginning to grin, which seemed to irritate Rattling Hooves. Barclay wondered if he perhaps hadn't gone a little too far, but he was in too deep to back out now. "Goddamn, afraid that if I get some food I'll be too mighty to handle. Afraid you'll get me back to your town and I'll prove the stronger, robbin' you and your people of your pleasure, and showin' you to be the faint-hearted skunk you are."

Barclay was not sure how much of this Rattling Hooves was getting. Sure, the warrior had talked to him in English before, but he had no idea of how strong the Arikara's grasp of the language was. The others seemed to understand, or at least get most of it, since they were laughing a little and saying things to Rattling Hooves. Barclay figured they were gibing the leader.

Rattling Hooves suddenly grabbed Barclay's knife, which he had taken from the soldier earlier, and with a quick flick, threw it at Barclay. It landed in the log on which Barclay was reclining, less than an inch from his arm. "Eat," the Arikara ordered. "And shut goddamn mouth."

"I want some coffee, too," Barclay demanded. He figured he had come this far, he might as well go all the way.

"One goddamn cup."

Barclay nodded. Because his hands were tied in front of him, he had a little trouble slicing off hunks of deer meat without them falling to the ashes, but he managed. By the third time, he was pretty adept at it. He saved getting coffee until he was full of meat, wanting to savor it. When he finished that, he pondered pressing Rattling Hooves for another cup, but decided that he felt somewhat better now, and he did not want to jeopardize that. After he had eaten and had his coffee, he slouched down and pulled his hat over his face again. He wasn't sure he could sleep, but if he at least pretended to, perhaps the Arikaras would leave him alone.

Once he was doing so, however, he wasn't sure if this had been the best idea. In the quiet, with his eyes closed, he could think—and in thinking, he pictured in his mind the Arikaras doing all kinds of horrible things to him. He began to sweat heavily, and not from the day's warmth. It struck him rigid with terror, and he had to fight with his own mind to try to regain some control over his emotions.

He finally managed somewhat—there was only so long his mind could dwell on such frightening sights—and he relaxed minutely. Once he did that, he began listening to the Arikaras. He wished he could understand their language. In his paranoia and fear, he figured they were discussing what they would do to him once they got him back to their village. The little bit of rationality he had left right now told him they could be discussing anything from the taste of the deer meat, to their families, or to the raids they had just been on. It was evident even to one as inexperienced as Barclay that they had been raiding. The number of extra ponies, the fresh scalplocks, the robes and other stolen plunder stacked against a small tree told the story.

Barclay was much relieved when the Arikaras turned in an hour or so later. Darkness had finally arrived, and with it came something of a serenity to the soldier. He figured that nothing would happen to him at night, and he could stop worrying for a while. He fell into a fitful sleep at last, his dreams peopled by savage Arikaras with big knives and evil intentions. Several times he awoke, sweating profusely, only to fall back to sleep and to more nightmares.

He awoke when one of the Indians kicked him. He was haggard and still drowsy, but the Arikara had been none too gentle in waking him. Since he did not want to encourage more such treatment, he roused himself. Without asking, he headed into the brush nearby to relieve himself, and then went to the river's edge, where he splashed cold, muddy water over his face.

Wondering what horror was in store for him next, Barclay went back to the fire. Without asking, he took some meat and a mug of coffee. No one said anything to him about it.

Before he was done, though, Rattling Hooves rapped him on the side of the head. "Hurry," the Arikara said. "We leave now."

Anger had surged through Barclay when Rattling Hooves's hard knuckles thumped his temple, but he quickly brought himself under control. This was, he decided right away, not the time to cross the Arikaras, though he had no idea of why now was different from last evening. Intuition, he supposed. He gobbled down a few more bites of meat, then sliced off a couple of pieces to take with him. Dashing out the last of his coffee, he tied the mug to his belt with a small buckskin thong.

"You take that pony," Rattling Hooves ordered, pointing.

"But—" Once again Barclay clamped his mouth shut to avoid bringing trouble down on himself. He just nodded and pulled himself onto the bony, sway-backed pinto. He suddenly could not resist saying something. "You're a poor bunch of goddamn horse takers, Rattling Hooves," he said haughtily, "if this goddamn piece of wolf bait is any sign."

Rattling Hooves's burst of laughter surprised Barclay, though the solider was pleased to hear it.

"That was Hollow Horn's doin'. Goddamn fool got no sense of ponies," Rattling Hooves said, joined in his laughter by everyone else, including Hollow Horn. "Sumbitch takes any pony he finds. Don't matter shit to him if it's blind or can't walk. He takes. If he can't ride 'em, he eat 'em."

Barclay shook his head in wonder. He had always seen Indians as little more than savages, and stoic ones at that. But here these men were laughing like any other group of men teasing a friend for his idiosyncracies. He relaxed even more until it suddenly dawned on him seconds later that he did not want to start thinking of this particular bunch of Indians as friends, or even as friendly. Not when he knew what they had in store for him.

The pony Barclay had been given had an agonizingly painful gait. Not having much in the way of flesh covering its bones didn't help matters. With each plodding step, Barclay was jolted, and parts of the animal's skeleton rubbed gratingly on the insides of his legs. Worse, the Arikaras had tied Barclay's feet under the pony's scrawny belly, so he could not even shift position to relieve the pain in his legs and buttocks. Within an hour, Barclay was quite certain that he would never be able to walk again, which posed something of a problem. He needed to be in the best shape possible, if he was to try to take advantage of any opportunity that arose to escape.

He realized, too, that it was probably why he was given this particular pony. It would slow the Arikaras some, but not too much, yet it would ensure that Barclay did not bolt, either on the horse or on foot. "Cunning bastards," he muttered when he came to that conclusion.

The war party moved slowly but steadily. They had no real reason to hurry, and the warriors did not want to lose their plunder—or their prisoner. Capturing this long knife and bringing him back to let him be tortured by all the village would gain the men on this war party much honor. And it would serve as the first retribution for the army's having shelled their town on the Missouri River a year ago, helping to restore a little pride to their people.

Barclay saw no opportunity to escape that day, or the next, or . . . By the fourth day after being captured, he was beginning to believe that he would never get a chance to get away. At least not in the daytime.

So he started considering trying to escape at night. That, he knew, would be highly risky. The Arikaras seemed to sleep like cats, waking at the slightest sound; he had no idea of where he was or where to go if he did get free, or where to hide when daylight arrived. The land they were riding through had turned increasingly barren, except along rivers and streams. In addition, he would be on foot again, unless he could steal one of the Arikara ponies, or one of the Pawnee horses they had stolen. But he did not think that likely, since the warriors guarded the horses every night. And he would be without food, water or weapons, and using legs that had gotten a little worse each day.

Still, a night escape seemed to be his only choice, and he decided that two nights hence he would make his move. He would use the two intervening nights to try to scrounge up whatever supplies he could. Then, when he sneaked out of the Indian camp, he would fool them by heading northwest, instead of straight back to the river, which he figured the Arikaras would suspect he would do. If he could get a few days away without being caught, he would consider his possibilities. He still had visions of catching up with the keelboats and becoming a trapper. He certainly couldn't go back to the fort.

That night he filched some meat, using his best sleight of hand—which even he had to admit wasn't very good; it was the darkness that allowed him to pull it off—to slip pieces of meat into his shirt pocket as often as he could. He still had a folding knife in his small leather belt pouch; the Indians didn't know about that. But that was about all. As he went to sleep that night, he figured that the next night he would steal more meat and try to pilfer a fire-making kit. That would be difficult, but having one would be vital to his survival. With those "comforting" thoughts in mind, he nodded off.

Because he had not been sleeping well since he had been captured, and because he was planning to be up all the next night when he escaped, Barclay tried to doze on horseback while they traveled the next day. It was difficult, given the horse's stiff, jarring gait, but he caught a few winks here and there.

At least he did until in his half-stupor he sensed something different in the Arikaras. His eyes opened blearily, and he stared around. He could see nothing out of the ordinary—except a new agitation in his captors. He thought that strange, but he was not too concerned. Not yet anyway. He would wait a bit to see if whatever was bothering the Arikaras revealed itself to him.

They traveled on, covering several more miles. Despite an intensifying irritation and worry evident on the Arikaras' faces, Barclay could see nothing untoward. The undulating prairie still rolled on till the ends of the earth, its grass bending in the constant breeze; the blue sky still untainted by clouds.

Finally the war band stopped, and the warriors conversed amongst themselves for a bit, sometimes heatedly.

Barclay could stand it no longer. "What the hell's wrong, Rattling Hooves?" he asked evenly.

"Shut mouth," the Ree leader said in a surly voice. He turned his small war band more northwesterly and stepped up the pace. The Arikaras crowded closer, keeping the stolen ponies with them. They were alert and tense.

Barclay had no choice but to go along with them, wondering all the while what had spooked the Arikaras. He kept his eyes busy, still trying to find out what was out there. But he saw nothing. So that began to worry him. If he was so unaware of potential danger, how would he ever survive out here? He realized now that he had been on the easy part of his original journey so far, and already he had been in a battle with Pawnees and captured by Arikaras. It was bound to only get worse the farther into the wilderness he traveled. Perhaps, he wondered, it was time to reassess this dream of his. Perhaps it was a half-baked idea.

Because of that, he tried to be even more alert, scanning the landscape constantly, searching. But still he saw nothing, though the Arikaras grew increasingly tense.

He finally found out what was bothering his captors when, less than an hour later, more than a dozen Indians bolted up out of a coulee only thirty yards away and swept rapidly down on the Arikara war party.

18

As all hell broke loose around him, Barclay sat there in dumbfounded fascination. He had never seen anything like this, not even during the Missouri Legion expedition.

The attackers—Barclay thought they were Sioux, though he could not be sure in all the confusion—charged up, shooting arrows. The Arikaras fired back, trying to protect themselves and their stolen plunder.

The Sioux stopped in a cloud of dust and slid off their ponies. Except for the three guarding the horses, the Sioux edged up on the Arikaras on foot. Their bows were slung over their backs now, and they advanced with war clubs, lances or tomahawks in hand, counting on their shields to protect them.

The Arikaras also dismounted in a hurry. Leaving one to guard their ponies and plunder, they headed toward the Sioux, prepared to defend themselves and their property, even though they were well outnumbered.

As the clash began, Barclay came out of his stupor. He grabbed the folding knife out of his pouch. Holding the handle in his hands, he pulled the blade open with his teeth. It was not easy, considering that his bony horse was shuffling and snorting, made nervous by the conflict around him. He finally managed, though, and then he bent and sliced through the horsehair rope tying him to the pony.

Just as he finished, the horse reared in fright, dumping him to the ground. Barclay lost his knife as he rolled frantically to get out of the way of his horse, which lost its balance and toppled, just missing him. But the activity had startled the other ponies even more, and they were stomping and shuffling. He was not about to wade in there to get his knife. Barclay didn't know how he managed to get out of that melee of hooves without getting hurt, but he did, and he was not about to question it.

He sat up and looked around. The two bands of Indians were battling furiously, though it was apparent even to Barclay that the Arikaras had no chance of winning. He moved into a crouch and froze, suddenly incapable of making a decision. He simply didn't know what to do. The Sioux had always been friendly at the fort, and that one he had saved back in the Missouri Legion expedition had certainly seemed grateful, but he didn't know who these Sioux were, and he was not certain at all how they would look upon a lone soldier in their midst.

Then it came to him, as his brain started functioning again. There was, of course, only one thing for him to do: run. Get away from the Arikaras and the Sioux. He wished that the ponies were calmer, so that he could grab one and get away on horseback, but it was a tornado of nervous activity among the animals.

With a pronounced limp, he began making his way around the maelstrom, figuring to stick to his original escape plan and head northwest, keeping away from the river for a while. When he was just about to start running, he took one last look back, and regretted it.

A little away from the main battle, Rattling Horn had just clubbed one of the Sioux down with the shaft of his spear. He was about ready to plunge the lance into the Sioux chest.

"Hey, Numb Nuts!" Barclay shouted. It was all he could do right now. There was no way he could run the twenty or thirty feet separating them before Rattling Horn killed the Sioux.

Rattling Horn looked back over his shoulder at Barclay and sneered.

"Come and get me, Numb Nuts."

Rattling Horn spit in contempt.

"Scared again, Numb Nuts?" Barclay challenged, fright sitting regally in his chest and stomach. He moved up a few steps. "Hell, look, my hands are still tied."

"You not worth it," Rattling Horn smirked.

"We'll see about that, you son of a bitch," Barclay said under his breath. He charged, running as best he could on his gimpy legs.

Grinning, Rattling Horn squared around to face Barclay, lance at the ready.

Barclay had no intention of running into that weapon. When he was still about six feet away, he dove and twisted. He hit the ground rolling, and his torso slammed into the Arikara's shins, knocking him over.

Barclay scrambled to his feet. He had hoped that his maneuver would have forced the warrior to drop the lance, but he hadn't, though the Arikara did look somewhat dazed. With a muttered, "Dammit," Barclay charged again, hoping to catch the Arikara by surprise.

But Rattling Horn had baited him. The Arikara war chief suddenly sat upright and jammed his lance out.

Barclay gasped as the sharp iron point tore through the meat of his left breast, just above the heart, and then out the back. "Oh, sweet Jesus," he moaned as he staggered back a few steps, and Rattling Horn held onto the lance, tearing it back out of his flesh. Barclay fell on his rump and sat there, weaving, right

hand unconsciously covering the wound, trying vainly
to stanch the blood.

The Arikara leader rose. He stood there, butt of
the lance on the ground, and laughed for a few
moments. Then he hefted the spear and took a step
toward Barclay.

The Sioux on the ground, who had appeared to
Barclay to be either unconscious or dead, suddenly
swung a leg out and kicked Rattling Horn behind one
knee. The Arikara fell to his knees, but used the lance
to catch himself. He also used the spear to push himself
back up to his feet. He spit in Barclay's direction, figuring he would dispatch the soldier in a few moments.
He turned toward the Sioux, angry now, and ready to
kill. He growled a few words in his own language.

Sitting a few feet away, Barclay thought that
everything was moving too slowly to be real. He also
wondered where the rest of the Sioux were, and why
Rattling Horn seemed to be all by himself here except
for his two wounded enemies. There was no way for
Barclay to know that the Sioux, thinking that they had
killed all the Arikaras, were on the other side of the
horse herd, already divvying up the plunder. Of
course, Barclay was not at all sure he wanted the Sioux
over here anyway, since he still was not certain how
they would look on him.

These thoughts took place in less than a second,
though Barclay felt as if he had had an eternity to dwell
on them and sort them out. But they were gone before
Rattling Horn had even taken a step.

Moving like an automaton, Barclay surprised himself when he rose and suddenly ran forward, heading
for the Arikara. He felt no pain now, not in his sore
legs, not in the vicious wound to his shoulder. It was as
if he were whole once again, full of piss and vinegar
and ready to take on the world. Then he jumped.

Barclay landed on Rattling Horn's lower back, his

legs spread. In the excitement, he felt no pain in his groin from the hard landing. As Rattling Horn began falling forward, Barclay shoved his still-tied hands over the Arikara's head.

When Rattling Horn hit the ground, Barclay was ready. He caught himself on his feet, instantly stuck his right knee in the middle of the Indian's back, and shoved down with it. At the same time, he got the horsehide rope binding his hands around Rattling Horn's throat and pulled back for all he was worth. Barclay was aware of the shoulder wound tearing open some more, but he still felt no pain from any of it.

Barclay came to his senses after a while—he had no idea of how long it had been—and looked down. Rattling Horn was dead under him, his bound hands still imbedded in the Arikara's neck flesh. Barclay heard a sound and he looked around. He was surrounded by Sioux warriors, and he suddenly became afraid. Then he passed out.

Barclay was pretty disoriented when he awoke. He had no idea of where he was, how long he had been out, or how he had gotten to wherever he was, or even what had caused him to be here. Odd smells and sounds tickled his senses, deepening the mystery.

Deciding that he had to solve this puzzle, despite his confusion, he pushed himself up. Or tried to. A searing agony tore through him, blinding him momentarily. He didn't know if he made any sound or not, but he didn't really care. All that mattered to him at the moment was the incredible pain that ripped down to the core of his being. He found it hard to believe that it was real. Nothing could be that agonizing. He expected to wake up for real any moment now, back in . . . back in where?

The pain, as horrifying as it was, helped to jolt his

memory once it had ebbed somewhat. Then things began to trickle back into his consciousness: his leaving the fort, his travels, the fight with the Pawnees, his capture, the battle between the Sioux and his Arikara captors. And the lance in the shoulder. He tried to smile but found it difficult. At least he knew that the pain he had felt moments ago was real.

And these realizations went a little way toward explaining where he was. He figured he had to be in a Sioux camp of some sort. Whether it was a real village or just the warriors' camp, he couldn't be sure. That would also explain the odd aromas and sounds.

That, however, presented another set of posers. Where, for instance, was he, geographically speaking? But the more important question was: Why was he here? He didn't really want to contemplate the possibilities that went along with that question, though he had to admit that they were not all bad.

Gingerly he reached up and touched his wounded shoulder. It was bound up with rawhide, he thought, though he wasn't certain. There seemed to be some kind of poultice material there, too. That was encouraging. Barclay didn't think the Sioux would go through all this trouble if they were planning to kill him. But why would they bring him here otherwise? he wondered. They could've brought him back to the fort, since his uniform gave him away as a solider, despite its being so tattered.

All this thinking and worrying about things he could do nothing about were giving him a headache. "Hell with it," he mumbled, and he went back to sleep.

When he next awoke, he was cognizant of what had happened, so he did not try to move. He still wondered where he was and how he had gotten here. He lay there a while, the remembrance of the torturing pain making him afraid to move. It didn't take him long to get bored, and not much longer for him to start to really fret about being confined with nothing to do, unable to do anything.

He must have dozed off again because the next thing he knew there were several dark faces looming over him. He almost jumped out of his skin with fright, but something calmed him; something familiar about these faces.

"How, kola. You one good sumbitch," one of the faces said with a grin.

Barclay blinked several times, then tentatively smiled. "Hey, you're that Sioux I helped a little down at the Arikara town last year, ain't you?" he asked.

The faced bobbed. "Damn right."

"Your name's Walkin' Thunder?"

The face pulled back a little more and became more realistic looking, less like a mask. "Yes," he said with dignity. "What's your name?"

"Miles Barclay."

"What you do out here?"

Barclay shrugged, and instantly regretted it. He didn't make a sound, but he screwed up his face with the burst of pain in his shoulder. He was a little surprised to see the sudden look of distaste on the Sioux faces. "I was headin' west," he finally said, "tryin' to meet up with General Ashley's keelboats—or anyone else's for that matter."

"You not a long knife no more?" Walking Thunder asked.

Something in the Sioux leader's eyes and bearing killed the lie that was building on Barclay's lips. "I was supposed to stop bein' a long knife, but they tried to keep me there, so I left," he said simply.

Walking Thunder nodded solemnly. Such a thing was perfectly understandable to him. A man could not allow others to rule him in such a manner. "You left the long knives' log lodge alone?" he asked. His

English was still heavily accented, but it wasn't quite the exaggerated gibberish he had spoken before.

"Yep," Barclay said with a touch of his old cockiness. He was rather proud of it, now that he thought about it a little. It might've been a foolish thing to do, but it certainly took courage.

The Sioux warriors were impressed. They were men for whom bravery was one of the main virtues, and they were not shy about letting others know about their courage. They appreciated it in others, too.

"Where am I?" Barclay asked when he realized that the Sioux were not going to say anything.

"In our village along Crow Creek. We brought you after fight with the Rees."

"I'm obliged," Barclay said truthfully. "But why?"

"You helped me a winter ago. And you saved Striking Arrow from the Rees," Walking Thunder said.

"Strikin' Arrow?" Barclay responded blankly.

Walking Thunder pointed to a young, rather handsome warrior sitting opposite him on the other side of Barclay. "Don't you remember?" The older warrior seemed a little concerned.

Barclay nodded. "I remember. I just never got much of a look at him in all the fuss," he said without apology. He looked at Striking Arrow. "I hope you're doin' all right. You seemed to be ailin' some last I saw."

"I'm well," Striking Arrow said, surprising Barclay with his lack of accent. "And you?"

"Shoulder hurts like a son of a bitch," Barclay said with a grimace of annoyance.

Walking Thunder's face suddenly hardened. "We don't complain about pain and such things," he said sternly.

Barclay's eyebrows raised. He thought that over for a moment, then said arrogantly, "Well, as obliged as I am for you helpin' me as much as you have, I got to say this, Walkin' Thunder: I ain't one of you. And I wasn't complainin' as such. Not really. Just kind of commentin', like you might about poor weather or somethin'." He figured he had just signed his death warrant, but he was tired of playing meek. If they respected arrogance and fearlessness, well then he had just shown them some.

A grin tugged at Walking Thunder's lips. But all he said was, "You're right."

"How long've I been here?" Barclay asked after a respectfully brief pause. "Or maybe I should ask how long it's been since I went out after killin' Rattlin' Horn. I did kill Rattlin' Horn, didn't I?"

"Yep. You been here only seven suns."

"Hell," Barclay said with a small laugh, "no wonder my shoulder still hurts."

Walking Thunder smiled. "You'll have to move it soon," he said firmly.

Barclay nodded a little. "I know. Tell you the truth, though, Walkin' Thunder, I don't look forward to it. That might not be the courageous thing to say, but it's the truth."

"Speaking with a straight tongue is important, too. And you got enough bravery to do what you need to."

"I think so, too," Barclay agreed.

"Hungry?"

Barclay nodded. Now that Walking Thunder had mentioned it, he realized that he was ravenous. He hadn't had a real meal since just after he had been captured.

"Someone come in soon with food."

"Obliged."

19

The young woman of his dream knelt next to Barclay, and he was sure he had died now. And gone to heaven, though he knew damn well he didn't deserve that. There was no other way to explain this picture before him. No worldly explanation for it anyway.

The young woman's face was wide and very round, with a high forehead. Her eyes were big, somewhat slanted and almost black. Her skin was smooth, uncreased by care or age, and the rich color of a burnished penny. Steam from the bowl of soup she held wreathed her face but could not disguise its attractiveness; in some ways it increased her beauty by giving her countenance a shimmering, almost ethereal quality.

She said something in Sioux, and Barclay shook his head, partly to let her know he didn't understand her, but partly, too, to rouse himself from the trance her beauty had put him in.

She pushed the bowl out a little farther, and nodded at it, then at him. She said a word in Lakota.

Barclay caught on then. He nodded. "Eat? Yes." Sucking in his breath, he prepared to push himself up. He remembered what Walking Thunder had said about not showing pain, and of how a Sioux man should act, and he did not want to come across as weak to this Lakota woman. No, not at all. He wanted to impress her more than anyone he had ever met before.

This was the woman in his dream, and he intended to have her, no matter what it took.

The only sign of the agony that tore through him when he shoved himself up into a sitting position were the beads of sweat that suddenly erupted on his temples and at his hairline. Then the pressure on his wrecked shoulder was gone, though the pain was not, and he was sitting, even managing to smile at the young woman.

She returned the smile, though she would not really look at him. He wondered why that was, and worried that perhaps she didn't like him, or objected to having to help a white man. He even had the thought that she was married, and so off limits to him, and that she was trying to indicate that to him. Those thoughts did not please him.

Holding the bowl momentarily in one hand, she handed him a horn spoon with the other. When he took the utensil, she went back to holding the buffalo-horn bowl with both hands. Again she said a word in her own language, and then nodded, still not looking at him.

He dipped his spoon into the bowl she held, and tasted the soup. He didn't know what was in it, nor did he really care. It was the best thing he had tasted in a long, long time, and he ate hungrily.

As the soup dwindled, Barclay reached out his left hand and touched her right hand to steady to the bowl. A shock raced up his arm and hit him straight in the heart. He glanced at her sharply. She was not looking at him, but he would swear that she had felt it, too.

He finished the soup, but was not really cognizant of it. He never took his eyes off her face or his hand off hers, even after he had finished. She did not object.

Walking Thunder and Striking Arrow entered the lodge, almost breaking the spell. "Good, hey?" Walking Thunder said.

With his eyes still locked on the woman, he nodded, then said. "Goddamn right."

"Want more?"

"Plenty."

Walking Thunder spoke in Sioux, and the young woman finally rose, though to Barclay she seemed reluctant to do so. She went to the fire and returned moments later with another bowl of the soup.

Barclay dug into that one—he was mighty hungry—with gusto, too, though again he held the woman's hand lightly, ostensibly to steady the bowl. And he focused on her, pretty much ignoring the two Lakota males in the tipi.

But he could not make the meal last forever, and eventually the woman rose and left the lodge. Barclay suddenly felt bereft. Having Walking Thunder and Striking Arrow come to sit nearby did not help fill the emptiness.

"How, kola," both Sioux said.

"How do," Barclay said absentmindedly, his mind still on the woman.

"Feelin' better after food?" Walking Thunder questioned.

"Yeah." Barclay hesitated only a second. "Who's that woman?" he asked.

Walking Thunder's eyebrows rose, though he knew he shouldn't have been surprised. Any man—white or red—who wasn't attracted to that particular young woman had something wrong with him, Walking Thunder figured. "My niece," he said. "Night Song. Daughter of my brother, Badger."

Barclay nodded, not seeing the twinkle of interest and wariness in Walking Thunder's eyes. "This might be presumptuous of me," Barclay said without hesitation, "but is she married or engaged?"

"Engaged?"

"Pledged to be married," Barclay corrected.

"No," Walking Thunder said, then added, "but she has many suitors."

That bothered Barclay, though it certainly came as no surprise to him. He wondered why she wasn't attached, though. She was old enough, beautiful enough, and if her caring for him was any indication, wifely enough. He decided that since she had so many suitors, she was just taking her own sweet time in making up her mind.

"Why'd you ask?" Walking Thunder questioned.

Barclay hesitated, then remembered that he had done well so far in being himself—cocky, almost arrogant, unafraid. He had seen how much Walking Thunder and Striking Arrow respected that. "I want her," he said simply, staring hard at Walking Thunder. He was surprised to see that the Lakota would not look him in the eyes. He thought that odd, and he wondered if perhaps the Indian was afraid of him for some reason. The thought was ludicrous but he could think of no other explanation for it right now.

Walking Thunder did frown, though, and his face hardened. "Not possible," he said flatly.

"Why not?"

"You not right for her."

"Why not?" Barclay responded again.

"Because . . . " Walking Thunder paused. He was not afraid to speak. He just had to figure out a way to say what he needed to say without insulting his guest, and form the words in English. "You get more sleep now. We'll talk about it later," he ended gruffly. He rose and moved out of the lodge, without waiting for more argument. Striking Arrow was right on his heels.

Barclay slid down until he was on his back, but he couldn't sleep, not for a while anyway. Too much was roiling around in his mind. But he finally came to a few conclusions, and then he was able to drift off. When he awoke again, he heard voices. He looked over and saw five Sioux warriors—including Walking Thunder and Striking Arrow—sitting around the fire. "How, kola," he said quietly. He had already figured out that that was a greeting.

The others greeted him and then gathered around him, squatting or sitting cross-legged. "This is Badger," Walking Thunder said, nodding at one of the other warriors. "Night Song's father and my brother." He pointed to the two others, "Elk Horn Bow and Talks Loud."

"Come here in a group to tell me why I can't have Night Song," Barclay said bitterly. "It ain't very brave of you, Walkin' Thunder."

Walking Thunder grew angry at the challenge to his courage, but then he relaxed. Barclay was a guest, and did not know the People's ways. "I bring them so you understand why Night Song's not for you."

"I know why you think she ain't for me," Barclay said harshly. It was one of the conclusions he had reached. He pushed himself up, evidencing none of the pain he felt. He nodded thanks when Striking Arrow put a willow backrest behind him. "It's because I ain't Sioux, ain't it?" Barclay asked astutely. When Walking Thunder and the others nodded, Barclay said, "I can understand how you'd feel that way. But hear me out, Walkin' Thunder. I ain't sayin' I want her for just a night or somethin' like that," Barclay added earnestly. "I don't know if that goes against your people's ways, but it goes against my grain. I want that woman for my own—for my wife." He paused, hoping that the five Lakota understood what he was trying to say. "I've seen her before," he continued, not sure at all if he was making sense. "In a dream. I—"

"A vision?" Walking Thunder asked, eyes wide, though still not looking directly at his guest. He seemed mighty interested all of a sudden, as did all the others.

Barclay nodded vigorously. "A vision, yes. That's it. I saw her in my vision, and she was with me. She was my wife. We were together, in a camp by a mountain stream. I—" He stopped when the warriors began talking urgently among themselves. He wondered what this was all about now, and he worried a little bit.

Finally the Sioux quieted. Without looking directly at Barclay, Badger asked, "What have you to give for my daughter?"

Barclay felt a burst of excitement inside. It seemed as if they were about to let him marry Night Song. He had heard that Indian fathers wanted horses or something in exchange for their daughters, but had not been sure whether to believe it or not. It had always seemed a somewhat barbaric practice to him, if true, but now it made more sense. His hopes were dashed, however, when he realized that he had nothing he could give. He shook his head. "I have nothing," he said. He kept his face expressionless, though he was sick inside, with shame and a sense of loss. After all he had been through to find the woman of his dream, he was about to lose her before he even really got her.

"That's bad," Badger said, voice thick and accented. He rose.

"You wait till I heal up, Numb Nuts," Barclay snapped. "Then I'll get you plenty to give for Night Song."

"Maybe wait. Maybe not," Badger said with a sneer.

"Sit, brother," Walking Thunder said soothingly in Lakota. "We'll talk this out like men."

Badger frowned but retook his seat. "There's nothing to talk about," he replied in his own language. "I don't want my daughter marrying this white devil."

"He's no white devil, brother. You know that. And speak his tongue, so he can understand."

Badger shrugged. "Why let Night Song marry this

pale-skin—a long knife?" he asked in his accented English.

"Why not let him marry my niece?" Walking Thunder countered.

"Many men want her for a wife. They got much to give."

Walking Thunder nodded at the truth of the statement. "But how many've saved the lives of Night Song's uncle and brother?"

"None who's done both," Badger admitted.

"And who of the People has had a vision about my niece?"

"None," Badger growled, angry. He could not deny these things, but he did not have to like them. He still did not want his daughter marrying a white man. He had little respect for any pale-skin. They had no manners, little courage; they complained of the smallest travails; they seemed to have no ways or customs that were proper for men.

"Then what's the trouble?"

"We don't know nothin' about him. Not ancestors, not habits."

"Are you trying to anger the spirits?" Walking Thunder countered, going back to his own language so that he could express himself properly. He looked a little worried. "If Saves Men Twice has had a vision, who are we, as mere men, to deny what it has shown?"

"He lies," Badger snapped, also speaking in Lakota. "All pale-skins lie."

"It might do you good to have a pale-skin son-in-law," Walking Thunder said, ignoring the insult to his friend and guest. "Someday the pale-skins will be too many to count. With a pale-skin in the family, you'll have it better than many of the People."

"That might be so," Badger said thoughtfully. "But he must give something for Night Song. It's our way. I'd look like a fool otherwise."

"He has given you something," Walking Thunder said simply. "A greater gift than any of the People have given you."

"And what's that?" Badger asked suspiciously.

"What the hell're you two talkin' about so long?" Barclay interjected. He felt like an idiot not knowing what was being said.

Walking Thunder explained it briefly, then said, "And I was just gonna tell him what gift you gave that's better than all others."

"So?" Badger asked impatiently. "What's this great gift?"

"The lives of your brother and your son."

Badger had suspected that, since he knew it was the truth, but he did not want to accept it. "That wasn't his gift," he insisted. "It was strong medicine. Yours and Strikin' Arrow's. Nothin' more."

Striking Arrow wanted to object, to disagree with his father, but he kept himself in check. Such a thing would have been disrespectful of his elder, and that was unacceptable to a true Lakota. But it was difficult not to say anything. He was grateful to Barclay for having saved his life, and in just the little bit he had talked with the soldier, he had come to like him.

"Hah!" Walking Thunder scoffed. "If I'd had strong medicine that day, them Rees wouldn't've snuck up on me. And if Strikin' Arrow's medicine was powerful, he wouldn't've been flat on his back at the mercy of the Rees. The spirits gave you—and all the People—a powerful gift in this goddamn long knife who ain't a long knife no more."

"The spirits gave you a gift. And my son. That damn long knife ain't the People's savior. The People don't need any saving."

"That your last word about it?" Walking Thunder asked. He was angry, but did not show it in any overt way.

Badger nodded with finality.

"How many ponies you want for the woman?" Walking Thunder asked. "Ten?"

"Twenty-five."

"Twelve."

Badger pondered that a bit, then said, "Fifteen."

"Done," Walking Thunder responded. "Saves Twice'll bring 'em to you when he's better."

Barclay's heart sank, and he was glad none of the others was looking at him. He was afraid he would not be able to keep the hurt and disappointment off his face.

"From the long knife, I won't take less than thirty ponies," Badger snapped.

"You agreed to fifteen," Walking Thunder reminded him.

"That was your price."

"I was askin' for Saves Twice."

"Who the hell is Saves Twice?" Barclay asked in annoyance.

"You," Walking Thunder said, without looking at him. "It's the name I gave you."

Barclay was taken aback, but recovered quickly. "I ain't got no thirty horses, nor fifteen. Hell, I ain't got a one."

"You got as many as I say you got," Walking Thunder said tightly.

"Like hell," Barclay insisted. "I can't let you give me all those horses."

"They're my gift to you. You give me a gift—my life—and so I got to give you the best gift I can. It's our way. So I'll do this for you."

Barclay decided to shut up and see what happened.

"So, brother?" Walking Thunder asked.

Badger was trapped, and he desperately tried to find another way to extricate himself and his daughter. Only one thing came to mind. "We got to ask Night Song," he said. "She'll decide."

"That suit you, Saves Twice?" Walking Thunder asked.

"Yes," Barclay said with suddenly dry mouth. "I'd not want her if she don't want me." Actually he would want her every bit as much, but he would not force himself on her. He worried that she would reject him. After all, why should she want him? They had just met, and not really spoken a single word to each other. He was a white man and one in pretty poor condition right now, and she had plenty of Sioux suitors, all of them, he assumed, brave and resourceful warriors. He caught a gleam of hope in Badger's eye, and he figured the warrior was having the same thoughts—but with exactly the opposite outcome in mind.

20

Night Song entered the lodge tentatively. She looked like a frightened antelope ready to leap away, racing for safety. She walked over to where Barclay lay surrounded by Lakota warriors. She sat between her father and brother, her legs out to the side a little, the way a good Lakota woman should sit.

Walking Thunder translated for Barclay as Badger and his daughter conversed, though he kept the sneering out of his voice, unlike Badger. He figured Barclay was astute enough to hear it for himself, even if he didn't understand the words.

"This long knife wants to marry you, daughter," Badger said. "He says he's brave and trustworthy. I think he speaks with a snake's tongue, like all pale-skins. Your uncle wants me to push this union, since he feels he owes this long knife something. But it's your decision. If you want to marry him, I won't stand in your way." His voice made it evident even to Barclay that he would despise that choice. "If you don't want to marry him, there're plenty of other—better—men to choose from."

Night Song sat there for some time, eyes down, head bowed. She did not know what to say. She knew her father wanted her to have nothing to do with this white-skinned stranger, but she felt a strange attraction to him, as if they were meant to be together. How that was, she was not sure. She did not know this man. He looked funny with hair covering his face, and his voice and accent were so odd. He knew nothing of her or her people, none of their customs or ways. Yet she still felt as if he and she were brought together, no matter how briefly so far, for some reason.

She was certain that it was not just that she had felt an instant quickening of the heart when he had touched her hand that first time, or the rush of desire at the thought of mating with this exotic man whenever she looked at him, no matter how obliquely. She was convinced there was a higher purpose. And, if it turned out that such wasn't the case, what of it then? She could do much worse among her own people, she figured. She had heard how this white man had proven his bravery twice over, saving her uncle at great risk to himself, and saving her brother despite the terrible wound he had suffered. And he had the cockiness of a true Lakota warrior; she had seen that just in his bearing.

What put Night Song in a quandary was having to tell her father that her mind had been made up since she first saw Barclay. She never expected to be given a chance to voice her opinion, but now that she had a chance, she wanted to grab it. The trouble was, her father was so adamantly opposed to it, and she did not want to go against his wishes or hurt him in any way.

"Well?" Badger demanded.

"I agree to accept him," Night Song said shyly, not lifting her head or eyes. She could feel the heat of her father's anger on her, and she finally did look at him, avoiding his eyes. She spent the next twenty minutes wheedling, cajoling, flattering her father, trying to get him to understand why she had agreed to be Barclay's wife.

Walking Thunder translated some of the fiery exchanges between Badger and his daughter, but not all. He let Barclay know that Night Song truly did want him, and that she felt they were meant to be together. "Another part of your vision perhaps, Saves Twice," Walking Thunder said quietly. "It all goes together."

I hope so, Barclay thought, but he said nothing, just nodded.

Since his sister was disagreeing so fervently with their father, Striking Arrow decided he could add his opinions. Barclay and Walking Thunder wisely decided to keep quiet and stay out of the family matter.

Between his two children, Badger slowly became convinced to accept Walking Thunder's wishes. He still didn't like it, and he worried that his daughter would be hurt by the situation, but he could not argue with Night Song or Striking Arrow any longer. He finally capitulated. "But," he said firmly, "the marriage won't take place until Saves Twice is well enough to bring me the ponies himself. Only then will we start the planning."

Walking Thunder, who had translated, asked, "That acceptable to you, Saves Twice?"

Barclay nodded, showing no emotion. He was boiling inside, though, with the desire to have Night Song here and now, and the sense of wanting to be pretty well recovered so that when they did come together it would be good. In his weakened condition, there would be little enjoyment.

"Then it is done," Walking Thunder said. He asked Talks Loud to get his ceremonial pipe.

Night Song left the lodge as the pipe was filled. Then it was lit, and the men all smoked briefly from it, the acrid smoke purifying and sanctifying the deal that had been formed.

It was more than two months, and deep into the heart of summer, before Barclay was sufficiently recovered to get married and thus take on the responsibilities of married life. During that time, he had learned a large amount of the Sioux language, surprising himself at the ease with which he had done so. It had never occurred to him that he might have an inherent facility for languages.

He had also learned many of the Lakota customs, though not nearly as well as the language. As he did, many things were explained—that it was uncouth for the People to look one another in the eyes; that it was even more barbaric to show affection in public. Because of the latter, Barclay was in a way glad that his marriage to Night Song had been delayed. He was sure he would have embarrassed them both by doing something in view of the rest of the People, something that would have insulted both his bride and his hosts.

He also found that he did have things in common with the other men—that his natural haughtiness fit in well with the Lakota male's view of himself. They were arrogant, cocksure, vain. At least in public. He wasn't so sure how they acted when they were alone or just with their lovers.

Seeing how the other men handled pain and strife made Barclay want to get up and about as soon as possible, the agony be damned. But he had enough sense not to want to ruin his shoulder permanently by pushing himself too early. It was, therefore, a week more before he actually rose and walked around the lodge a little. He was glad then that he had waited. He was weak, and his stomach rolled as he lurched a few steps that first time. He felt like vomiting, but he clenched his teeth until his jaws ached to keep from doing so. He would rather have died than to puke in front of Walking Thunder and the others.

It got easier after that, though, and within a few days, he was strolling around the village. That was as uncomfortable as anything he had ever done, at least for a while, since he was the subject of a fair amount of scrutiny by the People. He never showed his discomfiture, however, trying his damnedest to honor his host by acting as a Lakota man would.

Much of what Barclay learned was imparted by Walking Thunder, but Barclay found he learned a lot more from Striking Arrow. The young Sioux was about the same age as Barclay, and they grew as close as brothers. The two were impressive as they walked the village. They were about the same height and weight, one dark with a plump, fleshy nose and high, protuberant cheekbones, the other pale with an aquiline nose and wide forehead. Both were broad of shoulder, strong and determined looking.

Barclay had felt almost overwhelmed in the young Sioux's presence for a while, especially when Striking Arrow related his tales of derring-do during his battles with Crow and Pawnee. But then Barclay realized that he, too, had his own stories to tell, and did so with gusto. Following the Sioux lead, he did not exaggerate his deeds, but on the other hand, he did not shy away from the important role he had played in saving Walking Thunder the previous summer, or in his battle with the Pawnees, or in saving Striking Arrow while killing Rattling Hooves, despite being so seriously wounded. His bravery, candor and arrogance made him even more accepted among the People of Walking Thunder's village.

By midsummer, Barclay was feeling mostly back to normal, and he was prepared—actually, extremely eager—to take Night Song as his wife. Badger was still opposed, though he would say nothing against it directly. Still, Barclay was bothered by his prospective father-in-law's obstinance, and he thought that perhaps he should do something to try to change Badger's attitude toward him. He just didn't know what. He talked it over with Walking Thunder, who had adopted him in a very public and exuberant ceremony. Barclay came away with some thoughts, and soon after, talked Walking Thunder, Striking Arrow and several other young Sioux into going with him on a hunt.

He had no idea of how well he would do. Striking Arrow and Walking Thunder had been showing him how to use a bow, as well as a lance, but he was not proficient with either. But he had no other choice—guns, muskets mostly, were at a premium in the village—until he was surprised one day by Walking Thunder. The war chief quietly presented his "son" with his stolen "common rifle" and two pistols, as well as the accoutrements. Walking Thunder had traded five horses for them, Barclay found out later, to the warriors who had picked them up as plunder after the battle with the Arikaras.

Barclay took them almost reverently and looked them over. He smiled at Walking Thunder, and said seriously, in Lakota, "I'm honored, Father. Soon I'll offer you a gift as well."

Walking Thunder nodded, proud.

Properly armed, Barclay led off his small hunting party several days later. With the exception of his beard, one could not tell Barclay from the others. All were dressed in long, fringed buckskin shirts, leggings and moccasins; all had long hair, with at least one feather tied to the flowing, loose locks. Just outside the village, however, he let one of the other Sioux take over. He had no idea where he was or where to find buffalo, so the others would guide the group. The rich country teemed with game, including buffalo, and so it was only a matter of an hour or so before they found a vast number of those animals grazing stolidly on the lush grass of the prairie.

The men sat on a ridge waiting for Barclay to give the order to charge, but the soldier was in no hurry. He was still amazed at the bounty and beauty of this land—the sparkling bluish-green of the ocean of grass

meeting the stark, severe blue of the sky on the far
horizon; the undulating brown currents of thousands
of buffalo; the rolling of the land as far as the eye could
see. But sight was not the only sensation treated to a
feast here, not by a long shot. There was the caress of
the constant breeze that helped carry the hawks and
eagles overhead, and the smells of fresh grass and the
scent of flowers; the acrid, familiar stench of buffalo
droppings; the high-pitched, haunting screech of
hawks; the deep, almost unnerving grunt of bison. All
these glorious sensations filled Barclay with a feeling
bordering on the mystic, and he suddenly understood
some of the spirituality of the Lakota people.

"Something wrong, my son?" Walking Thunder
asked, concern in his voice.

Barclay smiled at the war chief and shook his
head. "No, Father," he said in passable Sioux. "I'm just
enjoying being here, and thanking the spirits for all
they provide." That surprised him. He had never
thought in such terms before. But it was the truth, at
least right now.

Walking Thunder beamed, proud of his adopted
son.

There was more to his delay, though, than Barclay
was willing to admit to the others. He was not certain
what to do. Sure, he had discussed the hunt with his
father and his friends, but that was not the same as
actually being out here. He did not want to make a fool
of himself, or embarrass his family and friends. Then
he decided that he could wait no longer. He found that
he was eager to do this, and he could see that the others felt the same.

Barclay looked from one to the other. "We go,"
he said, kicking his—well, actually, Walking
Thunder's—buffalo pony into motion. The well
trained horse gained its full stride in moments, tearing down the grassy slope. Suddenly Barclay found

himself screeching and shouting like a wild man. He did not feel foolish about it.

Barclay let the pony do much of the work, since it was far more accustomed to these hunts than he was. The horse angled toward a galloping buffalo—a cow, Barclay noted after a moment—and quickly paced the big, powerful beast.

Knowing he could not wait long, Barclay lowered his rifle, until it was brushing the side of the shaggy bison. It was a little awkward with the size of the rifle, but not too bad, Barclay decided. He fired and the animal fell. Without having to be guided, the pony jerked out of the way and raced after another buffalo.

The killing went on for almost half an hour. Lost in the thrill of the chase, Barclay wasn't even sure how many animals he had killed. He didn't want to stop this exhilarating run, but the buffalo pony began to flag, and Barclay retained a sufficient thread of sense to know that he didn't want to run the horse to death, so he finally pulled up. He wasn't sure who was breathing harder, himself or the pony.

Barclay looked around at the carnage, and smiled. Big, brown carcasses littered the rolling landscape, widely spaced. Barclay waved at Striking Arrow, who was a couple hundred yards away. The gesture was returned.

The men gathered in groups of two, and went about butchering the buffalo. Mostly they took the best cuts, but Barclay took all he thought the pack animals could handle. He had learned well from his Lakota hosts, and had plans for the plethora of meat.

The men spent several hours at the task before heading slowly back to the village. Barclay was still euphoric from the hunt; could still feel his blood pounding in his veins. It was an indescribable feeling. As they neared the village, however, Barclay forced himself to calm down some. There were things to be done, and he did not want to appear giddy during it.

With a great show of largesse, Barclay passed out almost all of the meat he had taken, given with pride to several families who were poor, or who had no young man to hunt for them. The people accepted the gift with gratitude in their eyes, though they made no display of their thanks. Barclay didn't mind; that was the way of the People.

That done, he finally headed to Badger's lodge. He slapped the buffalo-hide tipi and called for Badger. When the pudgy, stern-faced warrior came out and stood with arms across his big chest, Barclay held out a bloody piece of buffalo hide, rolled up. "A token of my appreciation for you, Father," Barclay said solemnly in Sioux. "To let my Father know that I hold no hard feelings despite our small disagreements of the past."

Badger's eyebrows rose. He stepped forward and peeled open the hide that Barclay still held. In it he found five fresh buffalo tongues, several livers and a number of various other organs. Badger covered the meats again and nodded. He indicated that his wife should take the bundle. "I take this with pride and respect. And I agree we must put our past differences behind us."

Barclay was surprised—and excited. He had hoped that Badger would come around and not be so against Barclay's marriage to Night Song. It seemed as if Badger was beginning to change his mind a little. "As men, we should be able to do that," he said hopefully.

Badger nodded. He still was adamantly opposed to the marriage, but he knew he could not hold out, and he decided just now that perhaps Barclay was not as bad a man as he might have thought. He would have to consider making the best of the impending marriage. The thought still galled him, but the thought of angering the spirits worried him much more, and this union certainly seemed to be blessed by the spirits.

Happy, Barclay left. Two days later, he brought fifteen of Walking Thunder's best ponies to Badger. Not long after, Badger and his family—with Night Song riding on one of his new horses—arrived at the site Walking Thunder had selected to give the feast to celebrate Barclay's wedding.

Eager to get the formalities and the celebrations over with, Barclay sat, trying not to show his edginess. He thought he did a good job of it. And finally, finally, darkness came, and he and Night Song were able to steal away to the small lodge that had been set up for them near Walking Thunder's.

Suddenly nervous, Barclay entered the lodge just ahead of Night Song. He stood and waited for her, looking around the inside of the tipi as if he had never seen one before. He tried to keep his eyes off the pile of plush, soft, inviting buffalo robes toward the back and off a little to one side. He had waited a long time to get to the marriage bed, he figured he could wait a few more minutes.

21

Barclay was uncertain of himself, unsure of how to proceed. Yet here he was with a Lakota woman, and so he could not appear to be unsettled. As a man—a Lakota man in Night Song's eyes—he must appear to be strong, self-assured, arrogant even here. Yet he had never been in such a position before. Yes, he had had women before, but never a wife, nor a woman he loved. And he was sure he loved Night Song, despite their short time—moments really—having been together. After all, their meeting was predestined, as far as he was concerned. He suspected she felt the same about him, and about their meeting.

Deciding that he had better do something, and soon, to show her that she had not been wrong in marrying him, Barclay cupped Night Song's small, round chin in one hand and tilted her face up. "I'm not sure how you're going to take to this, Night Song," he whispered in Sioux, "but I'm going to kiss you anyway." He eagerly did as he promised. The soldier didn't know if the Sioux or any other Indians made a habit of kissing; he had not seen anyone in this village do so. That didn't mean they didn't do it, just that he hadn't caught them at it—not surprisingly, considering their reticence at any public displays of affection.

He was glad when Night Song responded. It was tentative, to be sure, as if she really didn't know what she was doing but was all for trying it out, but it was responsive. Her lips and tongue were warm, moist and sweet; her body pressed against his, softly rounded, urgent, insistent.

Barclay could delay no longer; he felt as if he had waited far too long already. Cupping her firm buttocks in his hands, he hiked her up a little. She played along, wrapping her legs around the backs of his thighs as best she could—her long dress made it somewhat difficult.

Barclay didn't care. He lurched toward the bridal bed, his lips still locked on hers. When he got there, he let her down to her feet. Both stripped hastily, hunger for each other in their eyes, in the heat of their flesh. Then they were on the robes, coupled tightly, writhing and thrusting, bringing Barclay to heights of pleasure he had never thought possible. It was over far too soon for Barclay, though, and he rolled off Night Song onto his back. His chest heaved, and he still felt tingling throughout his body. He smiled up toward the smoke hole at the top of the tipi, full of himself.

Night Song brought him back to earth when she slid her sweat-slick body up onto his. "That's all?" she asked.

"What do you mean is that all?" he countered, surprised.

"I need more," she said shyly but firmly.

"More?" Barclay was surprised again. "You mean you like doing what we just did?"

"Don't you?" Night Song responded.

"Of course I do," he said, wondering what was wrong with her. "All men do." He was glad he had learned the Lakota language as well as he had. He still spoke with a thick accent—or so Striking Arrow was fond of telling him—but he understood it quite well.

"Women don't?" Night Song asked, eyes wide, though she still tried to avoid looking directly into his eyes. She was shocked.

"No," Barclay said with earnest solidity. "Of course not. Any woman who likes—" He sputtered to a halt. After a moment, he continued. "You mean Lakota women like to do this?"

"Some, yes," Night Song said with a nod. "Some, no." She paused, then grinned. "Most yes."

"I'll be damned," he breathed in English, startled anew. "White women who enjoy doing this—even if they're married—are looked upon poorly," he said in Sioux.

"No!" Night Song gasped, more shocked than surprised.

Barclay nodded. "That's the way among the pale-skins," he said, realizing for the first time in his life just how foolish that was—and sounded.

"Well that's not the way it is here," Night Song said with finality. "And I'm not like the pale-skin women."

"I suppose I'm in trouble now," Barclay said, only half in jest, "having to satisfy you."

"I think you're up to the job," Night Song said with a giggle, her hand reaching down to his groin.

Both of them were right.

They quickly fell into domesticity. Barclay spent much of his time with Walking Thunder and Striking Arrow, learning more of the People's ways, hunting, talking. But he began to have a desire to be on the move, to be doing something, to be with men of his own kind again. It wasn't that he had anything against the Sioux; he was happy here, and had made some good friends. It was just that his dream—his vision, as his Sioux friends insisted on calling it—was not yet complete. It would not be complete until he was in a mountain camp, with Night Song of course, and maybe some white trappers. He finally mentioned it to his "father."

Walking Thunder nodded, but sat, thinking it over. "Your vision's a good one, my son," he said seriously. "But these things take time to come about. And winter's not a good time for chasing a vision."

"It's not winter yet," Barclay said unconvincingly.

Walking Thunder smiled. "It'll be here soon."

"I know, Father," Barclay said with a sigh. "I just don't feel I'm fulfilling my vision."

Walking Thunder nodded. "Even if you left now, though, you'd never find the boats, or the men you seek. Not before being trapped by winter."

"So I stay here for the winter?"

"Is that so bad, my son?" Walking Thunder asked seriously. "You have friends here. Family. A good wife."

Barclay laughed a bit. "I suppose I could be content to stay the winter here."

Walking Thunder nodded. "You can join us on the hunt before winter comes. And," he added pointedly, "maybe you'll join me and some of the others in a raid."

"Against who?" Barclay was intrigued.

"The Pawnees perhaps," Walking Thunder said, but he could not stop a grin from rising. "Or maybe the Rees."

"I wouldn't mind paying the Rees a visit, since I'm not sure they've been punished quite enough for what they've done to me."

Barclay wasn't sure about leaving Night Song behind as the small war party rode out of the village. But he was not about to let the other men hear it, or see it in his eyes. He didn't even look back, just rode with head held high. He wondered if the others felt about their wives as he did about Night Song. He supposed he would never know, since they were no more going to talk about that than he was.

There were only six of them—Walking Thunder, the leader; Barclay; Striking Arrow; Elk Horn Bow; Talks Loud; and Badger. They were a fairly tight-knit group, and not given over much to talking. Though Barclay was new to this, the men acted in concert, as if they had been doing so for years—since, except for him, they all had. Barclay found he fit in well. He knew the Sioux language sufficiently, and enough of their ways that he was not too out of place. He fell into doing what camp and other duties were required of a young man on his first war party, and he did it without complaint. That, in turn, helped gain him more respect from among his companions.

In less than a week of steady traveling, they spotted a small—only eight lodges—Arikara village. After the bombardment of their town along the Missouri, the Arikaras seemed to have had little enough time or heart to construct another; they had simply taken to living in buffalo-hide tipis, like most of their neighbors.

Throughout that day the Sioux war party lay low, resting and waiting at a spot several miles from the lodges. They ate a little, talked quietly, napped. Well past midnight, they roused themselves and headed silently—on foot, walking their ponies—toward the village. Just outside it, they split up. Barclay and Striking Arrow turned toward the horse herd; the others spread out some, taking up positions in an arc around the village. While they were here mainly to steal horses, the actual task of it would fall to the two young friends. Then they all waited again, Barclay and Striking Arrow prone in the withering, prickly grass. The two had allowed their ponies to drift off and mingle with the Arikara horses. No one would notice, and they planned to get them back when they stole the herd.

Just as dawn's reddish glow eased over the rough land, the Sioux war band attacked. All the warriors—except Barclay and Striking Arrow—screeched war

cries to draw the Arikaras' attention away from their
horse herd. When they heard the sounds of their
brethren, the two young men leaped up and raced forward, silently, each heading toward one of the two Ree
horse guards.

The Arikaras were distracted, wondering what
was going on in the village a couple hundred yards
northeast of the herd, so they weren't paying much
attention. Barclay plowed into his target, and both
tumbled to the ground. When they had scrambled up,
Barclay's wounded shoulder ached like hell. He had
almost forgotten about the wound, but its presence
was brought back with a vengeance. He also found
himself with a hell of a lot more to handle than he had
expected.

The Ree was no taller than Barclay, nor much
heavier; he just seemed to the soldier to be made of
iron and had the strength of an enraged grizzly. The
Arikara slammed a forearm into the side of Barclay's
head, knocking the soldier down again. The butt of the
rifle slung over his shoulder hit the ground, jerking the
sling tight against him, adding insult to injury.

"Damn," Barclay muttered, shaking his head. He
felt as if he had just been run over by a buffalo—a big
buffalo. He got up again, and was promptly pounded
down again. Barclay was getting groggy, and the
Arikara seemed to be having a good time. And Barclay
began to think that he was in well over his head. But it
was only when the Ree pulled a flint and antler war
club and moved in for the kill that Barclay's brain
started working again, and he remembered his pistols.

Barclay yanked one of the weapons out and
cranked back the hammer with his left hand. But so
anxious was he that, when he fired, all he managed to
do was to blow a hole in the Arikara's war shirt.

"Oh, damn," the soldier mumbled, as the Ree
stopped for a moment and laughed. Trying to calm

himself some, Barclay dropped his pistol and shoved himself backward with his feet, scraping his buttocks across the rough ground. When he got a little distance, he stopped and pulled his other pistol. He cocked it and then took his time before firing.

The smirk dropped off the Ree's face fast when the ball slammed into his abdomen and plundered his innards. But it only stopped him momentarily. Then he presented a sickly grin to Barclay and advanced once again.

Barclay was more confident, however, now that the warrior was considerably slowed by the lead ball in his guts. The soldier pushed himself up to his feet and pulled his knife. He dodged the Arikara's feeble swipe of his war club, stepped up and jammed his knife into the Ree's chest.

The Arikara slumped against him, and Barclay shoved the warrior away. The Arikara fell. Barclay didn't really care if he was dead or not. He was out of action, and that was all that mattered right now. Barclay scooped up his two pistols and shoved them in his belt without bothering to reload them. Then he turned and raced for the horses. The whole thing had taken less than a minute, though to Barclay it had seemed an awfully long time.

Striking Arrow was already on his own pony, having dispatched his foe with no trouble, and waiting for Barclay. He had been about to go help his friend when the soldier managed to kill the Arikara. "Hurry!" he shouted, pointing.

Barclay glanced behind him and saw several Arikaras, armed with lances and bows, running toward him and his friend. He turned and ran, then jumped, slapping his hands flat on the nearest pony's rump and leaping onto the animal's back. Then he and Striking Arrow screeched and shouted, spooking the horses, and sending them running across the prairie.

The two young men got the herd moving in the desired direction, and kept on pounding across the undulating land. Several miles on, they slowed down some and in another mile, the two men got the horses down to a walk. They did not stop.

It was midafternoon by the time Walking Thunder, Badger, Elk Horn Bow, and Talks Loud caught up with them, and then they halted.

"Were you followed?" Striking Arrow asked.

Walking Thunder shook his head, grinning. "How could they follow us when they have almost no ponies?" he countered. "You two young men did well."

"We did fair," Striking Arrow said. "We left some horses behind. We should have gotten them all."

"And a good thing you left some," Talks Loud said, living up to his name. "If not, we'd not have been able to take many things from the cowardly Rees." He chucked a thumb over his shoulder at the several extra horses laden with furs, hides, a fair amount of dried meat, a few old muskets and other odds and ends.

"And no one was hurt," Elk Horn Bow added.

Walking Thunder laughed. "That's because the Rees, being the cowards they are, thought all the Lakota were attacking them, and so they ran away. We had almost no resistance from them. Of course, I did manage to count coup twice."

"I can attest to it," Badger said. He felt no loss of prestige in not having counted coup on this war party. And it was only right that he be the one to verify his brother's claim.

"Well, I counted coup, too," Striking Arrow said proudly. "And took his hair."

Barclay decided there was no reason for him to be shy around these men. "He wasn't the only one counted coup out there." He put a slightly sad look on his face. "But I didn't have time to take that yellow belly's hair, though." Silently he gave thanks for that.

Had he had time, Striking Arrow might've expected him to scalp the dead Ree and he would've been in a hell of a dilemma then.

Striking Arrow laughed. "My brother Saves Twice has an unusual way of counting coup," he said. "First, he lets the enemy knock him down several times—perhaps to make him overconfident. Then he fires a shot into the air, maybe as a warning. Only then does he shoot the enemy, while he himself is sitting down resting from all the advantages he has given the enemy. Finally, he gets his lazy rump up off the grass and finishes the job."

"This is true?" Walking Thunder asked, looking at Barclay with wide eyes.

Barclay was flushed with embarrassment. "Well, I suppose it might seem that way to someone like Striking Arrow," he said, an embarrassed smile on his lips, but wanting to give as good as he got. "Especially when one like Striking Arrow is so frightened of the mean old Ree that he takes unfair advantage of the poor man and kills him right off."

"At least I was able to handle my enemy," Striking Arrow countered with aplomb. "Unlike you, who thinks it best to let the enemy kick you around like a mangy cur until he tires out and you can best him."

"Oh, so now you're not only afraid of the enemy, you're also afraid to let someone hit you, since you'd go down to stay the first time."

It went on like that for some little time, as the elders sat there bemused by it all. But finally the two friends ran out of insults and desire to continue this nonsense, and so they ceased. They had work to do anyway, such as putting up their small camp. Once that was done and they had eaten, they were assigned to guard the herd of horses through the night. The elders figured the two were young enough to be able to recover from several days of little or no sleep a lot easier than they were.

Four days later they rode back into the village to the acclaim of all. When the plunder was divided up, Barclay and Striking Arrow each got sixteen horses; the other four warriors who had been along got four each. The hides, meat and furs were split, with the four older warriors getting the lion's share of those items, as well as all the firearms they had taken.

Barclay turned right around and gave Walking Thunder fifteen of his horses. He was pleased that he had paid his father back for having loaned him the ponies in order to marry Night Song, and still had one horse left that he could call his own. He was surprised a couple of days later when Walking Thunder gave him two ponies. Barclay didn't want to take them, but Walking Thunder insisted.

"You know enough about the People now that you know I am giving you a gift because you gave me one. So you can't argue. I'm also giving them to you because I am proud of my pale-skinned son."

Barclay nodded, accepting the praise—and the horses. But on the night he returned to the village, he also gave away virtually all the meat and other plunder he had been given for his part in the raid. He kept enough meat for him and Night Song to subsist on for a day or two—until he could get hunting again—and one robe.

Night Song was mighty proud of her husband for having done that, as well as for his success on the war party. She showed him just how much that evening when they were in the robes inside their lodge, making love as the drums pounded in the victory celebration.

22

A few weeks later, the band went on its annual fall hunt, to make meat for the long, bitter winter that was fast approaching. This was a far different hunt than the one he had been on when he had first recovered. This one was much too important to everyone in the band to hunt so haphazardly. And this one was highly policed by the Tokalas—the Kit Foxes—one of the warrior societies of the tribe.

For a while the scouts sought buffalo in vain, and the People began to worry. The elders discussed the matter over their fires in the evenings, trying to determine who had broken a taboo and cursed their venture. Some thought to blame it on Barclay. After all, he was a newcomer to the Lakota, and a pale-skinned man, too.

Walking Thunder, Striking Arrow, and others—including Badger—argued against that notion, reminding everyone how Barclay had saved both Walking Thunder and Striking Arrow; and they talked of his generosity, of his success and trustworthiness in the raid on the Arikaras, of his devotion to Night Song and to those he called friends.

After five nights running of listening to himself being castigated on one hand and praised highly on the other, he went to Walking Thunder's lodge. When he was seated at the fire, he said simply, "I think I'll leave the band soon, Father."

"Why?" Walking Thunder was not surprised. He knew Barclay far better than the soldier thought he did.

"The People've been very good to me since I came here," Barclay said quietly. He had learned pretty well, and kept his eyes downcast. "And I would do nothing to hurt the People. If they blame me for bringing poor medicine on this hunt, then I can't stay here any longer."

"A foolish idea, my son," Walking Thunder said tightly.

Barclay shrugged. "It's the best thing I can do for the People right now," he said seriously. "The survival of the band is a lot more important than having one sore-shouldered, trouble-making long knife on your hands."

Walking Thunder was proud beyond words of his adopted son, but that did not mean he was about to let Barclay leave the village if there was anything he could do to stop him. And he planned to try everything at his disposal to do just that. "Where will you go?" he asked.

Barclay shrugged. "Find some place I can hole up for winter. I can't make it upriver to find some trappers' camp, and I can't get back to the fort, even if I wanted to. So I'll find a place down along the Missouri. There're plenty of caves along some parts, of course, and they'd make a fine lodge for the winter. There'd be wood nearby, and plenty of water, and I expect there'll be more than enough game to keep me fed."

Walking Thunder nodded. "You could find that," he said quietly. "But what about Night Song? Badger won't be happy about you taking her to such a place. Not when the village and all her friends are here."

"I thought I'd leave her here. Life in a cave's not right for a good woman like Night Song." He was close to tears at the thought of losing Night Song, but he managed to hold them back, with great difficulty.

"She might not be here for you when you get back," Walking Thunder warned.

"I know," Barclay whispered. He felt like shooting himself. The thought of living without Night Song was almost too much to bear. Yet he was caught in a powerful dilemma. If he stayed here, he'd have Night Song, but the People would not have any food to get them through the winter. Not the way things were going. If he left, Night Song would be fed, but he wouldn't have her. He could, he knew, take her with him; she would be glad to go. But he did not want to endanger her. Despite his inherent cockiness, and the arrogance born of having become Sioux, he was not at all sure he could provide for Night Song on his own.

"You'd leave her to someone like Crow Foot?"

"Better that than the People should starve on my account," Barclay said, almost choking on the words.

"Have you discussed this with Striking Arrow?" Walking Thunder asked, now grasping at anything.

Barclay nodded. "He tells me the same things you do."

"Then he's a wise young man," Walking Thunder said firmly. "And you should listen to him."

"I can't do that, Father."

Walking Thunder sighed, defeated, though he did not let on. "Then do this, my son," he said after several minutes of thought, "don't leave yet. Wait just a short time. If we have found no buffalo in seven suns, then you can go. I'll help you as much as I can then."

Barclay pondered that a bit, then nodded. "I can do that, Father." Saddened and heartbroken, he headed for his own lodge, where he had a fitful night's sleep, despite Night Song's kind ministrations.

He rose in the morning well before anyone else, he thought, and prepared his pony. It was cold in the

darkness, but he knew it was just a mild prelude to
winter, a season he did not look forward to. With his
rifle and a small buckskin bag of supplies slung across
his back, he jumped on the horse. He and the pony had
become used to each other in their several weeks
together. Then he rode out of the village, heading
southeast. In the pale glimmer of the moon, he could
see the plumes of breath as the pony snorted and
shook its head, happy to be on the move.

Just past the last lodge, Barclay caught a movement to his left. He grabbed a pistol and half-turned
that way. Then he shook his head and put the pistol
away. "What the hell're you doin' here, Strikin'
Arrow?" he asked, voice filled with displeasure. He
spoke in English. As Striking Arrow had tried to
teach him Lakota, he tried to teach the warrior
English.

"Goin' with you," Striking Arrow said cheerfully,
with surprisingly little accent. "Make sure you don't
do nothin' stupid."

"I don't want company," Barclay snapped. "And I
don't need some nosy bastard tailin' my ass all day."

"Better get used to it," Striking Arrow said still
cheery.

"Dammit, you dumb bastard, you weren't supposed to take what I told you in confidence and then
come and use it against me." He was quite angry at
Striking Arrow. He had told the warrior of his plan,
thinking that Striking Arrow would not use the knowledge in any way. Now he was sitting here.

Striking Arrow shrugged. "Your friendship means
more to me than ignorin' what you tell me about such
important business."

"You ain't gonna have my goddamn friendship
much longer, you keep actin' like this, damn you."

"I'll take that goddamn chance," Striking Arrow
said fatalistically.

"Just keep up, goddammit," Barclay growled before trotting off.

The two men were out all that day and night, all the next, and part of the day after. But they finally found what they had been seeking, and then they turned and galloped toward the point where they estimated the slowly moving village should be. By the time they did, it was late afternoon, and the light was almost starting to fall.

A disheartened band of Lakota had begun setting up their nightly camp when the two young men raced in. Many of the People stopped momentarily to look darkly at Barclay. A growing number of the band members had begun to believe that the pale-skinned warrior was, indeed, the source of their poor luck in finding buffalo. Usually this country was teeming with the shaggy animals, ones grown fat after a summer of feeding on rich grass. But this year the beasts were nowhere to be seen in their usual haunts, and the People were edgy.

Striking Arrow stopped in what might be considered the center of the village. He was aware that he, too, was being looked on with some disfavor for his support of and close friendship with Barclay. But he didn't care. He figured these things would work themselves out, especially when the People learned of his and Barclay's news. Still on his pony, Striking Arrow called for a council of warriors.

They met less than ten minutes later, all the warriors gathered at one central fire. Women and children sat beyond them, listening intently. When everyone was quiet and waiting, Striking Arrow stood. "Our troubles are over," he said haughtily. "Saves Twice and I found the buffalo. Many of them. We'll have plenty of meat for the winter."

"Where?" Badger asked.

"Less than a sun's ride west."

There was a soft rumble of eager conversation among the Sioux.

Then an older man stood, holding a red blanket around his chest. "This is good," Long Strider said. "We'll move there tomorrow." He sat.

Angry, Striking Arrow rose again. "That's all you have to say, Grandfather," he said, mostly courteously.

"Is there more I should say?" Long Strider asked.

"Yes," Striking Arrow snapped. "I don't mean any disrespect for you, Grandfather, but you led those people who would put our troubles on my brother, Saves Twice. And on me for being his friend. You built up the fires of anger at us, and now you have nothing to say."

More than one listener gasped at Striking Arrow's rudeness. It was almost unthinkable among the People.

"Sit and say no more," Walking Thunder snapped. "You've shamed yourself and your people. Your disrespect is offensive to us all."

"Then perhaps someone else should apologize to Saves Twice for the shame heaped on him," Striking Arrow said firmly. "He vowed to put the good of the People before his own health and happiness, leaving here so that our band would have good medicine again. Yet no one thinks to take back some of the disrespect he faced. Not even when he decided to go out and find the buffalo our scouts couldn't. Not even when he found those buffalo, so that now the People won't starve during the winter moons."

Striking Arrow glared around the circle of faces, trying to avoid looking straight into anyone's eyes, despite his fury.

"Sit down," Barclay said quietly, tugging on his friend's legging. "You're making a fool of yourself."

"No," Striking Arrow snapped. He had made up his mind and was going to see this through to the end.

Barclay was about to say something else, but Long

Strider once again got laboriously to his feet. His long, heavily graying hair was loose, and flicked about in the wind. "We will wait until we see these 'many' buffalo," he said in a strong voice that belied his age. "Then, perhaps we might rethink things a little." He sat.

"No!" Striking Arrow roared, "You'll do that—"

"That's enough!" Barclay said equally loudly. He stood and stepped in front of Striking Arrow, staring directly at his friend. "Now sit."

Striking Arrow was suddenly uncomfortable and he cast his eyes down. Then he sat, though his anger was not lessened a bit.

Barclay hesitated a moment, considering whether he should apologize to Long Strider for Striking Arrow's behavior. But he decided that such a move would be almost as shocking as had his friend's discourtesy to the old chief. He simply turned and took his seat again. He and Striking Arrow kept quiet as the other warriors began making plans for the move in the morning—and for the long-hoped-for hunt.

The bison were a little farther off than they had been the day before, but they were easy for Barclay and Striking Arrow to find again. Joyous, the band made its camp a mile or so from the herd, not wanting to drive it away. The warriors of the Kit Fox society, which had responsibility for policing the hunt, made it known that they would be enforcing the rules to the fullest.

No one exactly apologized to Barclay, but almost every warrior who had spoken out against him came to his lodge at one time or another that evening. Each said about the same thing, telling the soldier that they were glad that he had found the buffalo, and that they were proud to have him a member of their band. They would eat a little and then depart. Seconds, or perhaps minutes, later, the next would show up.

Barclay treated them all with respect, and acknowledged all of their kind words courteously. He wanted to laugh in their faces, but he could not bring himself to do so. Truth be told, he couldn't take any of this too seriously, since he was too happy to worry about it. Since he had found the buffalo, it meant he would be staying with Night Song. Right now, that was all that mattered to him.

The hunt the next day went off with no problems, except for those normally encountered in such an important and dangerous undertaking. One man was killed and two others seriously hurt, and several ponies had to be destroyed as the men of the band drove the herd of buffalo over a cliff.

The tribe spent more than a week in the area, butchering and smoking meat for the winter. They took everything from the animals, horns to be made into bowls and spoons; hooves for making glue; the sinew for sewing; hides to be used as robes or to be made into clothing or tipis; entrails, sometimes eaten raw, right on the spot, others to be eaten later; bones for the marrow and for the pack of dogs; stomachs and scrotums to be used as pouches; the tightly curled fur to use for making pillows or as warm liners in moccasins.

While they worked, they gorged on fresh meat, including many of the organs, consumed raw and hot from the newly killed buffalo. At night they ate until they vomited and then went back for more. There were dances and feasts and celebrations. With the success of this hunt, there should be little trouble with the entire band being well fed, well clothed and well sheltered for the winter.

But at last the band moved on. They had tons of jerky and tons more of fat-rich, berry-spiced pemmican. They moved slowly, not wanting to overtax the animals carrying the life-giving burdens. Besides, they were in no hurry now.

Scouts went out soon after, looking for a good place for the band to winter, and, though it took longer than any of them had expected, no one blamed Barclay for it. They were too happy, particularly since they were still taking fresh meat just about every day, so they did not have to dip into their stores of preserved meat.

A good spot was found eventually, and they all began setting up their lodges amid the cottonwoods and willows along Eagle Creek. There would be all the water they could use, though soon they would have to chop through the ice for it, sufficient wood, and there was still a fair amount of game in the area.

Happy, Barclay settled in with Night Song, looking forward to a winter spent in her company with no worries. It was the first time since he could remember that he had had such peace.

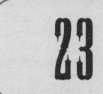

23

Barclay and Striking Arrow squatted on a short bluff overlooking the Missouri, waiting for a keelboat to come downriver. There was a good place nearby for one of the craft to pull to the bank. Barclay didn't know how long it would be before a boat would show up, but he was prepared to wait. Back off the bluff, downriver just a little, was a small camp amid the trees and brush. Walking Thunder and his family were there, as were Striking Arrow's wife and two children. And Night Song was there—the main reason Barclay didn't mind waiting.

It had taken a lot of thought over the winter to get Barclay to this spot. The winter had been bitterly cold, and the snow had fallen often and deeply, but Barclay, who had a warm lodge, plenty of meat, and a new and loving wife, was content. Though he knew spring would eventually arrive and serious work would interfere in this somewhat idyllic existence, he was comfortable to have it last as long as possible.

Reality intruded earlier than he expected, however, when Walking Thunder asked him one evening what he planned to do when spring did arrive.

"Wait for one of the keelboats coming upriver," Barclay said with a shrug. That was still some time off, so he wasn't all that concerned about it.

"Maybe you should take one of them going down-river?" Walking Thunder suggested.

"Why would I do that?" Barclay asked, surprised. "That'd be mad."

"Why?"

"You know why, Father. Any keelboat that comes down the river'll stop at the fort. As soon as it did, I'd be in chains again. I got too much going for me here, and out there—" he pointed west, "for me to throw it all away with one stupid move."

"Have you looked at yourself lately, my son?" Walking Thunder asked. When Barclay shook his head, the Sioux pulled out a small, wood-backed mirror and tossed it to his adopted son.

Barclay peered into the small tin mirror without much interest. He saw the man he was used to seeing. Or did he? His interest increased. From what little could be seen in the looking glass he had turned into a bearded, hard-eyed savage. There were some lines on his young face, where it was not covered by hair, lines from pain and suffering, hardship and weather.

He pulled the mirror away and looked down at himself as if seeing himself for the first time. He was dressed, as he had been almost since he had arrived at the Lakota village, in a plain, fringed buckskin shirt that hung to his knees; simple side-seam moccasins; unadorned buckskin leggings and a wool breechcloth cut from an old blanket.

Barclay also thought he had put on some weight. After the meager pickings of army food, he had eaten heartily of fresh buffalo, fat-rich pemmican, tangy antelope, roasted dog.

"They would have a hard time recognizing me, wouldn't they," Barclay mused as he handed the mirror back to Walking Thunder. He was even convinced of it himself. "But, still, Father, why would I want to risk it?"

"What'll you do for supplies if you head to the mountains now?"

"Get them from General Ashley, like I'd always planned to do." It seemed so simple for Barclay, and so didn't need consideration.

"Then you'll start out in debt to this man?" Walking Thunder asked.

Barclay nodded and shrugged. "I don't have much choice. I suppose if I had some money of my own, I might go downriver and see about picking up my own supplies. But I don't." He was fatalistic about it all.

"We have many furs, you and I," Walking Thunder said quietly, as if speaking to himself.

"You have many furs," Barclay corrected. "I have but few."

"The People're known for their giving of gifts. I'll make a gift of these furs to you."

"But I have no gift to give you in return, Father," Barclay said somewhat sadly.

"You will have one some day," the Sioux leader said.

Barclay knew that to be true, and knew that his adopted father was not worried about it. Barclay was torn, however, by the proposal of heading downriver. It would, of course, allow him to get his supplies on his own, which meant he'd pay far less for them than if he purchased them on credit with a company. And he had to admit there was a certain thrill in the thought of going by Fort Atkinson again, and running the risk of being discovered. The element of danger made that part of the proposal intriguing.

On the other hand, Barclay liked his life here, and had even begun thinking of just staying with Walking Thunder's band permanently, giving up his thoughts of turning trapper. He was uncomfortable with the thought of going upriver, taking Night Song with him, because of the men they would encounter along the way. And he was not sure how she would be accepted, if at all, when he got to some trappers' camp up in the mountains.

"What about Night Song?" Barclay asked suddenly. "If I go downriver, I mean."

"She'll be cared for," Walking Thunder said matter-of-factly. "She has her father to care for her. And your brother, Striking Arrow."

"But—"

"We'll come along with you to the great river," Walking Thunder said soothingly. "Whoever wants to make the journey with us. When the keelboat comes and you leave with it, we will come back here for the spring hunt. When that's done, we'll go back to the Missouri and wait for your return. From there, Night Song will go with you."

Barclay thought about that for a while. He didn't like the thought of being away from Night Song for any amount of time, and he wasn't sure that would even be necessary. The risk of him being found out at the fort, and arrested, no matter how slim, had to be considered. Because if that happened, he didn't know how long it would be before he could get back.

Still, he was not a shy man, and the thought of seeing old friends such as Schellenberger and Watrous again was a good one. The risk of capture might be worth that, especially when he likely would be getting his supplies much more cheaply.

"I'll think about it, Father," he finally said. There was no need to make a decision right now. Both he and Walking Thunder knew that. His adopted father had brought it up now so that he would have time to consider the proposal, and all its ramifications, and still have plenty of time to get to the river for the keelboats.

Walking Thunder nodded, and their talk turned to other, less important matters.

That night in the lodge, however, Barclay brought

up the proposal with Night Song, wanting to see how she would react. He didn't know what to expect, really, but he had not foreseen a complete and utter silence on his wife's part. He sat quietly, not saying anything either, listening to the pop and hiss of the fire, to the rush of the wind as it swept across the steep slopes of the lodge. Finally he shrugged, rose and went to the robes. He shucked his bear-fur coat—which he had not gotten around to taking off earlier—and slid into the warm buffalo robes.

It seemed like a long time, but Night Song finally joined him in their bed. "Why do you want to leave me to go down the river?" she asked, her voice as cold as the tempest blowing outside the lodge.

"I never said that," Barclay countered, surprised. Maybe his Sioux wasn't as good as he thought it was, if he had not made himself clear to Night Song. "All I said was that my father made such a suggestion," he added, speaking slowly, trying to make sure his language was as precise as he could make it. "I mentioned it to you to see what you thought of the idea."

"I don't like it." Night Song's voice had not warmed an iota.

"I don't like the thought of leaving you either," Barclay said. "And I told Father just that."

"So, why didn't you just tell him no?"

"There's a lot to be said about such a plan is why," Barclay said. He explained some of it—mostly the part about getting supplies. He avoided the part about the thrill of the danger, and he was glad when she didn't really ask about what might happen if he stopped at the fort.

"How long would you be gone?" Night Song asked, tones thawed minutely.

"Maybe two moons. The men on the keelboats can't afford to waste time."

"And you're not leaving me for some woman in

the east?" Night Song asked, voice cold again. "A pale-skin woman?"

Barclay said nothing for a bit as he tried to sort this all out. He could not understand how Night Song did not see his great love for her; the ache in his heart when he even thought of leaving her for a day or two, let alone a couple of months. Finally he turned on his side, so he was facing her. He touched her smooth, slightly flushed cheek with a finger. "There ain't no one but you for me, Night Song," he said in English, not trusting his Lakota for this.

"But what if you find another woman there and don't come back to me?" she asked in a whisper, speaking her own language.

"If I don't come back, it's gonna be 'cause I'm dead or so stove up I can't move," he responded in English. The two had no trouble understanding each other. "It ain't gonna be because of no woman."

"I believe you," Night Song said, kissing Barclay on the nose. After a few seconds of silence, she asked, "Then you want to go?"

"I'm not sure," Barclay answered, reverting to Sioux. "I need to think about it some, which is what I told Father. Will you fuss if I do?"

Night Song hesitated only a moment, then said, "No. It wouldn't be right for a woman to act so with her husband. I won't like it, but I won't stand in the way."

"You won't divorce me while I'm gone?" He held his breath waiting for the answer.

"No," Night Song said, shocked that he would even think such a thing. Didn't he know she loved him more than anything else?

"That's a relief," Barclay muttered.

"What?"

"I love you," he responded with a smile.

* * *

So now here he sat on the bank of the Missouri, as he had for almost a week, waiting for a keelboat. The weather was still cold and miserable, the skies leaden gray more often than not. Snow still fell with nerve-dulling frequency, and the wind climbed up the river-bank from the water with a bone-numbing chill. Chunks of ice ran down the river, as if hurrying to get somewhere. The only thing that made the waiting bearable was the small camp, and having Night Song waiting for him in the lodge.

It was four more days, but finally one of the large, flattish craft appeared up the river. Barclay scrambled up to the bluff and made sure his rifle was ready. When the boat was still fifty yards off or so, Barclay fired his rifle into the air.

A few moments later, oars appeared on the keel-boat, and slowed its progress in the swift river. Barclay waved his arms and, as the boat came alongside, he cupped his hands around his mouth and shouted, "Hello the boat!"

The craft turned and made its way to the bank across the river. A man stood on the low, flat box in the center of the boat and shouted. "Who are ye, and what do ye want with us?"

"I'm a trapper looking to take my furs downriver, and then hitch a ride back upriver."

"Ye alone?"

"Got some Sioux friends here. They won't be goin' along, though."

"Who're ye workin' for?"

"Been free trappin'. I plan to sign on with General Ashley soon's I can. He's told me he'd hire me on."

The man on the boat knelt and conferred with a few other men, then stood again and shouted, "We'll take ye on, mister."

"There's a landin' spot about half a mile down-river. This side. You'll see a small Sioux camp there."

The man on the boat didn't answer, just said something to his men. Barclay and Striking Arrow turned and trotted down the bluff, heading toward the camp. Fifteen minutes later, Barclay had loaded his furs on the boat, and kissed Night Song a hurried farewell. Promising her he'd be back as soon as possible, he hopped on the boat, and it swung away from the bank and headed downriver on the fast current.

Barclay was surprised when he saw General Ashley on the boat. "I don't remember tellin' you I'd hire you on," Ashley said to Barclay, though he did not seem angry or put upon.

"You certainly did, sir," Barclay responded, feeling his Lakota pride rising up in him. "Almost two years ago now. At the fight against the Rees."

"You were there, boy?" Ashley questioned. "I don't remember you."

"I was part of the Missouri Legion." He smiled a little. "But I reckon I looked a bit different then. No beard, dressed in my army uniform."

"You were the one saved that Sioux war chief, weren't you?" Ashley questioned after a moment's thought.

"That's me, sir, yes."

"Well, by God, I did say I'd hire you on. And I'll be damned if I'll go back on my word." They were sitting inside the keelboat's cabin, with a candle lantern throwing the only light. Ashley had a pipe going; Barclay chewed on a piece of wood. "One problem, though, son, is that we don't plan to take the keelboats upriver no more."

"What?" Barclay asked, surprised.

"Plannin' a rendezvous, boy. A grand meetin' of all the trappers and traders in the mountains, at some central point. We'll be packin' supplies in on mule, if it can be done. Which I think it can. But you're welcome to come along with the pack train, if you want, and then hire on with one of my brigades once we're there."

"I'll keep that in mind, General," Barclay said thoughtfully. "But I'll have to ponder it a bit."

"I can understand that."

"Not that I'm against such a thing. It's just that . . . Well, let me ask you somethin', General. Would you mind if I had a Sioux woman along?"

Ashley rubbed his scruffy beard a bit, then shook his head. "I don't reckon that'll be a problem. Some of the boys've taken up with Indian women. Another won't make much difference."

"Well, that's good. Another question if I may, General?"

"Ask away, son," Ashley said with a chuckle. "I ain't goin' anywhere."

"Would it be all right to meet you on the trail somewhere?"

"I expect. Why?"

"Well, I'm supposed to meet my woman right there where you picked me up. We didn't know the boats wouldn't be plyin' the river anymore. Anyway, I thought I might ride back this way on my own, pick up Night Song, and then head out to meet you and the pack train."

"Don't see that such a thing'd cause me troubles," Ashley said. "But, now, my turn for a question."

"Yes, sir?"

"What's your name, boy?"

"I'm a mite reluctant to say, General."

"Trouble?"

"You could say that." Barclay hesitated, then decided he might as well get it out in the open. "I'm a deserter," he said flatly. "I was supposed to be mustered out, but the son of a bitch who ran my company wasn't about to allow it. So I left."

"And you're going right by there?" Ashley said, smiling a little.

Barclay shrugged. "You didn't recognize me. I'm hopin' no one else will either. Especially if I lie low—like in here," he added hopefully.

Ashley nodded. "I admire your spunk, boy," he said. "And since I ain't so fond of the army, particularly after that foolishness at the Ree towns that time, your secret's safe with me."

"I'm obliged, General. Another favor, though?"

"What's that?"

"I know I'm imposin' on your kind nature and all, General, but there's two men at the fort—Privates Schellenberger and Watrous—that're good friends. If you could find them and let them know I'm here. Maybe they can sneak aboard for a quick hello or somethin'."

"I'll see what I can do, Mister—?"

"Barclay. Miles Barclay. And I'm in your debt, sir."

"I'm not makin' no promises, though."

"I understand."

Two days later, the keelboat was racing up to the fort, and Barclay felt his tension increase.

24

Schellenberger and Watrous entered the keelboat's dim, small, blocky cabin. When they spotted the solitary, wild-looking figure sitting on a stack of furs, Schellenberger said, "General Ashley said somevon in here vanted to see us. Since you're the only von here, dot must be you." He paused an instant, then asked, "So vhat do you vant vith us?"

"Hell, don't you even recognize your old friend, Numb Nuts?" Barclay responded, unable to contain his grin.

"Miles! You—" Schellenberger exclaimed, eyes wide.

Barclay jumped up and slapped a hand over the German's mouth. "Jesus, Klaus, keep your trap shut," he hissed. "Damn, you're gonna get me arrested and thrown in chains again, Numb Nuts. Now shut up."

"Well, it's your own damn fault for springin' such a surprise on us, damn you," Watrous said quietly, but he was smiling.

"Good Christ." Schellenberger added, "I can't beleaf vhat I'm seeink. How are you, mein freund? Und vhat are you doink here?"

"I'm doin' just fine," Barclay said truthfully. Then he explained what he had been through. He did it quickly and quietly, keeping down the embellishments despite his self-assurance. He did not consider it embellishment when he gushed unashamedly about Night Song.

"Ach, an Indian voman?" Schellenberger said. "They as goot as ve've heard?"

"I can't say for sure except about one," Barclay answered thoughtfully. "But that one's the prettiest, finest woman this feller's ever met."

"Dot vasn't vhat I asked," Schellenberger chided with some glee.

A touch of anger slid through Barclay, but he battled it down. He would have been just as crude—and rude—had the situation been reversed. "I can say that Night Song's the best woman I've ever met in every way possible," he answered calmly.

"Sounds like you love her," Watrous noted.

"Does that trouble you?" Barclay responded somewhat defensively.

"Didn't say that, Miles. Just making a comment."

"Well, by God, I do. I ain't ever met a woman like her. Night Song's everything a man—well, this man, anyway—could need, or want."

"Is that wise, though?" Watrous asked.

"What's wrong with it?"

"Nothin' wrong, I suppose," Watrous offered. "I just think it might cause you trouble—if you plan to go back to her." The last was a question.

"I do," Barclay said defiantly, as if challenging Watrous.

But Watrous grinned instead. "Well, if your mind's that set on her, I ain't about to be the one to say nay to it." He grew more serious. "I'd be careful, though," he added. "There's many a folk who doesn't take kindly to the mixin' of the races."

"I didn't know you were one of 'em, Jay," Barclay accused.

"Like hell I am. You know better than that," Watrous said a little huffily. "I don't give a damn who you want to spend your life with. I just don't want to see a good friend hurt by some thoughtless goddamn fools. All I'm sayin' is just watch yourself, in case someone wants to make trouble for you over it."

Barclay nodded. "I'll do so," he said. He knew he should apologize, but his Sioux training was still strong within him. That and his own natural arrogance made apologizing something he was reluctant to do. He rose, reached behind the bale of furs and pulled out a small bottle. "That General Ashley's a good man," he said with a grin, holding up the bottle. "It ain't much, but he let me have this for nothin'." He pulled the cork. "To the future, boys," Barclay said, holding the bottle up in a salute. He drank and then handed the bottle off to Schellenberger.

It took but a minute for three big, thirsty men to polish off the cheap whiskey, and then they chatted for several more minutes. Then Schellenberger said with a sigh, "Vell, it's been goot seeink you, mein freund." He stuck out a big hand to shake with Barclay. "I vish you vell in your life."

"You ought to be gettin' out of this sinkhole soon, too, Klaus. What're you plannin' to do?"

Schellenberger shrugged. "Go back east to mein family und see about startink mein own."

"Why not come west? I'm sure General Ashley'll hire you on. You, too, Jay."

"Dot might be somethink to ponder, but it doesn't seem like the think for me."

"For me either," Watrous added, "but I'll consider it." He, too, stuck out his hand and shook Barclay's. "Good to see you, Miles. I also wish you the best. You'll do all right for—"

They heard a commotion outside, and Watrous stopped talking. Suddenly, one by one, six soldiers stormed through the door, crowding the small cabin. Then Sergeant Sven Noordstrom walked in, followed by Captain Willard Pennington. The latter pointed at Barclay. "Private Miles Barclay," he said in a grave voice, "you're under arrest. Men, disarm him. And arrest his two compatriots, too."

"They didn't know I was here, Captain," Barclay said hastily, as a soldier took his two pistols and big knife.

"Don't play me for a fool, damn you, Barclay," Pennington barked.

"I ain't, Numb Nuts," Barclay snapped. "If I was tryin' to do so, it'd not be hard." He paused a moment to let that sink in, then asked, "Do you recognize me?"

"No," Pennington said flatly. "One of the boatmen told us you were here. Why? What does that have to do with anything?"

"They couldn't recognize me either. Klaus and Jay just wandered in here. I think they were hopin' to find a jug no one was lookin' after and spirit it back to the fort for later." He half smiled, as if letting Pennington in on some grand secret. "I was holed up in here. I didn't think no one here'd recognize me, but why take the chance of finding out? When they came in, I hesitated, wondering if I should let them know who I was, since they had no idea. I finally decided to, and was just doing so when you and your boys burst in here."

"That true, Private Schellenberger?" Pennington demanded.

Schellenberger waited less than a heartbeat. "Yessir," he lied firmly. "Private Vatrous and I haven't had any vhiskey in a long time—all vinter. Ve thought there'd be some in here, so vhen novon vas lookink, ve snuck in."

"Private Watrous?" Pennington questioned.

"Yessir," Watrous fibbed glibly. "Just like Private Schellenberger said. We were mighty surprised when Miles told us. We didn't know how he got here or anything. Like he said, he just told us when you and the squad came in."

Pennington was certain the three were not telling the truth, but right now he didn't care about Schellenberger and Watrous. He could deal with them later, if he so chose. Right now what mattered was that he had Barclay in his hands—and he was going to see that the wild-looking creature was hanged for sure this time. "Take him outside, men," the officer ordered. "We'll shackle him on deck, since there's not enough room here. Then it's straight to the guardhouse with him." He turned and went out, indicating that three of the soldiers should follow him.

"Let's go, Barclay," Noordstrom snapped with an ingratiating grin. He was going to enjoy this. Barclay had made Pennington, and by extension, him, look like idiots when the company could not track him down.

Barclay shrugged. He kept his face blank, not letting on that he was enraged inside. He would have to find another way to escape this one. More self-assured now, with an increased cunningness, he was certain he would think of something.

As Barclay walked through the doorway, Noordstrom gave him a good, hard shove, making him stumble out onto the keelboat deck. The push was accompanied by a rough laugh and a growled, "Hurry it up, asshole. We ain't got all day."

Barclay recovered from his stumble, straightened and then stepped forcefully back, jerking an elbow out, up high, as he did. The elbow smashed Noordstrom's nose and sent the sergeant reeling back into the cabin, bowling over two soldiers along the way.

"Shackle him, men!" Pennington roared. "Quickly! Before he can cause more trouble."

Barclay glanced over and saw that Noordstrom was still trying to disentangle himself from the two soldiers. The other soldiers seemed to be hesitating, not sure they wanted to try shackling this wild man before their friends were out here to help. Barclay decided that now was as good a time as any to try making a break for it. He certainly wouldn't get a better chance if he waited until he was in irons in the guardhouse. He had gotten away from here once before, living on his own hook; he could do so again.

He turned and smashed a fist into the face of one of the soldiers. He grabbed the man's pistol as he fell, then spun, cocking the single-shot flintlock. "Tell the others to back off, Numb Nuts," he barked.

Furious, Pennington nonetheless did so. Then he asked, "Well, Private? The next move is yours."

"We can do this nice and calmly, Captain," Barclay said, "or not. It's up to you."

"If you expect me to let you go free just because you're pointing that pistol at me, Barclay, you're sadly mistaken. So make your decision."

Barclay was aware that Noordstrom was on his feet and would be outside here in seconds. Without hesitation, he fired.

Pennington was far more shocked by the fact that Barclay had actually shot him than he was by the power of the lead ball hitting his chest and ravaging his lungs. He had not really believed that Barclay would do it. He was still wondering about it as he hit the wood deck of the ship and died.

Barclay wasn't paying attention. He knew that even if he hadn't killed Pennington, the officer was not going to be doing anything for a good long while. He whirled and clubbed a soldier on the side of the head with the empty pistol. The trooper—like the first one he had hit, unknown to him and probably new at the fort—went down. Then Noordstrom plowed into Barclay's back, wrapping his brawny arms around the former soldier.

As the sergeant tried to squash the life out of him, Barclay kicked Noordstrom in the shins, then again, and a third time, which fractured his tibia.

Noordstrom yelped and eased his grip on Barclay. He did not let him go, however, since he needed Barclay to stay on his feet. It was much easier now, however, for Barclay to flex his shoulders, breaking out of Noordstrom's bear hug. He took a step forward and turned as the sergeant tottered, trying to keep his balance. Barclay kicked his good leg out from under him.

Noordstrom fell and Barclay jumped on him, knees landing on the upper side of his abdomen, breaking some ribs. He ruthlessly pistol-whipped the sergeant on the face and head.

Then someone pounded Barclay in the back of the head with a rifle butt, and he fell forward onto Noordstrom, unconscious.

Barclay came to in the guardhouse. He had an aching head and was disgusted with himself. He was so intent on taking care of Noordstrom that he had left himself open to attack by troops he did not know. Had the men brought by Pennington to arrest him been old friends from his company, he would not have had to worry about it; but they weren't and he should have, but hadn't.

There was nothing he could do about all that now. He would just have to think of some other way to get out of his predicament, though at the moment that seemed like a remote possibility. He certainly didn't want to die so young, but he could accept it, if there was no alternative. The real problem, however, arose when he thought of Night Song. Leaving her a widow, not having a life with her sickened him. Then his adopted father's words and teachings swept over him, and he knew he could handle anything. He was still sick inside at the thought of lost opportunity, but he would face his death like a man—a Lakota man, not a white one.

Besides, there was still the possibility of coming up with something to get him out of this. He didn't know what, and it seemed like it would be impossible, but as long as he was alive, he would not totally give up hope.

Colonel Henry Leavenworth was furious because an officer had been killed, even though he didn't particularly care for Pennington. That it came at the hands of a deserter only enraged him all the more.

Two days after the keelboat had pulled back into the fort, Barclay was in the Colonel's office, facing a court-martial board that did not look at all sympathetic. Before his buttocks had hardly warmed his chair, he was pronounced guilty and sentenced to hang three days hence. Then he was back in his cell in the guardhouse. The entire process had taken less than an hour.

Leavenworth would not allow Schellenberger, Watrous, or any of Barclay's other friends visit him, and only new men—ones who had no idea of who Barclay was other than a deserter and officer killer— were to guard him. As a result, Barclay could not make plans with anyone to escape, and his meals consisted of weak, foul gruel, hard bread, and water.

Barclay grew a little forlorn, but he battled the feeling, trying to keep himself under control. He was almost glad that his execution was only three days off. Had it been much longer, he figured he would've had too much time to think about his impending doom, and therefore fall into despair. Of course, with more time before his sentencing, he might be able to devise a plan. But that was not to be.

The evening before his planned execution, Captain Robert Quinellen of E Company and several of his men showed up at the guardhouse. The cell door was opened, and one of the soldiers tossed a sack inside. Then the door was locked again.

"Put those on, Private," Quinellen said. "And get rid of that damned savage clothing you're wearing."

"Piss off, Numb Nuts," Barclay said more snappily than he felt. He was really listless.

"Do it!" Quinellen thundered.

"What the hell for?" Barclay retorted. "You can't do any more to me than you're gonna do. Hell, I'm gonna be hanged tomorrow." He was even able to laugh at the thought.

"You don't, boy, and I'll have my men come in there and cut those animal skins off you, and then you'll get hanged naked."

"You're just a big enough sack of shit to do it, too," Barclay said, not too perturbed.

"You have three minutes, Private."

"I ain't no goddamn private, Numb Nuts," Barclay snapped, tugging the long war shirt off. A little self-consciously, but not showing it any, Barclay stripped down and then pulled on the uniform. He folded his buckskins and put them in the canvas sack and held the bag out through the bars. One of the soldiers took it and tossed it in the corner. Barclay bit back a spark of anger.

"We'll be back in the morning, Private," Quinellen said smartly. "Just before dawn."

"What?" Barclay said with a smirk, "no last meal?"

"Sure you'll get a last meal—same one you've been getting since you've been here. Don't oversleep." Then he and his squad marched out.

Barclay put on his best smug face when Quinellen and Corporal Mac Dunnigan came for him in the morning. He found he could even make some jokes with Dunnigan after Quinellen split off to join the ranks of hundreds of soldiers lined up to watch the deserter's demise in the swirling mist.

He was tied to the post, and the firing squad lined up. Then came the call of fire, and Schellenberger cutting the ropes behind him. As he hurried away from Schellenberger, heading for the stables, he shouted at his friend, "Try to get my buckskins back, Klaus. In the guardhouse."

EPILOGUE

"Miles?" Schellenberger whispered. "Miles, mein freund?"

Barclay shoved out from his fetid haven, brushing off the clinging bits of rank hay and horse manure. "Jesus," he muttered. He had spent most of the day in the abominable straw cave with his nose stuck down the front of his uniform. That had filtered out at least some of the stench.

"You all right?" Schellenberger asked. As before, he was whispering.

Watrous stood at the doorway nearby, keeping a watch out.

"I expect. I smell like shit and I'm so goddamn hungry I was thinkin' of eatin' some that hay."

"Ve'll get you some jerky or somethink as soon as ve get out of here."

"*We'll* get me some jerky?" Barclay questioned, surprised.

"Me und Jay decided ve're comink vith you," Schellenberger said. He paused, then added, "If you don't mind."

"Hell, no, I don't mind."

"We figure you're headin' back to the Injins," Watrous said over his shoulder, also in a whisper. "Will they mind?"

"I don't know, but I wouldn't think so," Barclay

said truthfully. "If they do, we'll mosey on westward on our own."

"Without your wife?" Watrous asked, surprised.

"Hell no."

"Didn't think so."

"Let's get the hell out of here, boys," Barclay said. "I've been in that shit pile all day, and I ain't real eager to spend another minute in this fort if I don't have to." He paused, thinking, then asked, "Just how the hell're we gonna do it, though?"

"Everythink's vorked out, Miles. As vell as ve could vork it out. Don't vorry."

"I ain't worried. Just curious."

"Follow us." Before leaving, though, he handed Barclay a rifle, which Barclay slung over his shoulder, and a knapsack with some supplies in it. He and Watrous were similarly equipped.

Barclay shrugged. "Lead on," he said. He followed the two dark figures into the night. As he moved along, he brushed more of his shelter's residue from his hair. They all edged along the wood walls until they were at the gate. Private Jim Baxter—a friend of the three—was waiting there.

Baxter and Barclay shook hands quickly, before Baxter eased the gate open just enough for Barclay, Schellenberger and Watrous to slip out. "Good luck, boys," Baxter said and he tugged the gate closed again.

Schellenberger led the way, again along the wall of the fort. Then, in the darkest corner of the fort, Schellenberger headed toward the brush and trees that lined the river. They pushed through the brush, the sticks and thorns tearing at their clothing. But it was the best way to go, Schellenberger figured. Some patrols were still out looking for Barclay.

Several hours later, they finally stopped. Barclay started to ask why, but Schellenberger snapped, "Shut up," when Barclay had gotten only one word out. Then

Schellenberger whistled the first four notes of *Adeste Fidelis*. He waited tensely, and then heard the next four notes waft softly back toward him. With that, he breathed a sigh of relief.

"What's goin' on, Klaus?" Barclay asked in a whisper.

"More help for us. Come on."

Barclay shrugged and tagged along again. A minute later, he and his two companions were in a very small clearing. A whipcord thin man crouched over a low fire built in a two-foot-deep pit. Barclay had been unable to see it until he was right on top of it.

"Goddamn, boy, ye stink," Jethro Greathouse said as Barclay neared him. "Even to this rank ol' feller."

"Hell with you, Numb Nuts," Barclay said with a grin as he squatted next to the fire. "Is that deer I smell cookin'?"

"I'm surprised ye can smell anything, bad as ye stink," Greathouse commented. Then he, too, grinned. "Sure it's deer, sonny. Dig in. Coffee's hot, too. Best fill up good, since we'll be on the move the rest of the night."

Barclay didn't need a second invitation. He dug into the meat and gratefully accepted the mug of coffee Watrous handed him. Watrous and Schellenberger were also wolfing down food.

As he ate, Barclay asked, "How the hell did you get mixed up in all this business, Jethro?"

"General Ashley, mostly. He'd seen that ye and I was friends on the trip downriver. And he met your two companions here. He saw what happened, and knew what ye had told him about desertin'. He knew ye'd be in a heap of trouble. So him and me concocted a plan. Then I went to your friends and saw what they thought of it. They was agreeable, and here we are."

"You were responsible for talkin' them into leavin', too?" Barclay asked.

"Nah. We figured on them jist helpin' git ye out. Them blamed fools come up with this foolish notion all on their own, so we changed our plans a bit."

"Ain't this gonna get you—and General Ashley— in trouble?" Barclay asked as he reached for more meat. He was so interested in eating that he could hardly smell himself any longer.

"Shoot, boy, how's it gonna do that? Ain't nobody from the army knows about us. Besides, who gives a hoot about the army? After Leavenworth's folly against the Rees, ain't a one of Ashley's men has any respect for the army. Or at least its leaders, who'd be the ones to cause the trouble if they thought of it. In fact, boy, havin' these two fellers come along made things a heap easier. If they hadn't, I'd of had to wait right there by the fort, riskin' discovery, tyin' me and maybe the General into all this. But since they've come along, I could stay out here, and nobody's the wiser about the General havin' a part."

"Well," Barclay said soberly, "next time you see General Ashley, I'd be obliged if you was to tell him how much I'm in his debt. And you can tell him I'll pay him back somehow for all his kindness, even if it means I have to sign on with his company for the rest of my life."

"Shoot, I ain't no messenger, sonny. Ye tell him yourself. Hell, you'll see him the same time I will."

"I will?" Barclay asked dumbly.

"Hell, yes," Greathouse said with a laugh. "I'm going with ye three, till we meet up with them Sioux of yourn. Then we'll head on to that rendezvous the General's plannin'. We git lucky, we might meet him on the trail somewhere. If not, we'll see him up around Burnt Fork."

Barclay didn't think that required an answer. He was still too hungry and concentrated for a while on his meat and coffee. Then he suddenly thought of something. "What am I gonna do about supplies, Jethro? And what about Klaus and Jay here?"

"Ve haff been taken care of, Miles," Schellenberger said. "Through Mister Greathouse, ve haff hired on vith the General. Ve haff enough supplies—ve hope— to get us to this rendezvous think. After dot, he vill supply us."

Barclay nodded, satisfied that his friends were to be taken care of. Then he looked at Greathouse. "What about me?"

"Ye got the same as me and the others. The General said he'd take your furs down to St. Louis and trade 'em in. He'll use what he gits for 'em to supply ye at the rendezvous."

Barclay nodded, almost content. He drained the last of the coffee in his mug—his third refill—and wiped his greasy hands on his foul army pants. "Well, we better get movin'," he said, rising. "We've got a long walk facin' us."

"Sit down, boy," Greathouse growled.

"But—"

"Christ, boy, this ol' buzzard ain't gonna walk all the way to Burnt Fork. Nor even jist as far as it is to git to your Sioux friends."

"You got horses?"

"Hell, yes, we got horses. The General stopped the keelboat less than a day's ride down the river and traded with some Omahas for horses. I stayed around the fort, hidin' out a few hundred yards upriver. One of Ashley's men brought the horses up here yesterday."

Barclay sat back down and started eating again. But fifteen minutes later, Greathouse decided it was time to go.

"Check your bag there, Miles," Watrous said. "We got those buckskins of yours. There's also powder and lead and such."

Barclay nodded. He dug into the bag and smiled

when he found not only his buckskins and the shooting necessities, but also two flintlock pistols and his own large knife. He had no idea of where his friends had gotten it, nor did he care. Barclay quickly shucked his manure-fouled uniform and donned his buckskins. He fashioned a belt out of horsehair rope and stuck his plain leather sheath in it as well as the two now-loaded pistols.

The four men mounted the ponies bareback, their knapsacks of supplies hanging off their backs. Each had one thin blanket used as a saddle blanket while they rode; it would also serve for sleeping. They pushed on through the night, moving out onto the plain where the going would be easier on both men and horses.

Two days later, Greathouse stopped and called the three others around him. "We're bein' followed, boys," he said without preliminary.

"Army or Injins?" Barclay asked. It had to be one or the other.

"Army."

"So what do we do, Jethro?"

"That's up to you, boy," Greathouse answered evenly. "We can try to outrun 'em, or try to throw 'em off our trail, or set an ambush for 'em."

Barclay had to think that one over for a bit. His first inclination was to just race ahead and leave the patrol in the dust. Setting an ambush would be dangerous, and likely would result in some deaths. He did not like that idea—he was not bloodthirsty, and he did not want to kill any soldiers since some likely were old friends. And trying to throw them off didn't seem to make sense, not when there probably were a number of other patrols out looking for him.

"Let's outrun 'em," he finally said.

They rode hard for the rest of the day, and then camped in a thicket along the river.

Just as dawn was breaking, they heard a voice out of the darkness: "Give yersel's up, laddies."

"That's Corporal Dunnigan," Watrous said.

"I ain't givin' up, Mac," Barclay said. "Not to you nor nobody else. You should know why."

"Aye, I think I do, laddie. But hear me out."

"I don't think I need to hear anything you have to say."

"Aye, ye do, lad." He paused, then said, "I'll tell ye what, Miles. Let me and Lieutenant Hodges come in to yer camp and chat with ye. I think ye'll find it in yer favor."

Barclay looked at Schellenberger and then Watrous. Both shrugged. "All right, come on in," he said.

When the Officer and the Corporal were seated, facing Barclay, who had his three friends just behind him and a little to the sides, Hodges pulled a piece of paper from his blouse and tossed it to Barclay. It landed in Barclay's lap,

Barclay glared at Hodges for a moment, then picked up the paper. It was his release from the army dated just over a year ago.

"Corporal Dunnigan brought that to me the day before yesterday."

"A little late, Lieutenant," Barclay noted.

"Maybe, maybe not."

"What the hell does that mean?"

"Well, it proves that Captain Pennington had kept that paper from you, which means you weren't a deserter."

"I know that, but how does that help me?"

"It shows that he tried to falsely arrest you on the keelboat," Hodges said. "Now listen. Surrender and come back to the fort with me. I'll demand a new trial. With that paper and everything it signifies, you'll have reason under the law to have killed Pennington. It won't excuse it, of course, but with this evidence, you'll get no more than five or ten years imprisonment, not executed."

Barclay could not help but laugh. "You got to be crazy, Lieutenant. Mad as a hatter. I killed that numbnut bastard because he's had it in for me since the day I arrived in this territory. That's why he held that paper from me. He deserved what he got, and I'll be damned if I'll risk my neck with the army's brand of justice again."

Hodges shook his head. "Then I have no choice but to arrest you and bring you back by force."

Barclay and his three companions tensed, and they eased their hands toward their pistols. "There's no call for doin' that, Lieutenant," Barclay said evenly. "It's only gonna end up in bloodshed."

"Look, Private . . . Miles, I like you. I always thought you were a good soldier. I know I couldn't do much while Captain Pennington commanded D Company. But now that I do, even if it might be temporary, I can do a lot more to help you."

"The best thing you can do to help me, Lieutenant, is to just leave me and my friends be. Pretend you never saw us."

"I don't think I can do that," Hodges said somewhat firmly.

"I think Miles has the right idea, Lieutenant," Dunnigan said.

"You, too, Corporal?"

Dunnigan shrugged. "To be blunt, sir, Miles dinna do anything that near all the other men're thankful for. He's a hero to just about every enlisted man who knew him at Fort Atkinson for killin' the captain. Ye may not want to hear that, but it's true."

"I still have to do my duty, Corporal," Hodges said sternly.

"Lieutenant," Dunnigan said wearily, tired of all

this business, "I don't think ye'll find one man out there
in the brush who'd be willin' to take Miles—or the
others—by force."

Hodges was bright enough to know that
Dunnigan probably was telling the truth, but he did
not want to back down. He figured it would make him
look bad in front of his men and would lessen his
authority in the long run.

Dunnigan guessed what Hodges was thinking,
and he felt a little sorry for the officer. Hodges had
finally gotten some real authority and it was being
undermined before he could wield it. "The men won't
hold it against ye, Lieutenant," he said quietly. "They
understand this is a special circumstance, and they'll
obey yer commands in all other instances. I'll see to it."

Hodges pondered it for several minutes, making
everyone else edgy. Then he nodded. "I'll take you at
your word, Corporal." He looked at Barclay. "Miles,"
he said, smiling just a little in good-natured surrender,
"go in peace." He stood. "Well, Corporal, let's go look
for those damned deserters."

"Yes, sir," Dunnigan said, rising and winking at
Barclay. "Oh, by the way, Miles, ye might like to know
that Sergeant Noordstrom lived, but he'll nae be the
same again. And I dunna think he'll do any more lads
any harm."

Barclay nodded. "You take care, Mac."

"Aye, that I will. Ye do the same."

The soldiers left, after most called out a greeting or
some good wishes to their former compatriots.

After a quick meal, Barclay and his three friends
rode out. Barclay was feeling better now, and his
thoughts turned to Night Song. He would be with her
soon, and everything would be fine, then, just fine. It
was long overdue, he thought, but his vision was on
the verge of being fulfilled.

AUTHOR'S NOTE

Most of *Fire Along the Big Muddy* is fictional, as are the majority of the characters. However, the fight with the Arikaras was real, although I have embellished many of the details. Also real are Fort Atkinson, Colonel Leavenworth, Joshua Pilcher, and, of course, General William Ashley.

Ashley went west with the *Yellowstone Packet* and the *Rocky Mountains* in these years, but I have taken license with Barclay's return to the fort and his dealings with Ashley on that trip.

At the time, instead of heading back east, Ashley remained in the west to make arrangements for the first rendezvous, which was held in the summer of 1825 near present-day Burnt Fork, Wyoming.

John Legg is a full-time writer and newspaper editor who lives in Arizona with his family.

$1,000.00

FOR YOUR THOUGHTS

Let us know what you think. Just answer these seven questions and you could win $1,000! For completing and returning this survey, you'll be entered into a drawing to win a $1,000 prize.

OFFICIAL RULES: *No additional purchase necessary.* Complete the HarperPaperbacks questionnaire—be sure to include your name and address—and mail it, with first-class postage, to HarperPaperbacks, Survey Sweeps, 10 E. 53rd Street, New York, NY 10022. Entries must be received no later than midnight, October 4, 1995. One winner be chosen at random from the completed readership surveys received by HarperPaperbacks. A random drawing will take place in the offices of HarperPaperbacks on or about October 16, 1995. The odds of winning are determined by the number of entries received. If you are the winner, you will be notified by certified mail how to collect the $1,000 and will be required to sign an affidavit of eligibility within 21 days of notification. A $1,000 money order will be given to the *sole winner* only—to be sent by registered mail. Payment of any taxes imposed on the prize winner will be the sole responsibility of the winner. All federal, state, and local laws apply. Void where prohibited by law. The prize is not transferable. **No photocopied entries.**

Entrants are responsible for mailing the completed readership survey to HarperPaperbacks, Survey Sweeps, at 10 E. 53rd Street, New York, NY 10022. If you wish to send a survey without entering the sweepstakes drawing, simply leave the name/address section blank. Surveys without name and address will not be entered in the sweepstakes drawing. HarperPaperbacks is not responsible for lost or misdirected mail. Photocopied submissions will be disqualified. Entrants must be at least 18 years of age and U.S. citizens. All information supplied is subject to verification. Employees, and their immediate family, of HarperCollins*Publishers* are not eligible. For winner information, send a stamped, self-addressed Nº10 envelope by November 10, 1995 to HarperPaperbacks, Sweeps Winners, 10 E. 53rd Street, New York, NY 10022.